Witches & Immortals

Stephanie Vorwald

ISBN: 9798493363429

Editing by Whitney Morsillo of Whitney's Book Works
Cover Design by Etheric Tales & Edits | Mc Damon

Second Edition 2023

This book would be nothing if it weren't for my Grandma Helen being born and raised in Lancaster, Wisconsin. Thanks to her, our family has traveled to the Mississippi River to take on the beauty of the land and catch all kinds of fish from the river.

Also, thank you to my kids, family, and friends for the tremendous support.

Welcome to my world of magic.

Contents

Stephanie
VORWALD

ESCAPE FROM REALITY
YA FANTASY

Chapter 1

To New Beginnings and the Past

Journal: June 4th ~

I'm trying, I really, really am trying. Isadora, my therapist, gave me this journal and thinks it'll be a good idea for me to write down how I've been feeling lately. She thinks she will have some kind of breakthrough with her appointments by having me write my feelings and thoughts down.

What a bunch of shit this is.

Honestly, I think the infinity symbol on the front cover of this journal is the only reason why I accepted it. I felt drawn to it because it reminded me of him. And anything to hold on to my memory of him will catch my attention these days. Maybe it was the leather-bound cover with twine that just made it seem kind of old and unique and like it was screaming to be written in. No, it was definitely the infinity symbol. I guess I just wanted it. Maybe writing things down will help. As of right now, I feel all over the place and don't really know where to start. Do I just keep jotting down what pops in my head first? Do I start writing how I'm feeling? I feel like the feelings and emotions part could take a while...

Isadora would be happy with the progress, but would I? I guess that's the part about journaling, you can write whatever you want down and it's yours. I could write a big fuck you across every page with no shame because it's mine. No journal will ever be the same word for word, which is kind of amazing when you think about it.

Maybe I should just start with the symbol and why it felt like I was supposed to take the journal. He had a mark on his upper left shoulder blade that looked like an infinity symbol. It wasn't really a birthmark, at least I don't think it was. I never really noticed it until a few weeks before he died. We grew up together, and I would've noticed it. Right? Never mind, it's just a stupid little symbol anyways, it doesn't mean anything.

Well, at least, everyone else seems to think I'm doing just fine, but Isadora on the other hand, thinks I'm holding everything back. I guess partially because I don't say much to her and also because she's never dealt with a situation like mine before. She doesn't know the feeling, I mean truly know, the feeling of loss. I mean, damn it's been close to two years since I started seeing her, but still, I think she knows more about my dad than she does about me. Supposedly, they knew each other from high school before she moved away to escape this small town, which of course, means she probably knew my mom too. I wonder what she thinks about her and what she's done to not only me, but to my dad too.

Now I'm just rambling. Maybe I am holding back from her. Personally, I don't like her too much. I don't really want to share my entire life story with someone when I haven't even lived much of a life to tell. My story is boring. I've barely lived at all, and she keeps making me relive the part of my past that I hate. ~~I'm ready to move on.~~ I can't change what happened. I wish I could, everyday I wish I could, but I can't, and I'm mentally exhausted after these sessions with her trying to make me relive it time and time again. I just can't keep doing this.

She just seems to be in it for the money anyways, which of course, my dad doesn't mind paying if he thinks it'll be good for me. I

just feel like it's none of her damn business. She's not actually going to know how I'm feeling. She can't help me escape my own thoughts. Plus, she has the perfect little life, good-looking husband, the perfect dog, the convertible, the mansion, and even the white picket fence. At least, that's what her photo shows on her desk, maybe there's more behind the polaroid. Really, I don't want to taint her pretty little life with my problems. I'll be fine. Besides, today is my 18th birthday and I'm handling things just fine. Yesterday would've been his birthday. I cried a bit and sent off a lantern for him, but I'm finally coming to grips that he's gone. ~~I'm starting not to miss him as much anymore.~~ **It's getting easier... I think.**

I knew I could make it, even with the sweat dripping from my brow. I wiped it quick and continued to run a little faster. Trying to stay focused for today.

Come on, just around the bridge, that's it. The last mile for the day.

I pushed the air through my lungs and fought on. I just needed to forget that I was running and instead focus on my surroundings and not the fact that my breathing was extremely uneven and the brow sweat was starting to burn into my eyes. I really needed to start running regularly again. I needed to make this more of a daily routine because it honestly felt so good when I was finally done. This was a good hobby to keep up with. Both physically and mentally. I knew I needed any sort of distraction to finish this run for today. I sucked in a deep breath and let my mind wander, aimlessly.

Just think, summer was finally here, which meant no more homework or tests. No more long nights of studying until the sun came up. It was time to enjoy the summer, and this summer was going to be different for me. It had to be.

I knew senior year had been far too busy with all the AP classes that had kicked my ass but I knew they were just trying to prepare me for the local college here in Crystal Rock, Wisconsin. Even though I had no major in mind and felt that college may not be for me after all. But until that day comes... all I knew was a break was definitely needed.

My dad had been pretty strict the last two years. My grades had been flawless, and I've been trying my best. Jim Chamberlain, my dad, made me get a job this past year at the Rendezvous, the only movie theatre in town. He's old friends with the owner, Jack. I guess they had grown up together, and he's now one of his favorite fishing buddies. I'm wondering if my dad will make me get two jobs this summer, to keep me out of trouble. He practically knows the whole town. He owns Swig and Jig, the only bar and tackle shop there is along the river. Business was always good from the dedicated locals, and even the outsiders that came to fish the Mississippi knew about our place by word of mouth.

In the small town of Crystal Rock, everyone seemed to know everyone along the Mississippi River where the bluffs fly high and the river flows fast. Any town or city close by is a minimum of twenty minutes north, south, east, or west. You can go up in the bluffs and get lost with the winding roads while having your ears pop the higher up you go. The bluffs are Wisconsin's very own mountains, only not nearly as gigantic. Once you are at the highest point, you can look over the bluffs and see the river flowing fast; the strong river is how these huge rock formations are even formed in the first place. You can look the opposite way and see fields of corn, cabbage, pumpkins, or whatever else is being grown, depending on the season. Driving up these bluffs could be both amazing and scary because you can see signs saying, "Watch for falling rocks" all along the winding roads. I knew I wouldn't want to play chicken with these enormous boulders on any given day. The higher up you go, the more the rocky bluffs turn into rolling fields of land with green hills or farming fields for miles with a house or a barn off in the distance with at least a mile-long driveway. Those driveways were no fun when the snow falls during the freezing winters, but other than that time of year, Crystal Rock is a beautiful piece of land to explore. It's really a place to visit if you're ever in the area.

I began to slow down with my legs starting to feel like Jell-O and my lungs were beginning to rattle. I slowed my pace to a jog until I came to a complete stop and drew my arms above my head, crisscrossing them to help open my lungs and catch my breath. Overthinking while running could make you lose track of time, which could be a good distraction or sometimes it could turn into a mindfuck. My running watch began to buzz, which told me that the fourth mile was complete. I swallowed hard and wiped my forehead with my forearm. The beads of sweat making me cringe and I knew it was time to head back home and shower. I looked down the road and groaned at the thought of another good mile walk back to the house. I really need to come up with a better running path that circles back home, I thought.

The more I thought about my past, the more I can't really blame my dad for wanting me to stay busy with work; I had put him through hell. He really wanted us to have a mutual agreement and live as normal as possible. He wanted us both to be happy. Ultimately, my goal was for him to trust me again. That meant that I needed to keep my job at the movies and attempt to stay busy, then hopefully, he wouldn't have to worry about me so much anymore. I completely could understand why he continues to worry so much, but it had been almost two years since it happened.

I know many parents worry and love their kids, but I also knew that I didn't deserve even that after what I did. Even Alexandra, my mom, had claimed she loved and cared for me. Which was still one thing that I had a hard time believing since she's been MIA for a while now. No phone calls or texts, not even for my birthday. She could've at least been a holiday mom and made the effort for special occasion, but instead... Nothing. Really, I couldn't care less about what words came from her mouth anyways. I used to believe that she cared for me when I was younger, but not as a growing adult. Maybe she found out about the accident and wanted nothing to do with me anymore, maybe she's ashamed of me. I still would've preferred a check-in phone call once in a blue moon to keep our communication line open, though.

At sixteen, my parents divorced. Alex swore she did everything she could to make it work. She told me they were just "trying" to stay together for me since I'm an only child. She claimed that young children with divorced parents would rebel, do drugs and end up in jail by the age of eighteen. And yet, here I was, beating her statistics. Where she got the idea that sixteen was a better age to divorce us as a family is still beyond me. Alex said they were just never happy, and she claimed he was nothing but an inconsiderate prick to her and that she needed to breathe. It was harsh to hear her say things like that. I swear I remembered my parents being inseparable and madly in love. She assured me that that was my own childhood imagination trying to show me a better picture to escape the true reality we were living. It still blew my mind because he still loves her to this day and would move mountains for her at any given time. I knew everything Alex had said was a lie. My dad didn't have an evil bone in his body. Plus, I remember Alex was always preoccupied with "work" or other men for years. She always had those late nights and was quick to leave for the day with clients. She was living a double life. Her hours were bizarre, even for a realtor. Whether or not she cheated, I would never know, but I will always assume she did.

I still hated that I have her name for my middle name, Freya Alexandra Chamberlain. At least I only have a part of my mother's name and nothing else. I look mostly like my dad. I have longer than shoulder-length brown hair with natural-looking highlights due to the summer's sun. The natural highlights helped make my hair very low maintenance which had always been a plus. I have hazel eyes to match his, but mine have more green and gold tints while he has a blue hue. A few freckles on my nose, from not enough sunblock as a kid. I'm pretty average in height and weight, or at least I think so. I guess being a little taller would be nice to reach the top shelves at the stores, but most girls my age are similar in height. Except, of course, for my best friend Aisling Meadows (Ai-s-ling, not Ash-ling, she hated when people called her that), she should be a model. Her name comes from an ancestor, Aislynn, that had been passed on to the first-born daughter of the family for centuries. Her favorite Aunt Lynn, decided to shorten her own name to help stop the confusion for Aisling at a young age with mix ups. Luckily, with her parents always traveling for work, her aunt has always treated her as her own and she has never been alone.

Some days I catch myself looking in the mirror, and I find a young woman staring back at me in disgust. Maybe it's because of the accident. Knowing what I have done and that there was nothing that I could do to change it. It was hard some days, knowing that the person staring back at me was actually me. I do feel like I have grown so much in the last two years and now I'm nothing like I used to be. The lady who stared back at me was a mixed version of who I was and the person that I was becoming. I really hoped the new part of me was a better version than my past. I didn't want to keep living with the guilt. I wanted to grow. The car accident really messed with my head. Luckily, I wasn't hurt physically in any way, just mentally broken down, piece by piece.

Aisling always swears that girls envy me and guys want to date me, but I think she just says that to reassure me that I'm not some broken girl who is unable to date again. I knew she was actually just describing herself, but I gladly took the compliment from her to try and help boost my self-esteem. It was really hard for me to believe that anyone would even want to be around me after the accident, especially with *him* being gone and most people knowing it was my fault. I still try to avoid his old street to not have the guilt of his empty house looking back at me as a reminder. Maybe someday I'll try a new relationship again. Just not yet. Plus, most guys are just too shy or too scared in their teen years to say how they really feel, and girls my age are too into themselves or wrapped up in social anxiety to realize a world outside of their own existence. Dating young doesn't usually turn into your forever person anyways, so dating isn't really my thing right now. I firmly believe that life is too short, and there's no point in holding things in these days when you're not sure if there will be a tomorrow. So, if you love someone, then love hard; and if you are unhappy, then don't stick around and make excuses to stay.

The week the divorce was finalized in court, Alex had already been gone from both my dad's and my life for weeks. She even brought a random new boyfriend to the final court date. She seemed to be in a hurry and wanted things to be over as fast as possible. She rushed the judge to get through with the bullshit speech and just let her sign the final papers. I remember looking at my dad, and he had tears forming at the corners of both eyes and was trying to choke back every heart-shattering feeling he was holding in. I remember that being the exact moment when I decided I wanted nothing to do with Alex ever again. She had done enough damage, and he would need time to recover. He really did love her, and for her to do that to him was low, even for her. It made me sick to watch her walk in with that nobody as if it was her first day of freedom. The woman was a lost cause, and there was no way in hell I'd live with her. That was the day I decided to live with my dad.

I'll admit, the divorce made me a little rebellious. I guess I could call them some of my darker days. Bourbon had its own hidden spot on my nightstand. I would suck it down, even with the lasting burn in my throat that it caused, just to help me feel nothing and fast. Sixteen-year-olds and liquor were not a good combination, but it helped numb the pain I was feeling. I guess it enhanced my feelings toward Alex, which were mostly hate and hurt. My dad started drinking heavily every day, since working at a bar, he had a never-ending supply of alcohol. Which made it easy to take a bottle from him when he was passed out. He would assume that he had drunk the entire bottle by morning and run to Swig and Jig for another one. I don't remember a sober day for the two of us for a while. Partying became a new nightly agenda for me. I met a lot of new people as a sophomore, mostly juniors and seniors. They were not a very good crowd I was hanging out with. I knew that, but I was angry, and my life felt like it was falling apart. The spiral started, and I was okay with it at that time. I was hurting, and I wanted to forget her. I saw my dad in tears almost every day, and I was angry with Alex for hurting him so much, and for hurting me. Although, I would never tell her that she had that kind of hold on my emotions. I would never let her back in.

Aisling, being my best girlfriend since diapers, decided to stick with me with whatever my choices were. She never judged me, just kind of went along with me. I didn't realize how bad I had become until one summer night I decided to go out to a party. Everyone was there from high school.

Looking back, I wish I would have stayed home because I couldn't have cared less about that party. Every day I wish I could take that night back. It made my stomach twist, and I still feel the anxiety of reliving that night over every time I think about it. If magic were real and there was a wishing well or a genie in a lamp granting me one wish, then this would be the wish I would make: to re-do that night. But I know it's the one thing I'll never get. This was life, and you don't always get second chances.

Jaxon Oakes was my best guy friend for seven years and eventually became my boyfriend. He had dark brown hair that always fell just how it should. The type of hair that he could wake up and go and always look stunning. His eyes were ocean blue, but they had the slightest tint of green streaks in them. He always seemed to look directly in your eyes just so that the green would almost shimmer. Jaxon had the most perfect smile that no matter what the situation was he would always be smiling back. He had a heart of gold and would always put everyone before himself. I will always love him with every fiber of my being. I know I am young, but he should have been my forever. We had this connection beyond anything out there. He was my first kiss in elementary school on the playground, by the monkey bars that were across from the kickball field. Back when life was simple. Then, he became my first real love up until the day he was gone. We were inseparable from day one of meeting. It was almost like we were drawn to each other, and I couldn't inhale without him exhaling. Of course, we would fight here and there about stupid, petty things that didn't actually matter. The fights would always end with Jaxon smiling and saying everything was going to be okay and that would be that. It was hard to stay mad at someone who would go out of their way to make you smile. Even when I would be wrong, he would take the blame just to stop the fight, and later, I would realize that it was me and not him and apologize to him for me being a mini asshole. He lived with the "each day is a gift, tomorrow isn't promised" motto and didn't like parting on bad terms.

He was the most exhilarating boy I had ever met, and I had fallen in love with him. I remember the exact moment that I thought I could spend forever with that boy. It was the night of the accident and the reason we had left the party. Unfortunately, I hadn't realized how real our relationship was until our forever was about to be taken from us. Obviously, he tried to help me through my parents' divorce as much as he could, but when I started to rebel, he couldn't stop me. Nobody could. So instead, he went along with everything I did, no matter how self-sabotaging. Now that I look back on those months, Ais and Jax had been babysitting me and not actually partaking in the partying themselves. I hadn't even noticed that I was the only one drinking my feelings away until that night. So, it was the three of us together through thick and thin. Inseparable. Until the night of the accident.

Chapter 2

The Accident

It was July, and I had recently tuned sixteen. And despite my dad's wishes, I learned how to drive behind his back. He wanted me to wait until I was more stable and my grades were better, but I was being selfish and childish. It was Trevor, the senior who had the most reliable car, who taught me how to drive on our lunch breaks in the school parking lot. He had an easy-to-drive SUV that his daddy's money paid for. He willingly taught me how to drive with the expectation of a relationship for exchange in return. Ultimately, I was just using him to teach me how to drive, not in a malicious way. The weekend had come, and I wanted to do the usual and go out to a party on a Saturday night. I was still very bitter about how my life was spiraling and that Alex hadn't even tried contacting us in months. Each day that went by, made me more and more angry that she could just give up on us that emotionlessly. I knew I said I didn't care, but it still hurts to think about. So pretty much, all of the seniors and most of the juniors were at this house party. I decided to sneak out of my bedroom window, which was my first mistake. I "borrowed" my dad's prized possession, a 1972 Chevelle he had rebuilt from scratch. It was dark green with black racing stripes, and it was fast. That was my second mistake. Then, I called Jaxon on my way out of the driveway at 11:29 p.m. I remember looking at the clock on the dashboard when I started the car and hoped my dad wouldn't hear it. Then, when I was sure I was in the clear because I saw him passed out on the recliner in the living room with the bottle of Bourbon in hand, I pulled out of the driveway stealthily and went to pick up Jaxon. My third mistake. We arrived at the party about ten minutes later after we parked down the road and walked to the house.

We both decided to drink the Wapatui mix that was concocted, which was basically pure liquor so you could get drunk fast, and a side of morning hangover would always come with it. By the end of the night, or early morning, I still remember Jaxon and me sitting on the roof of the kid's house looking up at the stars talking about my parents' divorce and how I was getting tired of living with this rebellious attitude. I was ready for a fresh start. Jaxon said he would help me get through it and help me come out as a better person. I remember looking at him thinking that he was never going to leave my side. He was going to help me through anything. That was the moment that I realized he wouldn't give up on me, even at my worst, he loved me deeply. I had loved him so much for that, and at that moment, I realized it was time for a do-over.

I was ready to leave the party and get home. I had

stopped drinking an hour or so before getting into the car to drive home at around four thirty a.m. I still can't figure out how Jaxon and I got past Aisling that night to head home. She was the one who called and invited us in the first place. Yet I barely saw her that night. Supposedly, she was upstairs with some junior she had been crushing on all school year. Usually, she would say things like, "Freya, what are you doing? Where do you think you're going? Don't leave me here all alone." We would fight over who would be better to drive, but that night was different. She wasn't my babysitter, and I was done with this place. So, Jaxon and I got in the car, and I remember him grabbing my hand and holding it very caringly and we were both excited with this new fresh start coming. As I was driving, a semi-truck, that wasn't supposed to be on the back roads at all but had been looking for a gas station since the last truck stop, he ended up running the stop sign, and he slammed right into us. I didn't think I was still drunk from the night, that I physically couldn't have stopped in time to avoid it, but I guess my driving foot didn't hit the brakes fast enough to avoid the collision. I remember the minute we collided and feeling the biggest jolt I've ever felt stream through my body. I felt instantly sober of any alcohol that did remain. I felt awake for the first time in my life.

The car went up in the air and flipped several times, then landed on its roof and was smoking with flames starting on the ground where the hood was. At least, that's what the eyewitnesses at Willow Winds Diner across the street had told the police. It was the only damn diner that stayed open twenty four hours nowadays. The ambulance got there quickly and so did my dad, who must've sobered up just as quick when he got the phone call. I knew I was in shock but had somehow managed to get out of the car, as I was sitting up next to the car, completely untouched, not a broken bone, bruise, or scratch on me. I was just clutching myself, and I remember the tears wouldn't stop. Every emotion I had been holding off had finally caught up with me, and everything came crashing down, literally. With not even a scratch, I could hear the cops telling my dad that I was the luckiest girl alive. *Alive*, that was the word that I didn't deserve that night. I was alive; Jaxon, on the other hand, was not moving, let alone breathing, and was still buckled up in the passenger seat upside down.

I remember now what he had said to me as we were pulling up to the stop sign. "No matter what happens in this life, I'm not going anywhere. We will get through this together." How ironic it was that the world seemed to think differently at that very moment. It was like the universe looked down at us and laughed saying, "Time to fuck this up for these young lovers." It's the one thing that turns on like a broken record in my head some nights when I'm trying to go to sleep. It was like, you know, those nights where anxiety and overthinking decided to join the party and make you think of that time when you said something stupid like "you too" when someone says "you're all set" instead of "have a good day" that you had prepared for them to say. But how could the universe be so cruel as to take his words and shove them back down his throat in a very instant? He had lied to me, he was gone, and I was going to have to keep my promise on this do-over all alone.

That was the last time I saw Jaxon. It was a closed

casket at his funeral, so it still seems unreal. His family packed up and moved a week after that. There was so much left unsaid. It's like I'm still waiting for him to walk into my room with that ridiculous smile. It has been hard because I feel like I never got to say goodbye. He was there one minute, and we seemed to be invincible, and then he was just gone.

I guess this would be the stuff that Isadora would want me to write down in that stupid journal.

Well, life seemed to kind of stop after that for a while. Everyone seemed to say the wrong things to me, and it would just bring me to tears and make me angry. Tears and rage were permanent emotions for me and nobody wanted to be around me, and no one, not even my dad, would mention his name. I had just lost the one and only person I ever felt whole with, and I knew it was entirely my fault. I wish I hadn't been drinking and driving and being completely irresponsible. I can't ever take back what happened, and now I have to live with the guilt forever.

Since we live in a small town, everyone knew about the accident by noon that day. The town was silent. I was told the semi-driver was at fault for blowing the stop sign, but with alcohol involved and being underage without a license, I was in deep shit too. The judge decided to be lenient on both of us because of the terrible loss that was already at hand. He felt sorry for all parties involved. Jaxon's family didn't want me to be in trouble too much because they felt like living with the guilt was punishment enough before they moved away. I definitely got off easier than I deserved. A lot of community work and a few fines and obviously no leaving the house without adult supervision for a few months. In my eyes that was not punishment enough. The only good thing that came from that night was that my dad and I completely closed off drinking alcohol in our lives. He emptied his stash and decided we both needed to do better. It was time to heal.

Chapter 3

Do-Over

Well, that was almost two years ago. A lot has changed since then. I became an "A" student in my senior year. I was on the honor roll every time the paper came out. My dad now knows where I am at all times. We're working on our trusting skills again. Today's my eighteenth birthday, and I'm actually excited to celebrate it. I have been saving every dollar I've made each summer for a while now, and I want to get my own car and conquer my driving fears. I already knew that it won't be the best car, but it will sort of feel like getting my freedom back. Shockingly, my dad told me I could have a birthday party with a few friends while he went on his annual fishing trip on the Mississippi River with his buddies. He said this was my chance to prove that he could trust me again, and I wasn't going to mess this up. I promised there wouldn't be any trouble, and everyone would bring their own tents to set up in the backyard so we could have a bonfire and swim and we wouldn't make a mess inside the house

"Hey, Freya, how was your run?" My dad asked. Lifting his fishing poles off the table and setting them aside. "This old man should really start going with you to keep me young." The small talk always made me smile, and I could tell he was ready to leave for the weekend to be with his buddies. He loved fishing the Mississippi River, it was definitely his happy place.

"It was good... always good for clearing my head." I pointed to my head and smiled, pausing to try and read him to see if he had doubts about letting me have a few friends over. "Dad, are you sure you don't want to stay for the party?" I asked with a smile, knowing that the idea of a group of teens getting together and being teenagers terrified him.

"Uh, no... I'd rather not be around a bunch of young teens unsure if they should ask the girl to dance or not." He smiled shyly. "Sorry, darling. Just make sure you have some fun and enjoy yourself. You've been so busy working lately. And you do deserve this."

I half smiled. Wanting to deserve this, but still knowing that I probably didn't. "Aw, come on, Dad, we can be fun when we want to be." I winked and we laughed, but he already had one foot out of the door, ready to leave with his fishing gear.

"Take care of the house, kid, and please be careful, nothing stupid, okay?" Anyone could look at him and see the look of concern across his face at that very moment. "Love ya, kid, and promise you'll call me if you need anything?" He walked back toward me and pulled me into a hug with his free arm. He pulled me back and looked at me with a smile. "Oh, and happy birthday."

I smiled. "I promise." And that was it, he hugged me tight once more and was gone for the weekend.

I had to admit that I was pretty excited to do something for my birthday. I called Aisling immediately once I saw him load up his truck and he pulled out of the driveway.

"Hey, lady, so my dad said I can have a birthday par—" was all I could get out before I heard her screaming with excitement.

"Oh my god! I'm already in my car. See you in two minutes." And just like that, the line went silent. Aisling had always just been a little too eager to plan everything. I loved the girl, but she had always been the most popular girl in school and was a planner and perfectionist. Aisling's beautiful blonde hair, usually held in loose curls, and bright green eyes attracted everyone to her. She inherited the taller genes from her dad. She actually inherited every supermodel feature there was. Tall, blonde, amazing glowing skin. I might even envy her a little, but I love her more. Of course, everyone in the school knew her and I'm sure they envied her too, but my favorite feature of her is her reliability. If you're ever lucky enough to be friends with her. I call her, and she's there with no questions asked. I looked out the window and she was already pulling up, and it had been less than two minutes since she hung up the phone. Living a block away definitely had its perks.

"Okay, so where do we even begin to plan this thing? Let's see, do you want to do something like a theme or what?" Aisling started talking too fast with excitement as she pulled out her planner and began to jot ideas down.

"I have no idea. I was hoping you had something in mind. This is kind of your department." I laughed nervously, not even thinking about a theme or even what kind of cake to get.

Do I even pick up a cake for friends, or is that a family function only thing?

"How about a masquerade theme? That way you can be the center of attention but still hide behind your mask if you feel uncomfortable." She winked and I smiled at the idea of being able to hide if I wanted to. She already knew that being the center of anything scared the shit out of me.

All eyes on me? Yikes!

"That sounds perfect, and my dad heated the pool so it's good to go." I looked at her and could already see the wheels turning.

"Done! That way Sadie can bring her craft stuff, and everyone can decorate their mask or be plain jane, which we know who those ones will be." We laughed, knowing that most of the guys wouldn't care about making a fancy mask and will just throw a plain one on. She started planning and talking out loud, but I stopped listening to her because she knew what she was doing and I was just ready for this new year of being eighteen and starting a new beginning. It was time for me to self-love and move on. This was going to be my year, and I was not going to let anything stop me.

"We can set up those twinkling lights across the backyard and set up the snack table over there, and it'll be great, just wait!" Aisling was not wasting any time. She had already started making phone calls. And all I needed to do was pick out an outfit, she said. I told her that I wanted to help, but she would not let me lift a finger. I let her get to it and went up to my room to find something to wear.

A little while later an outfit was picked out, which was not an overly "look at me" type of outfit but comfortable enough for me. I walked down the stairs to head to the backyard to see if she needed any more help with anything. I smiled in amazement when I turned the handle and saw the lights already hung up. There was literally nothing left to do. This woman needed to be a wedding planner in her future.

"Everything is perfect! You truly are the best, Ais, thank you so much!" I knew I didn't have to compliment her, but appreciation was never a bad thing for anyone. She had gone above and beyond, and I wanted to make her happy with my excitement. Plus, the last thing you wanted to do was upset her. She can sort of take some things personally. Maybe that was her flaw in her almost perfect lifestyle. She could be too sensitive if things don't turn out perfectly. Which could be good and bad depending on how you look at it. Appreciation was key to her happiness, plus she really did go above and beyond.

"I know, it totally came out perfect!" She smiled and pulled me close to hug me tight, making me lose my breath for a moment, but I didn't stop her. "Freya, get the lights, let's see them shine." She said, once releasing her death grip on me. I plugged them in and stood back to look, astounded by the view. The lights twinkled, looking extra whimsical, like a fairytale in my own backyard.

"Wow... Thank you, Ais! This is really amazing." She mirrored my smile with excitement.

The party started and everyone who came grabbed a mask to decorate when they walked in the door. A mask-themed party was a perfect idea. It was still me, but I could be hidden if I wanted to be. Besides the "Birthday Queen" sash and crown that Aisling was making me wear to make sure I stood out, as much as I wanted to hide. I should've just worn a spotlight because she was not letting anyone *not* see me tonight.

I looked around and smiled, realizing that the party was going great. Definitely more people than I had planned on made it here, but word spreads fast when Aisling made phone calls. The music was playing, and everyone was having fun and mingling. Every person I walked past said happy birthday and either hugged me or high-fived me for another year in the books. They seemed glad to have me back and mostly stable. It turned out that I was glad we planned this party, it was turning out to be a lot of fun. The only person that was missing for this to be perfect was Jaxon, of course, and Aisling's new undeclared boyfriend Declan Greystone was late. Declan had just moved right outside of Crystal Rock a few weeks ago with his single dad, but she had been spending all of her time with him lately when I'm too busy. I guess he had to work until eleven and then was planning on picking up another friend to bring to the party.

Sometimes in life, a happenstance occurs and in this very moment, the world seemed to be working with one. It was 11:29 p.m. when Declan walked in, with a friend who was someone from out of town too, I guessed, but looked somehow familiar. The time could've just been a coincidence, but either way, my heart skipped a beat, and I could feel my skin starting to get clammy. The air started to thicken before I felt my legs give out, the room started to go dark, and I hit the ground hard.

"What do you think, Aisl? Too much to drink, or is the sight of me just too irresistible?" Declan laughed, but no one else joined him. I could feel a cold compress on my head, making the room feel much colder than how it should've felt on a June night. I felt like my head was clearing and I was coming back to reality but I just needed a minute to focus my thoughts. Then, I heard a loud smack on someone's skin, which was too close to my ear. I assumed Aisling smacked Declan pretty hard. He actually made a whimpering noise, which made me want to laugh out loud at the thought of the big tough guy being taken down by a girl. But I was going to take these extra minutes to just rummage through my brain and decide what just happened.

"Shut up, Declan. I don't know what happened, she just collapsed... and no, she hasn't been drinking. She hasn't drank since, well... since you know when. I told you the other day." Aisling tried to never bring up the accident. And for that, I was thankful. She was there with me through everything and knew how it hurt me. Pain radiated from my arm, bringing me back to reality.

I was very aware of my bruised elbow, which probably saved my head from hitting the ground, so really, the ice on my head wasn't doing much at this point. I could hear a crowd of people chattering around me. I wished everyone would just leave at this point. This was so embarrassing.

What the hell did happen anyway? Was someone spiking drinks around here? Maybe I'm a little hypoglycemic, and I needed something with sugar to eat? I remember eating earlier today, though, but maybe that was it... Declan walked in and then everything was spinning.

I shook my head. *No, I saw something. No, I saw someone.*

Then, with that thought in my head, I heard a new voice join the crowd of gathered high school friends trying to see what happened.

"Hey, is she okay? She fell pretty damn hard?" A boy's voice that I faintly recognized, chimed in. "Here, I've got some fresh ice. I'll sit with her until she comes to."

"Yeah, okay, but I want to know the minute she wakes up. No excuses!" Aisling hesitated before inhaling sharply. "Um, what'd you say your name was?"

"Sorry, I didn't get a chance to introduce myself. I walked in and then all this happened. I'm Jay, Declan's friend." The boy said, while he cleared his throat.

Declan jumped in, "It's fine, you can trust him."

"Okay, well, like I said, come get me the minute she's up, okay?"

"Mmhm." The boy replied.

"Thanks, Jay."

I laid there for a minute longer trying to remember what happened. Plus I was feeling pretty embarrassed that everyone was making a fuss over a little low blood sugar.

I thought about the last few minutes: Declan had walked in with his friend and then I swear I had seen a ghost. But that was impossible... Jaxon died in the accident.

There was an accident, right? Did he have a twin that I never knew about, or am I going crazy?

I had to be crazy; it was an impossible thought. I had to stop overthinking with false hope and just open my eyes and look at the damn boy.

Chapter 4

Reality Check

I waited a minute longer until the chattering became silent and the room felt cleared out. How embarrassing, I thought. I opened my eyes and saw a boy sitting across from me, it wasn't Declan and Aisling was nowhere to be found. Of course, this boy followed the stupid party rules and already had a mask on. He must've grabbed one before reaching me, which meant hopefully, he didn't see me fall after all. His eyes were so familiar. I stared back at him and I could swear that I knew those eyes. He had beautiful blue eyes with a green shimmer to them, hidden behind the masquerade mask. Oddly enough, there was this feeling of comfort, and tonight, I didn't really want him to leave my side.

"She's alive!" He threw his hands up in relief and gave me a quick look over to make sure I was in one whole piece. "I thought for sure we lost a good one tonight, and on her birthday, what a tragedy that would've been." He paused and waited for me to react in any way. When I didn't speak up, he asked, "What happened anyways?"

I swear I know those eyes.

I swallowed hard, trying to find my voice. "Jaxon?" I regretted asking the minute the name floated from my lips. If he had missed me falling, now he would for sure think I was crazy for calling him my dead boyfriend. Well, it was official, the boy looked at me like I was some sort of escape victim from the psych ward.

"Jaxon?" he asked while his eyes squinted with confusion. He looked down at his wrist and back to me with questioning eyes. I felt stupid and as if I couldn't get a good read on his reactions at all.

"Never mind, I must've hit my head pretty hard." I sat up into an awkward position on the floor with my back to the wall and knees bent to my chest. "Yeah, I'm alive." I took a deep breath, trying to clear my head. "I'm so sorry, I have no idea what happened. That's not something I do often, or ever actually." I fidgeted with my fingers, trying to focus my attention on something in real life to not have thoughts running in my head. "What did you say your name was again?" My elbow was throbbing. I had definitely landed with most of my weight on it. I looked down at it, and sure enough, I had a large bruise starting. It was just my luck. When didn't I have an unexplained bruise, scrape, or scab lingering somewhere on my body? Only this time, I knew why my elbow was on fire.

He must've read my thoughts because he quickly handed over the ice. "Here, put this on your arm instead." He smiled. "Oh, and I'm Jay. I live across the street from Declan. I told Aisling I'd sit with you, so she could go and keep the party going. She seemed pretty anxious to get back to the shenanigans." He shrugged. "I mean, I hope that was okay?"

I nodded, thankful for the company. Slightly embarrassed that it happened to be a dark-haired, blue-eyed, broad-shoulder man sitting across from me, though.

"However... I did say I would let her know the minute you came back to reality, so we might want to go and find her." He stood confidently and held his hand out to help me up to walk with him. "That is if you're feeling up to it. I just don't want to get on her bad side, she seems like someone you want to keep happy." He laughed, but honestly, he was right. Aisling was not one you want to be on her bad side.

"Actually, I'm going to sit a little longer, she will understand." I just couldn't get over his eyes. He looked so familiar but different at the same time. "You're not from around here, are you?" It was quiet for a few seconds before he spoke again.

"You know you hit the ground pretty hard. How's your head?"

"Honestly, I feel fine. Just a little embarrassed," I answered truthfully. But I felt like he was avoiding my question.

"And no, I don't live here. I came with Declan. He said that Crystal Rock has more going on than Genoa does. So, I figured I might as well tag along."

I laughed, "Well, sorry to disappoint you, but there's nothing special here. Just the same stuff as any other small town. Everyone knows everyone, and there's one movie theatre, two small family-owned diners, and a few small convenience stores. That's about it. Of course, there's the bluffs to explore and the Mississippi River to fish, but that is it."

He smirked. "Well, you seem a *little* interesting." He pinched his fingers together leaving a few centimeters of space as his eyes studied mine, but I still couldn't get a good read on him.

Who was this boy?

"I'm sorry, you just reminded me of someone that I used to know. I know it's impossible, but I swear you could be his brother." He smiled and that was what finally did it for me. I could feel tears forming in the corner of my eyes and was thankful for the mask to help hide them a little more.

"Well, I'm an only child, kind of like you." I looked at him, confused as to how he would even know that. He seemed to have read my mind again and went on. "Looking at the pictures on the walls here. Your dad must be one proud parent. He has every wall filled."

I smiled, knowing that my dad was proud of me now and he did like to keep me on display. Obviously, we've had some rocky roads, but the walls did have a ridiculous amount of photos of me growing up. I guess I never realized that until you get a view from someone outside of your circle.

I laughed, "Yeah, I guess so. All of his favorite happy moments." I hesitated for a moment, "So, how long have you lived in Genoa?"

"About two years now, we've moved a few times in my lifetime. My parents seem to like it there, though. They feel it's a safe place to live."

"Well, they're not wrong. These small towns along the

river are pretty safe. Not too much ever happens around here, either." I noticed he was wearing a bracelet that looked like one of those survival paracord bracelets, but it almost looked entwined with dried leaves, and was that melted wax? That made no sense. It was summertime and the leaves outside were fresh and green. "That's an odd bracelet, I've never seen anything like that before."

He grabbed the bracelet and turned it around his wrist a few times. "I actually just got it. Kind of ugly, I know. I'll probably toss it after tonight. It's really not doing what I hoped it would." He shrugged and looked me in the eyes. I didn't understand what a piece of jewelry could do for anyone. Maybe he was the crazy one after all. "I do, however, like your necklace that you have. Ten times better than this bracelet for sure." He smiled, and I automatically grabbed the tourmaline pendant and started fidgeting with it. Jaxon had given it to me on my birthday before the accident.

"Thanks, my boyfriend gave it to me." I winced, knowing that I should not have said that. "I mean, my deceased boyfriend gave it to me a few years back. I guess I can't make myself take it off yet. Is that weird?" Feeling sheepish now because my heart had started to race, and there was just too much going on in my head, the last thing I wanted to talk about was a subject that made me sad and anxious.

The pendant was so unique, the way the tourmaline and amethyst crystals were wire wrapped together really made it one of a kind. Jaxon had made it in metals class at school. He said the crystals were supposed to be for protection, healing, calming anxiety, and love, and some other bullshit things. The metals teacher was some hippie lady who was a little cuckoo. She had helped him pick out the crystals and "energized" them with positivity from a full moon. I laughed inappropriately when he had told me, and his face turned serious. Then, I felt bad for laughing, but I didn't believe in any of that kind of stuff. I did really like the pendant, though. I remembered when Jaxon gave it to me, he was so serious about wanting me to wear it like it was some kind of family heirloom that was to be passed down to future generations.

"No, I think that's nice, actually. I'm sorry that happened to you. I'm sure he watches over you and would be happy to know that you are still wearing it," he said, quietly. "Well, let me help you up." He suggested and extended his hand out to me to help me off the floor.

"Thanks, Aisling is honestly probably preoccupied with Declan. She most likely forgot about me." I laughed and went to grab his hand for balance. Our hands touched, and the feeling of electricity shot through my body. The room grew dark again and the feeling of passing out came back. I held my breath and waited for the impact of the ground. Instead, I was taken back to a memory of the night of the accident.

Jaxon was there looking at me driving. Admiring me. I looked carefully out of the window and realized it was happening again. We were going to crash. I was going to lose him again. I could feel him looking at me, so I turned to see him, and instead he grabbed my hand. I could feel his fingers interlocking with mine. There was a bright light illuminating the car which brought my attention from his hand back to the windshield and then to the window where the light was beaming toward us. My body froze knowing that the light was the truck driver's headlights and he was coming toward us. The saddest feeling hit me, knowing there was nothing I could do to make it stop. Jaxon's hand felt like it was burning mine like a lightning strike had just occurred between us and my hand was on fire. I needed to let it go before the rest of us caught fire. I looked back to our hands interlocked and ripped my hand away before we ignited.

My eyes flew open, and we were back in my home, back to my birthday party.

What the hell was that?

Jay was looking at me with nervous eyes. Like a deer in headlights, only it was the truck driver's headlights ruining my life and taking Jaxon's all over again. I studied his eyes, and something in them scared me.

Did he feel that too? Did he see what I just saw?

His uneven breathing matched mine, our hands were no longer touching. He seemed nervous, or maybe anxious, and with that, Declan came walking into the room a little too quickly. Both Jay and I were standing awkwardly about six feet away from each other, confused. Declan's entrance broke our attention away from each other, and he turned toward him while I stayed staring hard at Jay.

"Hey, bud, we have to go. Sorry to pull you away, but my dad just called, and he wants me home right now," Declan exclaimed. "I don't know what he's bitching about, but we have to go." Declan looked at Jay and threw his arms up in a frustrated motion. Aisling came trailing right behind him with a sad puppy face, knowing that he was leaving way earlier than she was hoping for. Her mood changed when she looked at me and saw me.

"Freya, you're up! That's so great, are you feeling better?" She smiled was she examined me.

I didn't know what I was feeling, but I felt like maybe it was time to get some fresh air outside, just her and me. This boy was unexpected, and tonight was turning into an emotional mindfuck. I leaned my head down to break my stare from the boy, shaking my head and trying to get my thoughts clear.

"Yeah, I'm going to head outside, though, get some air. Nice meeting you, Jay; bye, Declan." I walked away before anyone could say anything more. I needed air, and the Wisconsin June night breeze was calling my name. I pushed through the back door faster than I meant to and it slammed open, letting my lungs collect the cool air as quickly as possible. My deep inhale of air hurt for a second before opening my lungs and finally letting the breath help cool me down from the inside.

Aisling came walking out behind me and dropped down to sit next to me by the pool. We sat quietly for a minute with our feet dangling in the water. People started to leave without making a scene as Aisling waved them off. She put her arm around my shoulders, pulling me toward her. It honestly felt nice and comforting to have her next to me. I looked at her to find her eyes staring back at me, worriedly.

"What happened in the house? You seem sad all of a sudden."

I swallowed hard. "Ais, I swear that Jay kid looked so much like Jaxon, and I just couldn't stop thinking about the past." I started to feel the waterworks coming, and Aisling saw them too. She hugged me tighter and said how sorry she was. Obviously, if it was Jaxon, she would have acknowledged that. Maybe it was time for the party to end and go to bed. Aisling must've been thinking the same thing, so she got up and walked with me to my room, waving goodbye at the others.

"Freya, I hope that your birthday wasn't a complete screwup because of Declan bringing his friend. I had never met him before. When he walked in, he went straight to the mask table, so I didn't even get to get a vibe on him."

I half smiled. "No, it's fine really. I think I'm just getting tired, to be honest. Thank you for everything you did today. I love you."

"I love you more!" She said, smiling wide before hugging me hard and helping me get under the covers like a child and leaving me to my thoughts.

That night my dreams were far too vivid but seemed to be a time-lapse where one dream began before another one interferred.

I was driving alone down Jaxon's old road and pulled up to his house, but the house was dark and didn't seem right. The house looked old, too old for our century. It didn't look like anyone had lived in it for years. Those shutters were dark and broken, hanging halfway off his upstairs bedroom window. The window was broken like someone had used the house as target practice with rocks. It almost looked charred, like it had been through a fire. This was not how his actual house looked. Then, from inside the house, there seemed to be this bright little orb that started to grow and almost became too bright to look at. I turned the car off and started walking toward the window to see what was happening. The orb was growing and started to outline a man's figure. I got to the window and realized the orb was now a full glowing man who had his back to me. My brain was telling me to run, but of course, I was dreaming, and my dream brain thought I was invincible, telling me to investigate further. I started walking up the front porch stairs, and the light from inside faded. I went to open the door, and before I could touch it, the door flung open, and Jaxon was standing on the inside of the house with his eyes meeting mine with sadness and longing. I gasped, and without hesitation, I flew into his arms. He caught me and wrapped his arms around me, kissing my head, which trailed down to my neck and landed on my lips. Then, Jaxon pulled away and looked piercingly into my wet eyes. "Find me!"

I looked at him confused. "I don't understand, I'm with you now. Find you where?"

"Freya, you need to wake up, you have to come find me. Freya, wake up!"

Then he started to fade, and I realized my dream was ending and another beginning.

I was running down my normal path, except the path was covered in dying vines and thorns, and with every step I took, the vines were enclosing around me. I looked down the path, and at the end, there was another orb glowing, and it was drawing me closer. Curiosity was getting the best of me, and I kept pushing through the vines and thorns when the orb transformed into a person. Jaxon appeared again, only he was looking away from me and at another woman. He looked terrified.

Who would be scaring him on this path?

He glanced back at me and screamed, "Freya, run!" Then, with the fear in his eyes and the trust that I have for him, I turned and started running, but was confused. I took one glance back, and they were fighting, but it wasn't a normal brawl of fists. She literally threw fire at him and then another ball of fire was coming my way. I stared in disbelief before my legs took off, and I was running as fast as I could. I tried to scream but couldn't because my throat was on fire, my voice almost gone. I turned quickly while I ran to see behind the flame coming my way. I saw her. I saw the woman that was causing the fire.

I whispered with what voice I had left, "Isadora?"

I woke up trying to say her name out loud, but instead, was covered in a pool of sweat and my throat was too dry to speak. I reached across my bed for anything near me to grab a hold of to make sure that I was awake and back to reality.

Chapter 5

This Is What Crazy Looks Like

J ournal: June 5th~

Well, that was a weird night. Welcome to age 18, Freya, here's to hoping this year is better than the past. First off, I am proud of myself for day two of this journal entry stuff, and secondly, I met a boy last night that brought back some memories. Ironically, Isadora was a fire-throwing witch bitch in my dream, which isn't too far from the truth, I'm sure. Jaxon was in my dreams, though, and that hasn't happened in a long time. I know they say that when people pass away they don't usually show up in our dreams, but in other's not as close to them. Maybe the dead can't get through the dream connections of those closest to them

because of restrictions of tampering or something. If that even makes sense. So, when he showed up in my dreams last night, it was a surprise, but then it turned into a nightmare. It was all wrong. He was a glowing orb wanting me to find him and then he was fighting fire telling me to run. So, that was weird...

I don't know what to think. To be honest, it all started with that boy last night. He was just so familiar. When he helped me up from the floor, after making me fall, there was just something that seemed natural. The tingling in my hands was weird, though. Must've pinched a nerve in my arm when I fell or something. Either way, I think I want to see him again. I just have this feeling inside me that is telling me to go see him. So, I think that will be on the agenda today. On another note, the next time I see Isadora I'm going to picture her as a fire-breathing dragon. Well, that's it for now. Call me crazy, but I'm going to go see Jay.

I called Aisling and asked her if she was seeing Declan today. He was working now, but would be done around three, and she was going to head over to see him then. I told her that I wanted to talk to Jay, who lives across the street from him. She hesitated, being protective but trusted my judgment. She said I could tag along and just take her car to the stores if he wasn't home or if I chickened out.

It seemed like days away until three o'clock, when in reality it was only a few hours. I had no idea what I was planning on saying to him. I just felt like I needed to see him and maybe explain that last night was not a normal night for me.

I stopped shuffling my books around on the shelf and shook my head. *Okay, I have re-organized this bookshelf twice now, first by the author and now by color. That's it, I need to go for a run.*

I needed to clear my head and figure out what I was going to say. I grabbed my running shoes and threw my hair up in a messy bun, while walking toward the door.

I ran down my normal path, where there were no vines or thorns anywhere. It was June and everything was green and blooming. The sun was shining, and everything seemed normal. I felt so stuck in my thoughts, that I barely registered that I was running down Jaxon's old road. Coming up quickly on his abandoned home, my heart started quickening, no longer in rhythm with my breathing. Even being close to his home started to trigger so many memories of our past that I wanted to turn around, but I had to see if it's the same house I remembered or if it was like the dream house that I saw.

As I made it to the front of the house, I slowed and decided to stop running to actually examine it. It was surely abandoned still. Nobody had purchased the house since they moved. It was a house that had been passed down in their family for years so who knows, maybe they still owned it and just didn't want to live in it. I understood that. Memories could almost be more painful to be reminded of than thinking of a future without that loved one. Looking at the house, there was absolutely nothing out of the ordinary. No bright lights, no old, damaged foundation. Everything was normal. Good, I thought, as I checked my watch. As it was time to head back home and shower.

Not long after, Aisling pulled up to the house as I ran down the stairs. I grabbed the house keys and locked the door behind me as I hopped down the stairs and jumped in her car. I inhaled heavily as we took off for Genoa.

"Are you going to ask him on a date or what?" She asked me.

I shrugged. "We will see what happens." I laughed, knowing that's the last thing on my mind. I just wanted to see him on a clear new day with a semi-rested head.

"Okay, but if you end up needing to head back home, just take the car. Declan can bring me back home, or I'll spend the night, which is no big deal either way." She glanced at me. I could see the worry in her eyes. "Sound good?"

I nodded. "Thanks, lady. Yes, sounds good."

The Mississippi River was calming to watch as we drove. The bluffs on the right side and the river on the left created such a narrow path, but it's the only path to take to get north. I really had so many questions, and if anything, Jay seemed like a nice enough guy to at least talk to me again. At least, I hoped so. We pulled up to Declan's house when he walked outside to greet Aisling, his eyebrows furrowed when he saw me with her. She must not have told him that I was coming with her, but I was definitely not planning on being the third wheel.

"Hey, babe, I didn't realize Freya was coming too. I thought we were gonna watch movies alone in the bedroom while my dad is away." He looked at me and back to her, seeming frustrated or disappointed. It was hard to tell which, with his tight jawline.

I laughed. "Don't worry. I'm not staying, I was just coming to town with her and stealing her car." He exhaled quickly, with relief. "I actually was hoping to talk to your friend Jay. I wanted to apologize for last night." Declan's eyes grew bigger as I continued to talk. "I was hoping you could show me which house was his. I know he said he lives across the street." Feeling a little bold now for coming out all this way to talk to a boy that didn't have a good first impression of me seemed pretty stupid now.

"Uh, yeah... Let me text him quick, and let him know." He grabbed his phone from his back pocket and started typing quickly.

Ding-Ding-Ding. His phone became a rapid firing machine as I turned around and looked at the far apart houses.

"I'll just walk over, let you guys have your space." I turned and started walking across the street. While Declan was still looking at his phone with his fingers flying across the keys before realizing that I was already walking up the steps of the house directly across the street. These houses were not side by side so it was obvious that this would be the house.

"Freya, hold up, wait—" Declan was cut off by the sound of the doorbell.

Footsteps on the other side of the door were followed by Mrs. Oakes answering the door with a gasp. She became very pale with a look of shock running across her face. And I'm sure my expression matched hers.

"Freya!" Mrs. Oakes practically screamed my name.

"What are you doing here? I mean, honey, how are you? It's been so long." Confused, staring at her in disbelief, then I glanced down the hallway behind her, where a young man stood staring back at me. I knew that young man.

It was Jay...

No, that was definitely Jaxon.

He was older, but it was him. There was no mistaking that. Jaxon was alive and breathing. He was here and he was alive... He'd only been a town away this whole time.

Wait, he's only been a town away this whole time and never came to see me? I believed he was dead.... There was a funeral. What the fuck was going on?

I turned quickly on my heel and ran down the stairs, across the street to Aisling's car, fumbling with the keys that had way too many keychains on them, to try and start the ignition. I dropped them. Then dug around the floor and successfully found them with my fingertips. I tried to start the car again. Only this time I was able to find the ignition.

Got it!

Declan started running toward the car with Jay or Jaxon or whoever the hell he was, trailing fast behind him as Aisling was standing on the front porch with her hand over her mouth as if she had just seen a ghost. I glanced one more time in the review mirror before putting my foot to the pedal and took off.

Chapter 6

What the Hell Is Happening

Aisling finally stopped calling after thirty-six missed phone calls and too many texts to count. I just needed to breathe and be alone for a bit.

Jaxon is alive, and for that, I am so grateful, but why would he not come and see me? Why would he wait this long? He let me think I was the reason he was dead, this whole time...

My eyes welled with tears. None of this was making sense, and at this point, nothing could make me understand this sick joke. My phone started to ring again, which if I wasn't feeling so numb, it would've made me jump. I glanced at the phone, expecting to see Aisling's name again. Instead a different number came across the screen, I shook my head and set it down, knowing it was probably a telemarketer or a scammer letting me know my car warranty is about to expire for the car I don't even own. It finally stopped, then rang again with the same number.

Scammers were persistent these days.

Decline.

I heard the gravel rumble as a car pulled up behind me. I was sitting quietly on a rock at the top of Wyalusing State Park, at the highest bluff looking over the Mississippi River that I could find, to come and think alone. I didn't bother turning around because no one would be able to see me from this spot. This had been my thinking space for years, and no one ever came here but me. Then, I heard the pebbles falling as someone unexpectedly climbed the bluff by me.

"Freya, please, can we talk?" It was Jaxon's voice. "I'm coming up." He was almost to the top and pulled himself up to sit next to me. He was careful not to get too close, to not invade my personal space, or maybe he was afraid that I'd push him over the edge for lying to me. Truthfully, I was still debating on it.

"You have to at least hear me out," he started. "Please, Freya, just let me explain things, then you can decide if you never want to see me again."

"Never see you again? An hour ago, I thought you were dead, and I have been trying to accept that for almost two years now." I yelled and anger filled inside me. "What could you have to say that would ever explain why you would leave the person who was supposed to be your everything?" I didn't know if I was in shock, or still numb but one thing was certain, not a single tear was being shed. Which scared me a little. I just felt very confused and very angry.

"Okay, well, I didn't know if I could be close to you after the accident."

Immediately I started to shake with emotions coming to meet the surface. The numbness was disappearing and my anxiety came full force. "You act like the accident was on purpose. I would never have done anything to hurt you."

"No, Freya, it's not that." He looked back at me with hurt.

"Then, what is it?" I screamed. My throat felt scratchy, and my voice started to crack.

He inhaled slowly and exhaled fast. "My parents made me leave after that night, they told me it wasn't safe to be around you anymore. They said that if I were to be near you, then I would end up killing you."

I laughed out of anger. "Killing me? What the hell, Jaxon? I know I had a spiraling after the divorce, but come on, I just needed time. My dad and I both just needed time. We're fine now." I couldn't believe that he would even think that going away during my worst moment was going to keep me safe.

"Do you not know anything yet? Did *she* really not come and explain things?"

"Did *who* explain what to me?" I asked, getting more irritated.

He stood up carefully on the boulder and looked out toward the river. "My mom was supposed to come and see you after the accident and tell you everything. If she didn't come, then she lied to me too," he said with a strained voice.

"Your family packed up and moved the week after your accident, and I haven't heard from them since. Except for the yearly Christmas greeting card that was addressed specifically to my dad and only him," I said in disbelief.

Did he really not know?

He sat back down and I finally turned toward Jaxon, and he looked as if he was going to be the one who would break, sadness filled his eyes. He looked as if he truly did not know that I had been left in the dark all alone. He looked back at me and started to tear up. Every emotion I had felt over the last two years came rushing back, and I started sobbing uncontrollably. Without hesitation, Jaxon grabbed me and pulled me closer to him. There it was again, that electric feeling. All of a sudden, I was no longer at the state park, instead I was seeing Jaxon after the accident. But it was not at a scene that I recall ever being at.

Jaxon was at home with his family a little bruised and banged up, but alive. He was yelling. "Mom, I can't leave her! I won't leave her like this, she needs to know what she is! I'm not going anywhere until I know she is going to be okay."

Mrs. Oakes calmly said, "I will go talk to her, I will tell her everything. Sweetheart, go upstairs and start packing. We need to leave by the end of the week, otherwise you will end up getting her and you killed."

The sound of the rushing river brought me back to reality, as my eyes tried to focus back on the view of the present. Jaxon was looking at me confused.

"Did you see that too?" I questioned him, scared that these time lapses kept happening to me. "I saw you, but it was after the accident... I think." I felt my voice start to quiver as I said it out loud, feeling crazy. "It was almost like a dream, or maybe a memory of yours? I don't know what the hell is going on with me."

He asked with worried eyes, "You're having visions? When did they start?"

"Visions? That's the second time that's happened. The first time, Jay, I mean you grabbed my hand at the party. I saw the car accident scene all over again. Only it was like new memories of it, or it was more clear." I paused, thinking about what I just said out loud. "Then, just now, I saw you again, but this time, I physically wasn't there with you to even know that memory." The confusion grew and my stomach started to turn. He looked at me with questions that I didn't have answers for. If it wasn't for his arms being wrapped around me, then I think I would've unraveled. It felt nice, it felt almost normal to have him next to me again. I had longed for this feeling for so long, this moment was everything that I have dreamt of having again. I just didn't understand how this could even be possible. An hour ago, he was just a distant memory.

"Jaxon, what the hell is happening to me?" I asked, feeling like I was going to have a panic attack. "I think I'm losing my mind." He didn't let go of me and waited for my breathing to become even and slow before he started to talk again.

"Freya, there's no sane way to say this without you thinking I'm crazy. Hell, I didn't even believe it at first." He hesitated before continuing. "Our families come from a long line of witches, and this whole thing has been a huge misunderstanding." My body froze at the word 'witch'. This was not going down a normal path. I laughed, wiping the tears away. Staring at him, waiting for him to join me. When he didn't, anger blossomed in me.

"You're going to pretend that some mystical magic bull-shit is the reason you have been gone for this long, making me think I killed you? Are you fucking kidding me?" I yelled, louder than I meant to. As my voiced echoed through the bluffs.

"My mom was supposed to come and explain this all to you." He hesitated, watching me closely. "Well, actually, your mom was supposed to be the one to tell you all of this, but she thought it would be better to leave with a clean slate. She must've hoped your powers would never be triggered." He waited for a reaction that didn't come. "She was obviously wrong. I didn't know about any of this magic stuff until about a month before our accident. It's all real. I don't know how else to say this."

My eyes bulged at the sound of Alex being brought up. "Wait, what do you mean my mom was supposed to talk to me? I haven't heard from her since the divorce," I asked with more annoyance now. "An even better question is... What magic are you talking about? Witches are not even real. So, if that's your story, then we are done talking right now."

He grabbed my arms and forced me to look at him. "Freya, spell casting, fire-throwing, hexing, crystal wearing, full moons and superstitions, all of it. Witches are very real, and you and I are both born from these bloodlines."

I laughed. "Right, and Alex is a witch? More like a bitch, in my opinion," I said with bitterness, thinking of the last time I saw her. "This is bullshit."

"Well, she definitely didn't handle things the right way with you," he said, knowingly. "But I guess neither did my mom."

He released my arms and we sat quietly for a minute while I tried to process this nonsense.

"Okay, say for a brief moment that I believe you. Does my dad know too?" I asked, still doubting every word.

"Not that I know of, he's just an ordinary dad. He doesn't have a Mark that I know of."

"What kind of Mark would that be?" My head began to throb as my reality of normal was exploding. I wanted to believe that there was a legit explanation for his disappearance. But magic was not one of them. Then again, these weird visions were blowing my mind, and maybe magic would be the only explanation. I wasn't sure what to believe, or if I was dreaming.

Am I dreaming? Will he still be with me when I wake up from this, or will he be gone again?

Jaxon grabbed his shirt collar and pulled it down from his left shoulder and showed me his infinity-looking birthmark. It almost looked like a light-colored henna tattoo that should've been long gone by now. "This appeared one morning after I started having nightmares of death. I woke up in a sweat and went to take a shower and saw it out of the corner of my eye. My mom just happened to be walking past the bathroom door and got a glance at it too. That's when she sat me down and started explaining." He watched every inch of my expression. "I thought it was all bullshit too, but then she showed me stuff that couldn't be explained."

"Your birthmark," I said, thinking of the journal's symbol that drew me to it. The infinity symbol did remind me of him. "That's odd. I wrote that down in my journal, there was something about it that I felt brought me closer to you." I looked at him as a smile started to form at the corner of his lips. "That kind of makes a little sense now." I couldn't believe my mind was letting me believe this at all, but something in my heart said to listen to him.

"Do you want me to keep going, or do you want some space up here? I know it's a lot to take in. You have just been kept in the dark for too long now. You deserve to know everything," Jaxon said with a heavy sigh.

"How did you get your birthmark? I mean, do I have one too?" I didn't recall any birthmark appearing randomly on me.

"Well, it's not a birthmark. We call them our Mark. We are not born with them, but every witch from our bloodlines has another witch that is bound to them, and we receive them when we are supposed to. There are not many of our kind left. We are a rare type of witch, or warlock, that has been on the verge of extinction for the last few decades now." He stared at me cautiously, waiting to see if I was going to push him off the rock. When I didn't say anything, he continued. "We have a second lifeline, or an Anchor, as we like to call them. We get second chances as long as our Anchor is still alive." He looked out toward the Mississippi and I took a minute to study his new, older features that I used to know and he let out another exhale. "To get your Mark, unfortunately, either you or your Anchor have to have a near-death experience. Which then makes an identical Mark appear on both witches. If both witches are killed within a small time frame of the other, then both will die." He looked back at me with the hope that any of this was making sense. "I know, it sounds crazy, but our car accident is an example." I looked at him, to warn him to speak with caution on that subject. "How do you think I'm still alive? How do you think you're still alive? That accident should have killed us both, but somehow, here we are."

"So, I'm your Anchor?" I asked, doubtfully. "Shouldn't that accident have killed us both?" I tried to make sense of this hypothetical realm he was trying to have me live in.

"See, that's what I couldn't figure out, either, then my mom explained that to me. We were holding hands when that happened. I saw the truck coming, and I must've somehow transferred a portion of my own magic to you as a shield to protect you, which is why she said we had to leave town. She said that the closer we were to each other, then we wouldn't be able to both survive a magic transfer like that. So, we moved to keep us both alive, or so she thought." He paused and in that very moment.

I panicked. Fear of him sitting next to me and he could be slowly killing us both. *If* this was real. "Wait, then why come to my house yesterday and risk it?"

"That's where all of this started to make more sense. You don't have my Mark." He shook his head and started to smile. "We have different Anchors, and it wasn't until a few weeks ago when Declan and his dad moved in that we realized that he and I share them. That's when I realized my mom had been lying to me, which I still can't figure out why." He shrugged. "Declan and I came up with a plan. He made me that ugly bracelet that was supposed to keep me unrecognizable to those that knew me. A simple glamour spell. I wanted to come, to check on you and make sure that you were happy without stirring up emotions if you had moved on or anything. Problem was that you knew me right away. The bracelet didn't work on you, but it worked on Ais, and that wasn't supposed to happen. At first, when you fainted, I thought my mom was right, and that us being close was a mistake. Until I realized why you fainted. It was because you had literally just seen a ghost." He stopped talking, and I stared back at him in disbelief. I thought literally nothing could explain him being so close and alive without me knowing, but a part of me started to believe him. Otherwise, he was going through a great deal to make it sound real. "Freya, I'm so sorry. For everything. If I could take the time back, I would. I never wanted to leave you. I thought I was saving your life."

I wanted to believe him. I wanted this to be real. But my doubts were twirling. "Can I just have a minute to wrap my head around this?" I asked. Thinking of different possibilities, in this unnatural, magical world. I waited a minute or so to try and process little by little. "What about old age and natural causes? Does that mean if your Anchor is still alive you come back? That's kind of fucked up."

"No, if one dies of natural causes, then it's just a normal final breath, but if it's something supernatural, then your Anchor lifeline kicks in. So, our accident included magic between us."

I nodded as if I understood any of this. I looked back out toward the river and then back at him.

"Jaxon, if it is really you, then this is all a little insane. The word 'magic' still has me kind of creeped out honestly. It's just a lot all at once. I just feel like I'm going to wake up, and all of this will be a dream or a nightmare. I haven't decided which one it is yet."

He laughed softly and shook his head. "No, I get it. It's a lot. I'll go down by the car to give you some space to think. Take your time." He awkwardly stood up, not knowing how he was supposed to leave this moment. I just nodded for him to let me think, alone. He understood, and climbed down.

I took a deep breath in and felt my lungs rattle with too much oxygen and exhaled slowly. I looked out to the Mississippi and tried to clear my head. Jaxon was alive. That was not a dream. He had been living a town away this entire time. Declan and Jaxon were witches. *Or do I call them warlocks?* I didn't know what the correct term for them was. This shit was not in my vocabulary yesterday. And Declan was the reason that Jaxon was alive because he is his Anchor.

So, I'm a witch too, supposedly, and I need to find my Mark to find my Anchor? How does life go back to normal after all this? Is Jaxon going to stick around now that I know this?

I had so many questions, and I honestly didn't have the energy to battle everything inside my head. I took another deep breath and looked out toward the water, watching the sun setting. The way the painted orange sky looked in the far-off distance was so breathtaking that time actually could stand still. Everything seemed normal and serene for a brief moment until I started to think about the recent events. This new reality was a lot to take in. I still didn't understand half of it, and that was going to take some time.

I whispered in the peaceful scenery, "Here's to being eighteen and new beginnings, I guess. When I said I wanted to start fresh, I didn't think it would involve supernatural beings."

I think I just needed some sleep to process everything.

Minutes passed as the sun had fully set and I looked back to see Jaxon waiting for me in his car. Aisling's car was gone, Jaxon must've called Declan and Aisling to come pick up her car so he could drive me home tonight. I took a deep breath as I jumped down from the boulder. As I reached his car, he hopped out and opened the passenger door of his car. Now that is the same old Jaxon that I remembered. Chivalry used to be his thing and I see that hadn't changed, which made me smile for the first time. I paused and looked up at him as I made it to the door. I just stared at him for a moment, still in disbelief that this was real. I touched his face and ran my fingers to his shoulders and down his arms, squeezing him a little tighter than I meant to. But I needed to feel that he is real and that my brain is not having hallucinations. I leaned in, breathing in his woodsy scent that I remembered and asked him quietly, "Will you stay with me tonight? I just don't want to be alone right now."

"I was hoping you would ask me that." He smiled, his contagious smile, and it was all I needed to realize that everything was going to be okay.

Chapter 7

Time to Conquer This Witch Stuff

The sun was just starting to peek through the blinds when I looked over and smiled, realizing that he stayed with me and was still laying beside me with his arms wrapped around me. Exactly in the same position we had laid down in last night. Honestly, that had been the best sleep I've had in a very long time. No dreams, no nightmares, and no waking up mid-sleep in a panic. Just blissful sound sleep, with Jaxon. I turned gently around to look at him just to make sure he was still real and that he was still with me. He was still sleeping, but as soon as I turned toward him, he started to stir.

"Thank you for staying with me," I whispered, not caring if he actually heard me or not. He looked so peaceful and so much like himself, only a little older, a little more mature, and a little more of a manly man. But at this very moment, everything was okay. I could lay here all day just to make up for the lost time, but I knew my dad would be coming home today from his fishing trip. I had no idea how to explain why there's a boy in my bed. A boy that he would recognize and may have a heart attack seeing.

"I told you I would stay," Jaxon woke and whispered back to me. I blushed knowing that he *had* heard me earlier. I rubbed his arm and stared at him in disbelief.

"You being alive, real or fake?" I asked, still doubting myself.

"Real," he laughed.

"I'm a witch... real or fake?" As if hearing it again was going to make it any more real.

"Very real," he said, pulling me back tight to him. With his body behind me, he started to kiss my shoulder and up to my neck, cautiously but with need. I didn't stop him so he kept exploring. I relaxed when I realized there were no electric visions showing up, only new excitement from feeling him close to me. His hand inched from my back around to my stomach, and he flipped me so my face was an inch away from his. I could feel the heat radiating off his lips, grazing mine. I looked up at his blue-green eyes, and they were looking back at me with such desire. Before I realized what I was doing, I grabbed the back of his head, and our lips locked. I started kissing him fiercely, and he didn't hold back either. Every part of my body wanted him, but the fear of getting close and losing him again was terrifying. His body started pushing hard against mine with so much need. I grabbed his shirt and started to pull it over his head before hesitating. When I touched his torso, I realized he had so much more muscle than I remembered. My eyes moved to his stomach and my fingers touched for another reality check. He paused and looked at me with a smile, reaching back to kiss my lips, but I stopped him. Realizing that it had been a long time between us. Fear of moving too fast came back to mind, then the thought of: *what if he leaves again?* My mind was still being cautious and a little distant. The want was there, but I needed more time to bring my guard down.

"Is everything okay?" he asked between panting breaths.

"I just don't want this to move too fast," I said. "It's just that we've lost so much time together. I just want to get to know you again," I added while catching my breath and feeling stupid for taking it this far. I felt my face flush with embarrassment.

"I get it, can we at least keep snuggling and maybe kissing?" He innocently asked.

I smiled, because even though so much time had passed, he was still the same sweet, gentle, and sexy man I remembered. I nodded my head in agreement and went back to kissing him.

Having him lying here with me again felt like nothing had changed. Except the obvious, that everything had changed. All I knew was that I was not going to lose him again.

It was time for me to get up, I looked over and he had fallen back to sleep so I was going to take advantage of this time, to shower and put a little makeup on after. Maybe just some eyeliner and mascara to make me feel a little pretty. Then, I knew I should really write in my journal. Only today my journal entry was going to be a happy, but bizarre one.

. . .

Journal: June 6th ~

Life can be weird and full of surprises, but today is going to be a good day. I found out some crazy news this weekend. I keep looking back to make sure he doesn't disappear. Jaxon is here with me. I'm not hallucinating, he really is here with me. He's alive and has only been a town away. Talk about a small world, I guess. My heart is full right now with him here. Not sure how to explain this to my dad when he sees him, but I guess we can figure that out later. I'm just enjoying this for a bit without all the complications that come along with finding him again. One of those complications includes me finding out something crazy. I'm a witch, not entirely sure what that really includes. I hope I don't have to do any sacrifices or curses or anything because I feel like that might not be my thing. Jaxon is going to have to fill me in on that part a little more. I guess I'm having visions, which is kind of freaky. I don't really know how they happen or why, but they are like little glimpses of the past. One was of my past, and the other time was of Jaxon's. Nothing happened when we were laying together through the night though, so I'm not really sure how they happen. Well, I guess it's time to conquer all this witch stuff and start being a magical badass, or I might be labeled as that crazy person.

"Hey, what are you doing way over there? Come back to bed. I'm not done snuggling you," Jaxon yelled at me from across the room. "I've got a lot of time to make up."

I smiled. "I'm coming back, geez, I'm trying to keep up my routine that I've made without you."

"Ouch, that hurts." His brows furrowed and his lower lip turned down into a pouty expression.

"I'm kidding, well kidding-ish. I have a new writing thing. I'm on day three and kind of want to keep it going. Although, I don't know how much witch stuff I should be writing down unless it's for one of those magic books." I laughed, still having a hard time believing this.

"You mean a grimoire?" he asked, in a know-it-all manner. When my brows furrowed in confusion, he continued. "It's a book of magic passed through generations. Don't even worry about that now, though. We will get to that." He smiled. "Hey, and get used to the "W" word stuff being said because I found your Mark while you were sleeping. Now it's official. I just haven't seen one like yours before. It's different."

"What? Where is it?" I stood, circling my own body in the mirror trying to see what he found.

"Here, stand still... let me show you." He tugged me closer to him, turning me sideways toward the mirror and lifted my shirt to the middle of my torso, then ran his fingers to the small of my back. And there it was. The lightest shade of beige that's almost too light to see, blended with my skin almost too perfectly. It was shaped like a symbol I didn't recognize, either.

"It looks kind of like a Unalome symbol with something else connected to it, off to the top here, but it's weird because it starts to fade here." He pointed to the fading point of the Mark. "It's only halfway developed. I've never seen anything like that before. Usually, it's a full symbol, and your Anchor will have an identical one. Yours is different from what I've seen in books."

"Go figure, I'd be an incomplete witch of all things." We both laughed.

His hand was still on the small of my back, when I looked up to meet his gaze with a half smile. He gently caressed my back.

"Freya, you look pretty perfect to me." My full smile came out to shine. I knew I was far from perfect, but today, I was going to take the compliment. Today was going to be a good day. And he promised to take me to an open field and show me some tricks.

We drove up to the bluffs and came to the most secluded area we could find. I told him I'm ready to see what this witch stuff was all about. I guess seeing would be believing in this case. Jaxon kept driving right onto a dirt path that looked like it had been abandoned years prior due to the greenery growing through, it was very unkept. We drove to the end of the road and had to walk the rest of the way to the open field. Nothing too special about the place, except that it was quiet. My dad would be home later today, and I wanted to be home when he got back there to show him that I could handle things with him gone for a weekend. Plus, I truly missed him and was ready for him to be back.

"Okay, where are the wands and cloaks?" I laughed. "Come on, I've seen *Harry Potter* enough times to know that I need my wand to choose me as its partner or whatever."

"No wands." Jaxon laughed and looked at me skeptically. Maybe he was questioning why he came back to me in the first place if I wouldn't take this seriously. "Just a lot of practice from within."

"I mean, it's just weird. Wouldn't I know if I had some kind of magical powers? Like, wouldn't I have accidentally broken a window or started a fire or something over the years?"

"Wait, have you? Maybe in your sleep?" He smirked and started to laugh. "Freya, it's not that simple. You have to be connected to your magic, you have to feel it within yourself."

"Well, then let's see something little. Something that proves to me that this is all real." I pressured.

"Okay, maybe you want to sit down for this? I don't need you passing out on me again," he smirked.

I rolled my eyes and sat down cross-legged and waited. He grabbed a yellow dandelion and lifted it calmly until it reached eye level. He furrowed his eyebrows, and by the time I blinked, the yellow weed transformed into the seedlings of a wish. My jaw dropped and my eyes felt like they were going to fall out of their sockets.

What the hell did I just see?

Jaxon was looking at me curiously. "You know, legend has it that if you can blow all the seedlings off in one breath, then the person you love will love you back." His eyes were still locked on mine as he went to blow them into the air. As he blew the seeds into the sky, they started circling like a mini-tornado and danced in the sky in front of me.

I was speechless but swallowed quickly before throwing a snarky remark back at him. "You missed a few." He laughed with me and my freak-out moment passed. He wasn't lying to me after all. "I, uh...um, can you do that again? I just wasn't expecting *that* and think I need to see it again."

He laughed. "Yes, I told you I would show you as much as I know. Doesn't mean I'm perfect at this stuff yet, but I'm learning. I'm still considered a newbie to my family. You see, my family specializes in Earth magic. We can call our magic from anything growing from the ground basically. Being in nature gives us more energy to use without feeling drained."

"Well, that was amazing! Seriously, I mean it's still hard to wrap my head around this idea, but I think I can definitely get used to this stuff. So, what kind of witch does that make me?" I asked as my imagination wandered.

He shrugged. "Honestly, I have no idea. But we might as well try and find out. I can give you some small stuff to try to test yours out."

With that being said, my phone buzzed. I looked down and saw Aisling's name cross the screen. I never called her back after leaving her yesterday. I sighed, heavily, feeling like such a bad friend. I just felt like so much had happened and was still happening that I didn't think about her and what I could even say to her about all of this? I had never kept a secret from her, and I didn't want to start now. I wondered if Declan had filled her in or if she knew anything.

"Hey, it's Aisling calling. I need to talk to her. But does she know about any of this 'witch' stuff?" I asked.

"She doesn't know any of this. Declan made it clear that he didn't want to tell her unless they were going to become a long-lasting thing."

I nodded, unsure how I felt about her knowing this either. "Okay, and what about you? Would Declan have filled her in on that whole thing?" I looked down at my phone, vibrating.

Aisling texted after leaving a voicemail.

Aisling: LISTEN to my voicemail NOW! Then call me back!!!!! Love you <3

I went to my inbox and found her message lingering there, waiting to be played.

My own panic grew.

What was it going to say?

VOICEMAIL: 1 NEW MESSAGE
AISLING

I hesitated and then pressed play with a shaking finger.

"Damn it, Freya! You do not leave me with the look of fear and confusion on your face before speeding off, in my car, without me! I am your best friend and can handle absolutely anything with you, but I cannot let you handle things this big on your own. I know that Jaxon is alive. It took me some time to understand why his parents would leave and want a fresh start with his amnesia and all. But, man, that was extremely harsh of them to keep him from you. Anyway, Declan told me that seeing you triggered his memories, and all of a sudden, he remembered everything. Thank God he is alive, which is an absolute miracle. I am just so happy that you can have this happy ending if you want it. I love you, girl! Call me back, I just want to make sure you're okay. Oh, and I drove by your house looking for you. There's a car parked in the driveway. It looks lik— BEEP... End of message."

So, an amnesia story. That's what Declan was going with?

That wasn't half bad. Maybe he was smarter than I first thought he was. Well, not every guy Aisling had dated had good looks and brains. He might just be a keeper. I decided to call her back and of course, she answered immediately. I stuck with the amnesia story and how Jaxon and I had spent the night together and were still catching up on lost time. The more I thought about it, the story should actually work for my dad too, which would be a good thing since I didn't like the idea of lying to the man who was finally starting to trust me again. He would feel sorry for Jaxon and be mad at his parents for the entire scenario but all would be good. Aisling talked for almost twenty minutes just to make sure that I really was okay.

"Well, babe, today is a good day. I hope you can feel as much happiness as you used to with him. Love you, I'll text ya later," Aisling said, and with that, we were off the phone.

Jaxon laid in the field across from me with his sunglasses on, looking up at the clear blue sky. The June summer breeze was lightly blowing his hair, and our body temperatures were nice and cool. He was just patiently waiting for me to finish my girl-talk time. Plus, I noticed he listened carefully to know the story that he had to stick with too. It was so strange looking at him again, right in front of me. It was like I was still waiting for him to disappear. I sat, watching him breathe, and for the first time in a long time, my life felt infinite.

Now that I was off the phone, it was time for more of this magic stuff. I wanted to at least levitate a flower by the time I had to head back home. Jaxon jumped up and plucked a leaf off the only tree in the middle of this abandoned field and handed it to me.

"Now concentrate on the nature of its being, feel the smoothness of it, the dampness of its consumed water that gives it life."

I held my hand out and felt the leaf.

A fucking leaf.

I chuckled at the idea of me being able to do anything to this leaf except toss it to the ground or throw it in the air and see how far it can freely fly. Jaxon looked at me with his serious look that I remembered, which hadn't changed much.

"Okay, okay, I'll try and focus more," I said, laughing. "I'm sorry, I'm still trying to wrap my head around this." I took a minute to collect myself. Staring in disbelief at the leaf, not entirely sure what I was supposed to do with it, but was assuming to try and feel its energy and then see if my feelings will do the rest for me. I closed my eyes to focus, and the leaf started to feel heavy as if it were to break my wrist. My eyes flew open, and all of a sudden, the leaf felt like a damn tree. I turned my wrist over and let it fall to the ground. I grabbed my wrist, rubbing it to make my muscles relax. Jaxon looked at me speechless.

"Whoa... I'm actually surprised you were able to do that on your first try, that took me weeks to even feel a connection." He said, almost ashamed of his own magic.

"But what happened at the end? Why did you drop it? You were doing so good."

"Good? It started to feel too heavy, I don't know. I felt like it was going to break my wrist."

"Well what were you thinking about when it started to get heavy?"

"Like the exact moment?" I questioned, unsure what that had to do with anything. "Well, I was thinking about how when I woke up on my birthday, everything was normal and there wasn't anything out of the ordinary going on. Well, and now everything has changed. I mean, for the better, I'm hoping."

He nodded. "Life, you were thinking about life. That's a heavy emotion. You basically tried to take on too much at once, and that's why it became heavy." He looked at the tree and grabbed a new leaf. "Okay, new leaf, a new beginning. Try it again. Only this time, think about Aisling, she has been a good constant in your life, and I think that might help."

I hesitated for a moment then decided, what the hell, let's give it a shot. Taking the new leaf and trying to focus on the softness again. Only this time I closed my eyes with the leaf rubbing between my thumb and finger and thought of Aisling. *My only constant.* I thought about when we were kids and how she was, and is always by my side. I thought of the time when we were giggling and playing in the sand at the neighborhood park. She was making a castle, and I was making the bridge and digging up the moat. I opened my eyes, feeling happy, and looked toward the leaf. It was not heavy at all anymore, instead it was glowing purple and sparkling in the sunlight. My eyes widened, and I looked at Jaxon in disbelief.

"I'm doing it!"

Then, I heard my mom's voice in the background in the memory, that it was time to go home. Of course, that was back in the day when life was normal, and Alex was still around. My hand started to tingle then started to get warm before becoming hot, fiery hot. I looked down at my hand. The leaf had caught fire, burning my fingertips and the flickering heat, inching for my palm. I panicked and Jaxon noticed my change of expression. He grabbed my hand and flipped it over to drop the leaf and stomped out the flames.

"Woah, what changed in your thoughts now?" He asked.

"Alex came to mind. I didn't realize how much control she still had over my mind, I guess." I shrugged. "Sorry again, but hey, can I just brag for a moment at how I turned it purple!" I smiled and felt excited for what was to come.

"Yes, you did, and please stop apologizing. This is all new, and I think you might actually be more of a natural at this magic stuff than I am. This is the start of a new adventure for you." He grabbed me and pulled me closer to him and let his lips crash down on mine. The butterflies grew in my stomach and my body started to tingle from the excitement coursing through my veins and the heat of his body touching mine. No visions this time as he lifted me in his arms and cradled me while still kissing me, turning toward his car. Walking at a fast pace, he sat me down on the hood of it and started kissing my lips, neck, torso, as if he needed me to survive, as if I was his oxygen. My hands started roaming his shoulders and pulling his shirt to bring him closer to me. I explored his abs with my fingertips, which were still tingling. Almost like electricity starting to course through them. I wanted him closer. Our breathing, became heavy and uneven. With the magic still coursing through my veins, I felt my blood flow intensifying, and all I could think about was that I wanted him, now. The moment felt exciting and right and then it was interrupted by my phone ringing with my dad's personally picked piano riff ringtone playing.

"Shit, that's my dad calling," I said in between panting breaths. "I have to answer that." Jaxon grunted with a slight growl in the back of his throat forming. He slumped, heavily over on top of me and sighed before handing me my phone. I took a minute to catch my breath and let the phone call end so I could call him right back when my voice would be more presentable.

I dialed him back and he answered before the first ring had even ended. "Hey Dad, I'm—"

"Freya, where are you? I need you to come home right now please." The urgency in his voice wasn't something I was prepared for.

I sat up quick, pushing Jaxon back from me. "Is everything okay?" I asked him, all playfulness now gone.

"Um, well, your mom is here." His voice broke and I could hear how she still had control over him, just as much as she had over my memories.

Damn it, what was she doing there? She had been gone this long, why even bother coming back now? Ugh, my poor dad, sitting there alone with her probably, not knowing what to even say to her.

My stomach went from Jaxon butterflies to Alex vomit

brewing. I had to get home. I couldn't let him face her alone.

"I'm on my way now. Did she say why she's there?"

"She wants to talk to you, not sure what about. Just come home, kiddo, see you soon."

"Okay, love you."

"You too."

Jaxon must've heard him through the phone because he seemed just as irritated as me.

"Let's get you home."

I sighed heavily when I realized that not only did I get Jaxon back in my life at eighteen, but now Alex was jumping back in too. I guess I had to take the good with the bad.

Chapter 8

Taking the Good With the Bad

We drove back to my home in silence as my mind was wandering. *Why would she come back now? What does she want?*

We pulled up to the driveway, and sure enough, a car was parked in the driveway with different state plates. It was definitely her, and she already thought she owned the place again. She had been here for a while, considering that my dad parked on the road from coming home from the fishing trip. He would've had to haul all his fishing gear through the front yard instead of just parking it in the garage to unload. She was already making his life more difficult, and it's been only a few minutes. I gritted my teeth at the thought of her hurting him again.

"Do you want me to come in with you?" Jaxon asked with concern.

"I'm thinking one person back from the dead might be enough for my dad today. Do you mind if I call you later?" I asked, sad to be parting ways after just getting him back.

"Of course, here I'll put my number in your phone." He

grabbed my phone and started to type, handing it back to me when he was done. It was weird thinking that I didn't even have his phone number. I leaned over and kissed him quickly before turning to get out of the car. He pulled me back to him and kissed my lips longer, letting our foreheads touch, lingering for an extra moment. "Don't worry, I'll still be here tomorrow for you." He nodded, and I smiled back from ear to ear, knowing that it would be true.

I walked into the front door of my own home feeling uncomfortable. I could hear the chairs creaking in the dining room, but they were not saying anything. I walked in, cautiously, to meet them, and my dad gave me a look as if I just relieved him of his third shift duty and he was ready for bed. He stood up, walking over to me, hugging me tight before stepping out of the room and leaving me alone with her. Geez, he could've at least made sure we didn't kill each other first. I looked back and he was gone.

"Wow, Freya Alexandra, you look absolutely stunning!" She looked me up and down and stood to try to come closer to me.

Was she coming in for a hug? Oh hell no!

I dodged her arms and grabbed the closest chair next to me to sit down.

"What are *you* doing here?" I asked with bitterness. Making sure she heard the disgust in my tone.

"Freya, I've missed you, darling. I needed to see you."

"See me?" I laughed. "You decide to just randomly show up to see me?" I yelled, but quietly enough so I didn't make my dad come back to this awkward situation. I could handle this. He couldn't. "Well, now you've seen me. You can go. We don't need you here."

She stared back at me in disbelief. She almost looked vulnerable and hurt. Her blue eyes seemed to actually be filled with heavy emotions. As I continued to stare at her angrily, I realized she had aged in the last two years. She was still beautiful on the outside, but fine lines had started at the corner of her eyes and lips. She was still aging gracefully, but aging. Sad how much time she's lost between us because of her own selfishness. I scrunched my nose in disgust.

"What, did your boyfriends run out of interest with you? Or did you go broke? What do you really want? Because Dad does not need this shit again."

"I deserve that." She said and briefly paused, examining my uninterested expression. "I need to talk to you about other stuff if you'll listen to me. I know I don't deserve your time, but I need to ask you some questions."

"What about?" I tried to keep my tone dry and uninterested.

"Your Mark," she said bluntly.

I felt my gut get kicked. "I don't know what you are talking about," I said defensively.

"Oh, please, Freya. It's very important for you to tell me what you know."

"I told you, I don't know anything."

She sighed heavily and put her fingers to her temples, talking under her breath. "She has no idea, this makes no sense. Why would Clara tell me differently? I wouldn't have risked coming here if she wasn't aware."

Interrupting her thought, "Clara? Wait, who's Clara?" Somewhere deep down the name sounded familiar, but from almost a distant memory that I couldn't quite recall.

A picture came to mind of a woman with long dark hair, oval leopard print glasses, and a short hourglass body at the park talking to Alex while I played with Aisling in the sand from the memory I thought of earlier today. I've seen that woman before a few times in my life. Randomly, I've seen her talk to Alex on other occasions too.

"She's a friend of mine, and she told me something triggered your Mark. She said it was time to come see you."

I flicked my tongue, annoyed that some lady had to tell her to come see me. "What could you possibly know that Jaxon can't tell me." My eyes rolled. "You didn't need to come back. There is nothing left here for you. So just go," I finally had said what I wished I could've had the strength to say years ago. Only getting the words off my chest did not actually make me feel better and her just sitting there, never taking her eyes off of me with each word I spoke.

This woman can leave now!

"The Oakes boy, Jaxon? But how? I thought he was in that accident?"

I froze. "How do you know about the accident? You were gone, and your phone number had been disconnected... Dad was never able to get a hold of you after that." My eyebrows furrowed, and my breathing started to speed up. I didn't know if I was angry or actually surprised that she may have had someone keeping tabs on me after all but never came to check for herself.

"That accident was no accident. They were trying to bring me back here." She looked up frantically and gasped at saying too much.

Who was after her? Who caused the crash?

My mind started to spiral in rage, and that was never a good thing for the mundane, let alone a new magic witch.

"Freya, you have to listen to me now. If Jaxon is alive, then we are not safe here." She took a deep breath before continuing, "Your accident was not an accident, okay? It was planned very strategically by them. I can't explain everything right now, but we need to get a move on now before they come for you or your dad." She started speaking in a panic.

"Woah, calm down! You do *not* get to come back into *my* life and tell me what to do. *You* need to leave, not me. So go!" I stood and yelled. I could feel my blood boiling and my chest filled with anxiety. A panic attack started as my pulse raced, and my skin became clammy. I felt the tingling in my hands start to course through my fingertips, and that was it, I was going to explode. I felt my magic working without my control. I turned toward Alex with my hands coming up in front of me with my eyes staring in horror. They were shaking uncontrollably with electricity running from my right to left hand. I was holding a freaking lightning bolt. With that, my dad came walking back toward the dining room, and Alex grabbed my hands and closed them together, a cooling sensation came over my hands. Just like that, the electricity was gone, and the rage was settling.

What the hell was that?

I felt as if my mood went from angry to relaxed after she touched me, a feeling of tranquility came over me. She made eye contact with me and it was a look of *you better start listening to me before you get someone killed.* I looked down at our cold hands touching and back to her eyes, and with a quick nod, I agreed to listen.

"What's all the yelling for? Geez, I could hear you from outside. I didn't think I would have to mediate a conversation between a mother and daughter," he said as I turned to look at him. His eyebrows were furrowed, and his face was saddened.

"No, it's okay, Jimmy. Sorry, we just had some catching up to do, and things got a little emotional. That's all. It's all good now. I think we decided to head out back by the pool to talk, though. I mean, if that's okay with you," she asked with her blue doe-eyes, they were so pretty that she could get anything she desired.

"Fine with me." He looked at me hesitating. "Whatever Freya wants to do is fine with me."

For the first time in two years, both my parents were in the same room, caring about what I wanted in life. It seemed strange to bring them together like this. I nodded and we headed out back by the pool.

The weather was still in the seventies, and the cool breeze was flowing through the trees. I was already feeling better being outside in the fresh air. I knew I was still in shock since I felt like I should just keep my mouth shut for a little bit and just listen to her.

What was I even going to do with that electricity in there? Would Dad have been caught in the middle of me losing control? What if I had hurt him?

I didn't know enough about magic stuff yet, but I would soon enough. Making my own mental note that I would never lose control again.

"Sit." We sat side by side with our legs dangling in the pool as if we're best friends catching up on boy talk. "So, you do know about your Mark."

I nodded. "To be fair, I just found it this weekend, and Jaxon was explaining some things to me." Considering that it was all new to me, I felt like I was taking it pretty well.

"Okay, so that's good then. You know about Jaxon and his family already. So, that's a start. Now you just need to know about your bloodline because he does not know any of that." She stared at me, almost debating if it was time to open that can of worms. "How would you feel about a little drive with me next weekend to my friend Clara's house? I promise things will make more sense if she's helping explain some of it."

I agreed without hesitation. If I was going to master being a witch, then I needed to know everything.

"I have to work the Friday matinee shift at the theatre, but I can probably get done a little earlier if we're not too busy." I hesitated for a moment but realized I had no vehicle to go anywhere. "Would you mind picking me up from there when I'm done? I can let Dad know that I won't be home right away."

"Yes, Friday afternoon would be best for Clara too. She lives about thirty minutes south of here." Alex paused and looked at my hands again before looking back at me. "Are they feeling better?"

I looked down at my fingers with my hands still slightly shaking and rubbed my thumb across opposite palms. They did feel better besides the adrenaline that was still coursing through my veins.

"Mostly," I replied

"Do you mind showing me your Mark?"

Without saying anything, I turned away from her and

lifted my top to my mid-back and let her examine it. She touched it gently, and all of a sudden, a vision started.

I was walking with a woman down by the river. Was it Clara? Only my hair was shorter and had chunkier blonde highlights throughout. I was picking up small rocks and examining each one carefully, then tossing them into the river. The lady was talking about a garden that I didn't know about, asking if I wanted to tend the herbs today and grab some veggies for dinner. I agreed and paused in the sandbank, reaching for a purple hag stone halfway sticking out of the ground. I plucked it into my hand, staring through the hole while looking over the Mississippi. Jumping up and placing it in my pocket to keep.

I looked around, and Alex was sitting next to me again. I was back to reality. I checked my pocket quickly to see if it was there.

Nothing. What was that about?

I knew that wasn't a memory of mine and my hair had never been that short. Alex looked up at me with questioning eyes.

"What was that? Did you have a vision?" She asked.

"I'm not sure, it must've been a memory or something. I think I was walking with Clara by the river. It was weird, though, I don't remember doing it or having my hair shorter." My face was full of confusion, and Alex noticed it too.

"Hm... well, I wouldn't lose any sleep over it. I can explain more to you now, but some stuff will have to wait." A twinge of disappointment washed over me. "If you are going to keep practicing your magic with Jaxon, then I say you just need to clear your head and let it flow. Magic is hard to teach, you just have to learn to control your emotions to control your powers. So, try and focus on an emotionally happy idea when practicing and listen to Jaxon. He comes from a good bloodline of very smart witches. That I can tell you. Some things will just make more sense next weekend, though."

"What does my Mark mean? Jaxon said that he comes from Earth witches with his infinity symbol that he and Declan share. So, what does this faded Unalome thing mean?"

"Unalome? That's what Jaxon called it?"

"Well, he said that it looked similar to one, but that it wasn't complete." I looked down at my feet dangling in the water and felt a little foolish.

"That's one of the strongest symbols a witch can get; it's only faded for now. Once you find your Anchor, then it will finish itself." Alex suggested. "Your Mark is known as an ancient Red-moon born Mark and the first I've seen in person in my lifetime." She smiled approvingly. She turned her head and showed me her Mark just below her left earlobe. There were three spirals connecting in the center.

"Can these symbols be seen by the human eye? I don't remember ever seeing that on you before." I inhaled heavily trying to consume everything I could.

"Once your Mark appears and your powers have been triggered, then you get an all-seeing eye toward things out of the ordinary. So, ultimately no. Only other witches can see these."

"I feel like before the accident with Jaxon, I noticed his infinity symbol, and I thought I imagined it until he came back. But my Mark hadn't appeared yet, so how did I see his?"

"I think your magic was pulling through right before the accident, but witches and magic didn't exist to you at that time, so how would you have known what to look for?" She shrugged. "We were trying to hide your magic for your own safety."

"Wait, who's 'we'? Does Dad know any of this?"

"No, of course not! For his own safety, he cannot know. Magic and mundanes do not mix weTHIll." I nodded in agreement. "Jaxon and you still have that special connection." I blushed as she said it. "That's good. There has always been a closeness to you two. I actually think he's the reason your Mark appeared again." I looked up at her with so many unanswered questions.

The thought of Jaxon made me wonder. "Do you know who my Anchor is?"

"Yes, I do. But that explanation will have to wait for this weekend," she said with another shrug. "It'll all make more sense... I think."

"You seemed pretty freaked out in the house about us being in danger, should Dad and I be worried?" My brows furrowed, feeling a little uneasy about putting him in danger by being around me. "You said my accident wasn't an accident, what did you mean by that?"

"No, I don't think so. I panicked when you said you didn't have your Mark, and I thought that they had set a trap for me. They're not after you anymore, they want me. I have something of theirs," Alex said calmly. "Your accident was a way to try and lure me back here." She stopped and took a deep breath before continuing. "There are both good and evil witches in this world, Freya, just like in the mundane world. Well, one of the bad ones tried to kill you and Jaxon in that wreck thinking you two were Anchors to each other. They were wrong, of course, and I believe they were trying to get me to come back for them. It's kind of a long story. They messed up, and the trap didn't work. They figured while they were at it, they tried to take out a pair of Anchor witches too, or so they thought." She paused and looked at me. My face must've became unreadable because she decided to stop discussing the already tough subject. Even though Jaxon was alive, the accident and the time after still traumatized me enough that discussing it gave me anxiety. I started to feel clammy and anxious. I felt another panic attack coming on, and even worse, was knowing that the accident was actually someone who was out to hurt me and Jaxon. That made me angry and I could feel my heart racing at the thought of it.

"How about we stop for tonight? Clara will be able to explain more with us this weekend about the bad ones. Just know that right now you are not in danger." She tried to reach for my hand but I retracted mine further. "I should get going, though, just to be safe, and so I don't overstay my welcome. I am so sorry I haven't been here for you and I am so sorry about that accident, that never should've happened." She looked at me with real sincerity, and all I could do was nod in agreement with her.

We sat quietly for a little longer before we both decided that next weekend we would discuss more. She needed to get back on the road for tonight. It was like she had become my business partner for new information and not my mother. I honestly was feeling a little better, or at least better than I thought I would've felt after seeing her again. When she went to leave, she awkwardly came toward me for a hug and paused when she saw me tense. She came to a halt and turned, saying she would just see me next weekend. I agreed with another nod.

When it rained, it poured. That's how I was feeling. The sun was setting, and it was a normal June day here in Crystal Rock for everyone else. But for me, this weekend had been an adventure. My life was changing, and hopefully, it would continue to grow for the better. There was just a lot to take in from everyone that had recently returned to my life.

I stood after taking a few deep breaths and looking at my non-tingling hands one more time before I walked inside the house. I told my dad that Alex and I were going to grab a late lunch after work next weekend at the diner and that I would bring him something home for dinner, which he seemed happy to be able to avoid awkward conversations at a small table at the Willow Winds Diner. He looked at me with questioning eyes, waiting to see if I was going to unravel and have a nervous breakdown.

"Dad, it'll be fine. I can handle her," I told him confidently, which I hoped was true.

"Are you sure that you want to spend more time with her? I just don't want you to go backwards, if I'm being honest with you." He half smiled and I could see his own emotions toward her trying to claw to the surface.

"I'll be fine, I will keep her at arm's length, Dad." I smiled to help reassure him. "Are *you* sure you're not going to spiral from seeing her?" I questioned him and waited for his sigh to finish.

"I'm okay, kid. I have you to keep me grounded." He laughed and I smiled. He walked over to me and hugged me tight. "I missed you this weekend. The guys are fun, but you catch way more fish than they do." We laughed. He ended up with a stringer worth of bluegills, a catfish, and bass and one catch and release sturgeon according to the photo his buddy took of him, and already had them filleted and on ice ready to fry up for dinner.

"I'll get the pan ready for frying if you make your special seasoning for the fish?" I asked, and he nodded. The discussion was over about the events that had just happened. Instead we were going to move on with life. A normal life for him and my life was going to be a little more complicated now, but I wouldn't let him be involved with any of it. Well, except for the Jaxon story.

We sat, quietly eating dinner, then he said with excitement. "Hey, I was thinking that we could go and look at some cars this week. I know that you've been saving, and so have I. What do you think?"

"Are you serious? Yes! 100% yes!" I squealed with excitement at the idea of looking at vehicles. I knew it wouldn't be anything too fancy, but if it had four wheels and got me from A to B, then I would be happy.

"Alright then, it's settled. We can go and look this week." He smiled.

I thought about bringing up Jaxon with the amnesia story but was a little hesitant about overwhelming him with too many blasts from the past. But really when else would be a good time, though? Either way, it was going to be a miracle to him.

"Hey, how was your little party on Friday? Everything turned out okay for you?" He asked, pulling me back to reality and out of my thoughts, and I realized this was my moment and I couldn't pass it up.

"Actually, Dad, you're not going to believe this…" I hesitated while he stared back at me, waiting. "Um, well—" I paused again. "Jaxon is alive. He showed up at the house during the party." His jaw dropped, and he nearly choked on his bite. "Long story short, he didn't die at the scene. He actually was revived and had amnesia from the accident, and his mom thought it would be best to start a new life elsewhere." He stared blankly at me and I couldn't read his expression, so I continued. I figured I might as well rip the Band-Aid right off. "His memories came back, and he surprised me at my party. It's been a weird weekend, to say the least."

"Jaxon?" He scratched his head. "As in… Our boy, Jaxon? He's alive?" I could see the realization growing on his face that this was a miracle or maybe he was ready to lock me in the psych ward.

I took a deep breath. "Yes, I actually fainted when I saw him. We ended up talking all night long about everything that had happened. He actually brought me home when you called, but I didn't want to freak you out with both Alex and Jaxon coming back in person on the same day, so I figured I should tell you first and let this one sit with you for a while. Considering that one came back from the dead, and one just showed up after a long time away. Though, at least we knew she was still on this earth."

His eyes started to swell with tears. Happy tears. He always had liked Jaxon. He always thought he was a good boy growing up. He had taken losing him pretty hard too.

He stood up from the table and walked over to me, hugging me from behind my chair.

"That is the best damn news I have ever heard in my life, kid," he said between sniffles. "You should've started with that!" He wiped his tears and sniffled again, kissing the top of my head, and walked back to sit down.

"Yeah, Dad it really is," I said and I felt so much relief to get that off my chest and to see a genuine smile on my dad's face with the news. I actually think he forgot about Alex being here earlier once he realized there would be another man around the house again, and that I would have someone to keep me well-grounded too. Jaxon was the better deal for both of us.

Chapter 9

The Never-Ending Week

This week was going to be the longest week of my life. Waiting on more family history and trying to distract myself until Friday was going to be tough. Jaxon texted me after dinner to call him if I needed him. I was going to be okay, though, I told myself. I distracted myself by cleaning up the kitchen until my dad went off to bed, then I decided to call Jaxon and tell him everything that happened between Alex and me. I let him know that he was safe to come over at any point now. Just as long as he knew that Dad may hug him and never let him go so he'll have to be prepared for that. He laughed and agreed to see me tomorrow before we hung up.

I decided to head to bed early too, my head started to ache. I think my brain really was on overload now, and my emotions were starting to burst at the seams. My journal would have to wait until tomorrow to catch up with life. I started to think that journaling might become a full-time job with all this new information I kept finding out.

I went to brush my teeth and washed my face. When I

got back to my room and by the time my head hit the pillow, I was out. Unfortunately, it didn't take long for another dream to start.

Dad and I were on the fishing float at the Lock and Dam. I had just walked to the opposite side of the rugged float to try fishing on the back end closer to the dam while he was at the opposite end, saving his lucky spot. A fish tugged on my line, and I set the hook, then started reeling. I yelled to him that there was a fish on. He came running toward me but seemed to be on an endless running journey. The float kept getting longer and he was getting further away. I looked down at the river, and the water started to turn blood red. My eyes refocused on the water, and again it stayed red. The river was bleeding, and the fish that I was reeling in was getting closer to the surface. I needed a net, but he was still too far away. A man ran up next to me with his own net and said he would help me. He was a tall pale man in a fancy suit, definitely shouldn't be fishing in that outfit. He had dark hair slicked back like a businessman, but his eyes looked almost demonic, and his teeth were pointed into spikes. My heart panicked at the site of him and I gasped. He was evil. My hand was still reeling while looking at him. The fish broke the water, and blood splashed up from the river onto both this man's suit and me, which brought my attention to the water again. I didn't have a fish at all. I had a journal at the end of my hook, and it was bleeding out of its pages. The journal was what caused the river to turn bloody in the first place because the minute I pulled it from the river, the water became clear again. The journal was still bleeding on the float. The man pushed me aside and grabbed the journal off the wooden floorboards and started running toward my dad. I screamed to stay away from him, but my throat couldn't scream loud enough to warn him to watch out. The demonic man grabbed my dad and flew away with both the bleeding journal and my dad.

I woke up in a pool of sweat with my hair soaked to my pillow and anxiety pulsing through my veins. My throat was on fire from physically trying to scream for my dad in real life, but with no voice to do it. I jumped up from my bed and ran to his room to make sure he was safe.

As I reached his door, I realized that I was being silly, and I could hear him snoring, so I cracked his door open an inch and saw him safely sleeping in his bed. I knew he was okay and I was just being a scared girl of an impossible nightmare. I thought of what Alex said, that we could be in danger and that might've been what triggered this nightmare. Now I was subconsciously worried about his safety. My biggest fear is to lose anyone that I care about. Now that I knew he was okay, I decided to walk to the kitchen and grab a glass of water. Slightly afraid that when I turned the faucet on it would bleed red, I was relieved when it didn't. This is what I get for not journaling tonight, my own journal is mad at me and gave me my own nightmare, I thought. I laughed, quietly to myself, shaking my head and looking at the clock. It was only three in the morning, and I was going to need more sleep than this to function.

I walked back to my room and grabbed the stupid leather-bound journal and started to write in it.

Journal: June 7th ~ (too early to be awake)

These dreams are getting weird. I'm going

to keep this short and simple in hopes that I can fall back to sleep. This week is going to be a NORMAL week. My brain needs a normal week. Alex is back for now, and I'm seeing her again on Friday. Life is going to be okay. It has to be.

I stared at the entry for a long while and debated about writing more, but honestly, I didn't even know where to start. This weekend had been one for the books, not just for a journal. Honestly, it's been such an adventure already, and I'm equally excited and nervous to learn more magic and to see what I can really do. There's no way I would be able to fall back to sleep tonight. I grabbed my phone and texted Aisling.

Freya: Hey lady, are you awake by any chance?

Aisling: Yeah, I'm up. You okay??

Freya: Can't sleep...

Aisling: I'm blaming Alex for this one. Do you have ice cream at your place?

Freya: Ice cream? Lol yeah we do. Why?

Aisling: Good! I'm bringing root beer over for floats and we can hang out in the pool. Yes?

Freya: Yes! You're the best!

Aisling: I sure am :)

I headed back to my room and changed into my bikini top and bottoms. Then, I went to the kitchen to grab the ice cream and mugs. After that, I headed to the bathroom for the towels, and I was ready to head out to the backyard. I heard Aisling pulling up out front, my mood instantly changed to feeling better knowing that I would not be alone in my thoughts anymore. She walked around the front and met me at the side gate, letting me unlock it for her and walked in.

"Hey, did someone text me asking for help with her overthinking?" Aisling laughed and came in with her hands full with a two liter of soda, her bikini, and a pink envelope. Juggling too many things at once but too determined to be an empowered, do-it-all woman. I grabbed the soda from her hands and started scooping the ice cream into the mugs.

I laughed, "Thanks for coming over, I just couldn't sleep. This weekend has been pretty crazy with Jaxon and Alex. You know?"

"Girl, I had my phone next to me all day waiting for you to text or call me and let me know how this Alex thing went. I saw her sitting in that car when I drove past and thought, 'Oh shit, what does this bitch want?' I even debated on getting eggs to toss at her car, or even at her before I realized your dad would probably be mad at me. So, I didn't, but it crossed my mind." We both laughed together, and I was so happy she was here.

Aisling changed into her suit and we jumped in the heated pool with our floats. I started to fill her in on Alex, and I told her how she wants to see me next weekend and talk about life. I left out all the witchy details for now. I would have to decide if it was something that I could tell her down the road, but until I knew more, then it was best to keep it quiet. We got on the subject of Jaxon, and I felt my face flush.

"He still makes you all fuzzy, huh?" she asked with a smile on her face. I knew she was picking on me but being nice about it. I scrunched my nose at her and we both laughed.

"It's pretty amazing to have him back. His mom was wrong for keeping him away, but he's back and remembers everything, so that is a miracle."

"Oh, for sure! I'm excited to see him in person now that I know it is him. I can't believe I didn't recognize him at your party. Must've been the mask that threw me off." She shrugged and let it go.

"We can maybe do a double date soon. I mean, if Declan and you are official now?" I questioned because they had technically not given themselves a title yet, even though I knew she wanted to.

"Well, official is such a title. But honestly, I would be mad if he was seeing anyone else. So yes, we're an official couple, which I should probably tell him that too," she laughed. "Which reminds me." She jumped out of the pool and set her drink down. She grabbed the pink envelope from the table and handed me a towel to dry my hands to give me the card to open.

"This was your birthday present, but when you mentioned Jaxon's name at your party, I thought maybe it wasn't a good idea to give it to you that night. So, I changed it up a little bit. Open it!" She squealed with excitement.

I opened the pink envelope and an eighteenth birthday card came out with a glittery front cover spilling into the pool. I read the card out loud about being best friends and how life is extraordinary, etcetera. I pulled out the folded sheet of paper and started to read the front of it. My eyes grew bigger at the words, and now I was the one trying to hold in my excitement so I didn't drop the paper in the pool.

"You got us airline tickets to Colorado? That is amazing! When do we go?" I squealed.

"Well, it's for next month. It was supposed to be a getaway for the two-year anniversary of the accident and how far you've come. So, I was hoping to get you out of here, but then when we found out about Jaxon being alive, Declan thought it would be a good idea for maybe all four of us to get out of here for a weekend." She paused to catch her breath and watched me curiously for my response. "Before you say anything, I already talked to your Dad and your work about it and everything is good to go!" Aisling said proudly. She was such a planner. This girl needed to do this for a living.

"I was going to say yes without hesitation! This will be amazing. Thank you so much!" A vacation was just what I needed to clear my head. This would be good.

"So, you will just have to tell Jaxon too. My dad had enough air miles to get the boys added with us. So happy birthday to you, and happy double date vacation to us!" She said with satisfaction.

I started feeling much better after the hours of having girl time with her, and my mind was feeling much clearer. The sun started to come up, and our fingers were becoming pruney from the pool, so we got out and sat on the gravity chairs with our towels and just kept catching up on life. We must've fallen asleep at some point because I woke up and was far too warm with the sun overhead. Forgetting to put the ice cream back in the freezer, we now had liquid vanilla, and I would have to buy my dad a new pint to replace it. Aisling woke up and saw me heading to the garbage with the melted slush. We both laughed. I told her again how excited I was for the trip and so thankful for her coming over last-minute. She hugged me tight and started walking toward the gate to head home.

"Morning, girls, you could've slept inside you know?" My dad chuckled and waved goodbye to Aisling.

"Sorry, Pops, we lost track of time. Your daughter is 100% cured now after our girls night... You're welcome!" Aisling said sarcastically and he smiled and thanked her before she left.

"Dad, I promise to get you more ice cream," I said. "We lost track of time talking."

He shrugged. "It's not a big deal, I'm just glad to see you smiling. What do you think about going car shopping today? Let's make this part of your birthday present and graduation present and you save the money that you've earned."

My eyes bulged and my face lit up. "Are you serious? Dad, no, I will pay toward whatever vehicle we find. That was my plan all along."

"Well, I'm older, and my plan was made first." He smiled. "So, go get ready, and we will head out to the car lots to see our options."

I hugged him and headed inside to get ready. I texted Jaxon excitedly, telling him about the car shopping, and asked if we could see each other later and head to the field to practice.

Jaxon: Will you be picking me up in your new ride?

Freya: Or you can meet me at the field after? To save time :)

Jaxon: Sounds good to me! Good luck car shopping little witch :)

Freya: LOL. Thanks, see you later.

Car shopping was not as easy as I thought it would be. I mean, geez, how many cars were actually in this world? We test drove multiple ones but, in the end, decided on the used navy blue Jeep with new tires for Wisconsin winters. It had 100k miles but was supposed to break 200k and still be reliable according to the dealer. This was the only one with zero rust under the body. I was beyond excited, and my dad would not let me pay a dime toward it. I felt overly spoiled and couldn't believe this was my life right now. Life was good, and not only was I getting a vehicle today, but also what this meant was even more special to me. This meant that he was starting to trust me again.

I decided to treat him to lunch at the diner since he wouldn't let me spend my money on the Jeep. We both drove to the diner and parked next to each other. I smiled when I got out next to him and hugged him again. I told him that I was going to meet up with Jaxon after lunch if he didn't mind, and he was happy to let me go. He made me promise that he would come by later so he could see him for himself. I promised him.

As I drove away from the diner and parted ways from him, I looked at my hands on the steering wheel and thought to myself that this was my fresh start. This was my freedom. I had the music down low with the windows rolled down and was driving up the bluffs in peace and happiness, getting ready to meet up with Jaxon. Driving alone in a vehicle was a little scary, but made me happy. I pulled up to the abandoned dirt road path I remembered taking yesterday, and Jaxon's car was already parked there waiting for me.

"Wow, a Jeep, huh? I like it. Very you. I mean, I think it's still very you," Jaxon said as he walked around the Jeep, examining it for himself. "This will be great for the winters here, a very nice choice."

"Thanks, I have to admit that the 'Life is Good' sticker on the back windshield caught my attention. So I decided to test drive it." I smiled.

"Good choice." He smiled back and nodded in agreement. "So, do you want to practice some magic today?"

I nodded, feeling awkward and hoping that I could make some progress today. We walked out to the open field near the only standing tree again. Today was a little warmer than yesterday. I could already feel the sweat starting at the nape of my neck. I grabbed a leaf off of the tree and twirled it in between my finger and thumb. Ready for the training.

"Let's try something else. We already know that you can connect with the magic, so let's try a different element this time... Water." He held out a bottle of water. He twisted the cap off and set the bottle on the ground.

"What am I supposed to do with that?" I asked, while I stared at the liquid.

"I want you to levitate it without spilling it."

I laughed nervously. "And how am I supposed to do that?" I rolled my eyes, feeling annoyed because that seemed impossible.

"Just focus on the liquid inside the bottle. Feel the connection to the element of water, and once you feel it, then just imagine raising it up to eye level to grab it and drink it." He made it sound so simple. Just point and shoot.

I focused as he had said to with my eyes open. I could feel that connection starting. It was almost like a tingling starting in my chest that was growing. Once I felt the tingling hit my fingertips, I pointed my palm toward the bottle, and the liquid started to vibrate. My eyes widened with excitement, and I pushed the connection harder. I felt like I was just about there, to lift it, when the bottle crushed itself, collapsing, and the water came splashing up in the air, and soaked both Jaxon and me. I fell to the ground and laughed, and Jaxon joined me. The water actually felt nice in the heat. So, I didn't complain one bit.

"Well, that wasn't how I expected it to go." He started wiping off his clothes as best as he could. "Maybe we should go back to the leaves for now. Unless you brought an extra pair of clothes," he said sarcastically.

"The leaves might be a better idea. I have a lot of catching up to do," I said. "It's crazy to think that some families grow up knowing their witch history and then there's me, not knowing anything, like this didn't even exist until now."

"Sounds like Alex was trying to protect you from something. I'm curious to see what she has to say this weekend too. I mean, how do you leave your kid behind without even a user's manual or a grimoire."

I felt the pain from his words and he noticed and seemed to want to back pedal but instead I kept the questions coming. "So, are those actually real?" I asked, and he nodded quickly. "They actually exist outside of movies?"

"Each family has their own grimoire, and it has new spells added throughout the generations before it's passed down to their kids and so on. I'm sure Alex has your family's to pass down to you eventually too." He didn't seem too confident with that answer.

"I wonder if Alex and I share the same kind of magic. Like, is it passed down genetically?"

"My family comes from elemental magic. Earth, specifically. There are all the elements: wind, fire, earth, and water witches. Then, there are tarot, intuition, and simple spell witches. Electric, telekinetic, and even telepathic ones." He paused when my eyes started to widen. "I mean, the list goes on. It just depends on the Mark you are given. With new generations of witches born, strengths seem to be mutating."

"What does my half Mark mean? You said you've seen it in a book somewhere."

"I looked into it more last night actually, and there's not much information on it. That's probably a better question to save for Alex. I even tried asking my mom, but of course she didn't say much. I don't think she likes us hanging around again. She just seems standoffish lately." He shrugged his shoulders as if he didn't care much of what she thought.

"Well, I mean, she did keep us apart for almost two years. If Alex supposedly has an explanation, then maybe your mom does too. I just don't understand all the secretiveness." I furrowed my eyebrows and felt like a child again, unable to know the truth. Soon I would know it all though, I hoped.

We decided to keep practicing our magic for the next few hours. Trying out all his little tricks, as I failed at most of them. It seemed like my magic was more of a connection to my emotions than to the earth. The sun started to get lower to the west, and it would be time to start heading home soon. Luckily, I got the hang of levitating small light-weight objects down with just a hand gesture and a strong emotion of forcing the small objects to rise. Each time was becoming slightly easier. Magic was not for the weak; I could definitely see where many people would give up without seeing fast progress.

"The sun is starting to set. What do you think about coming over for dinner with my dad?" I asked him, hoping that we could get the awkward reunion over with. "We can pick up dinner from the diner, so we don't have to wait on food because, honestly, I'm starving right now."

"That sounds good to me. Do you think Jim will mind?"

"I think he will be ecstatic." I smiled. "Let me try one more thing." I took the last bottle of water, took the cap off, and attempted to lift it. I focused on what I wanted and poured all my intentions under the space of the bottle to give it a boost. The bottle rose an inch off the ground, it shook but it did lift. I smiled at the small success and set it back down without spilling it. Jaxon smirked, and I jumped in his arms, kissing him with excitement.

We called the diner and had a to-go order placed. Jaxon said he could pick it up on his way over, so I could get a head start home to let my dad know about the extra company for tonight. I got home and walked in the front door and let him know that Jaxon would be joining us if he was okay with that. Without hesitation, he smiled from ear to ear.

"That's great! I was wondering when I'd get my hug with that boy." He laughed, wiping his happy tears away.

He really would be happy to have another man around. Especially since he actually liked Jaxon. Jaxon always would jump in and help him when he would come over without hesitation.

"Cool," was the only word that I could say.

Jaxon's headlights pulled in the driveway. Before I could even get to the door, my dad ran outside and half-picked him up before he even could get out of his car. Luckily, he wasn't holding the dinner, otherwise, he would've dropped it on the ground, and we would've had to settle for a frozen pizza. They embraced in a manly hug for just under a minute before my dad pulled him back to look at him from head to toe. They must've had a few "boy, have you grown" exchanges and so on before they walked into the house with dinner. We sat, ate, and laughed, and Jaxon explained the amnesia story to him. I made a mental note that this was definitely another good moment to write about.

After dinner, my dad decided to hit the hay early. Jaxon headed home since his mom wanted him home to discuss family matters, or that's what she had said on the phone. Jaxon looked annoyed by her demands but agreed to head home. I decided that some actual sleep would be good for me too. I would just wake up early and catch up on my journal entries since my therapy appointment is scheduled for Wednesday morning. I would have to bring the journal in and at least show her that I've been putting it to good use. I'd rather her not read any of it, but at least she can see that I've attempted to express my feelings. Although everything had changed, and I felt pretty good about it all.

The morning came early, I grabbed the journal and

began to write.

Journal: June 8th ~

So, a lot has happened. Where to even begin is the hard part. Dad bought me a Jeep for my graduation and birthday present and wouldn't even let me pay a dime toward it. He was able to meet Jaxon last night for the first time again. I think that is going to be a good combo. I keep catching myself smiling this week. One, I am happy, and two, life is a whole new adventure for me. I'm waking up with an excitement brewing in me each new day that I didn't think was possible. Jaxon and I have been practicing magic, and I actually think I might be getting the hang of it, or maybe not and he's just being nice to me.

I'm actually excited to see Alex on Friday. Not so much to see her, but to hear more about my family history. I feel like I have so many unanswered questions, and it seems like she may have the rest of the answers that I'm looking for. I kind of wish I would've known I was going to have a vehicle before I told her to pick me up from work. It would've been nice to have my own ride in case I needed to escape her quickly.

Oh, and Aisling got her and me Colorado airline tickets for a mini getaway next month, and now we are bringing our men with us! Our men, that's so weird writing that, or even

thinking that again, but I am not complaining. I really don't know how I would've survived my whole life without her. She makes me happy.

Well, I have my first therapy appointment since I started writing in this journal tomorrow. I'm thinking with the root of all of my "problems" coming back to me that these therapy sessions might be coming to an end very soon. It's a waste of my dad's money, and my time too. I might keep journaling, but honestly, I am feeling pretty normal right now. Well, maybe not normal because of the obvious fact of me being a witch, but more emotionally stable with the lost being found again? Who knows? I am just ready for Friday, and the rest of this week is going to drag on. UGH!

I looked at my watch and realized it was time to head to work. I had to keep trying to live a normal day in the life and a cashier at a movie theatre was a perfect cover story. Today we would only sell tickets to only a handful of people, who probably just wanted to sit in the air conditioning and not really wanting to watch the one-star rated film that came out.

I got to work and spent the next few hours sweeping popcorn in the theatres when the shows finished and decided to continue practicing my magic while getting paid for it. I took a handful of popcorn from the tub left behind and tried to swirl it in my palm while I was alone. The popcorn shuffled around my palm, and I laughed at the thought of magic in my right hand and a broom in my left. That really made me fit in with the witch role. I dumped the popcorn in the garbage and chuckled at myself for making my own entertainment. If anyone saw me, they would think I was crazy. Some of the unpopped kernels missed the garbage and landed on the counter above the can. An idea came to mind and I grabbed them and lined up the kernels, focusing my palm over each one before willing them to heat up. I focused on the energy of fire and closed my eyes.

POP, POP, POP!

No freaking way! It worked!

That was enough for today. I was trying not to push my luck. I had to get back out front, back to being "normal" again. I grabbed the film, headed upstairs to the booth and started to roll the film on the reels for the next flicks we had playing today. Magic would have to wait. Today was supposed to be just a normal day. I sighed heavily as I started reeling.

Yes, a normal day.

Chapter 10

Therapy Sessions and Date Day

Wednesday was here, and only two more days until I learned more. Just had to make it through the therapy appointment with Isadora and then work tomorrow. I could do this. I drove down the road to my appointment, bringing the journal with me in case she wanted to glance at my progress. I didn't want her reading it, but glancing would be fine. I'm sure she would start with, "How have you been feeling," and end with her second famous line of, "You have to accept circumstances before you can grow," type of bullshit. Either way, I was ready to be done with these appointments.

It was early morning, and my appointment was at eight thirty a.m. I drove through the town, parallel to the Mississippi, and looked at the fog hovering over the river with the cool air mixing with the warm day. The fog happened often on the river in the early hours but would clear before noon. It was kind of eerie, but also beautiful. The bluffs would become filled with the rolling fog, and again, it was slightly eerie if you weren't from around here.

I pulled up to the small office located in a decent-sized business park that included a local dentist and the only law firm in town. It truly sounded like it could be the start of a joke: a dentist, therapist, and lawyer walk into a bar...

Her office was the last one near the back and was probably rented out just to help pay the electric bill. It really looked like a walk-in closet with her desk and a lounge chair for the patient. When her door is closed, you have to sit outside the office in the only chair located next to the door. She would come and let you in when she was ready. She must've had another patient in there because the door was closed, but I could hear a man yelling. He must be going through a divorce or something because he sounded pissed. She definitely didn't have soundproof walls... *highly noted for any future appointments.*

The door opened, and a tall dark-haired man with a nice, tailored suit and a very defined jawline walked out with one hand in his pants pocket and his jacket tucked behind his arm showing off his undershirt and belt. He would've been a good-looking man, but his face was held in a furious position that gave him an unattractive look. He reminded me of someone, but I couldn't place where I recognized him from.

"Miss Chamberlain, I'm ready for you," Isadora said with a sigh as she shrugged her shoulders. "Some people just need to vent," she stated as her gaze followed after the man that stormed off.

"Yeah, I guess so," I said while looking back down the hall too. The man turned back toward us for a brief moment and I tried to look away quickly to not let him know I was watching him. I grabbed my journal and stood to enter the closet of a room.

"Well, let's start this session. How have you been feeling lately?" I rolled my eyes and tried to hold a smile in. There it was, her famous starter line.

"Um, actually, I've been doing good," I said and grabbed my necklace out of habit, twisting it between my fingers to distract myself. "I turned eighteen, and it seems like since then my life is falling into place, well, sort of." I wanted to keep things simple for her, and obviously, I wouldn't tell her anything witch related. I didn't know about telling her about Jaxon, either, at this appointment. I felt like if I told the amnesia story then she would call Mrs. Oakes, and she would suggest making an appointment for her crazy talk too and I didn't want to be in the middle of that.

"So you are happy about your mom coming back then?"

"I mean, I wouldn't say I am happy about seeing her," I said, eyebrows furrowed. "Wait, how did you know that? I didn't even mention her."

"Oh," she paused. "A little birdie told me, my dear."

"My dad called you?" I asked angrily. "Why would he do that? I thought that was a privacy violation since I'm an adult now." I could take care of these appointments by myself. I thought he was starting to trust me again.

She shrugged and said with her stupid smirky smile and her false lashes blinking, trying to make herself look innocent. "He may have told me; otherwise, honestly, it is a small town, Freya. There are not many secrets around here." Her blonde, curled hair, blue eyes, and high cheekbones made her look doe-like and, of course, beautiful.

Ugh, this woman drives me crazy.

"I don't like that. I want things to come from me. What... did he tell you about Jaxon too then?" Now I was even more annoyed.

"Jaxon and your mom are both back then?" She asked but didn't seem surprised as she nodded.

"Yes, it's kind of a long story, though, and a huge misunderstanding, but I'm sure you know about that already too."

"So, how does that make you feel? I mean, having both people you thought you had lost come back into your life?" She left it at that and didn't even question how it was even possible. She just continued her therapy session. She was probably writing down that I would need a psych ward soon or she really wasn't surprised by the information. Maybe she was in on the relocating with Margo Oakes. Although, I thought Jaxon's dad wouldn't be so cruel. His mom, sure, but Callum Oakes, never.

"I mean, I was happy about one of them," I said, quietly under my breath, but still being truthful. "It was a shock, and I still can't believe my dad would go behind my back and call you."

"Huge shock." Isadora avoided the accusation. "Is your mom going to stick around this time?"

My jaw dropped.... *Wow, that was a little blunt for a therapist.*

That actually stung more than I was expecting it to, making me feel angry toward both her and Alex. I took a deep breath to make sure my magic didn't ignite out of control again.

"Obviously, I never wanted her to leave in the first place, but that wasn't my choice." I shook my head, pissed at having to even say those words out loud and ready to change the subject. "Would you stop calling her my mom please? It's Alex, just Alex."

"Has *Alex* decided to come back for good?" She almost spat back at me.

I inhaled and waited to even my own anger. "I'm not sure, we are getting together for a late lunch after work on Friday. That's all I know so far. One day at a time."

"That's a good idea." She glanced toward my hands holding my journal. "I see you brought your journal in. Have you been writing things down?"

I lifted the journal, hugging it closer to my chest in a protective hold. Afraid she was going to pry it from my fingers to see what progress I had made, or better yet, what progress she has made with me.

"I have. Every day, I have written something down. It's more therapeutic than I thought it would be. I actually gave myself a nightmare the first day I didn't write enough down in it." I laughed, thinking how stupid that sounded out loud.

"It was most likely your subconscious trying to help you get stuff off your chest. It's a therapy trick," she stated matter of factly.

"Do you need to look at it or anything?" I asked, holding my breath, hoping to not have to share my secrets with her.

"Oh, no. What's yours is yours. You only tell me things you feel like telling me. I won't invade your space unless you ask," she said sweetly, changing her tone from being annoyed back to being paid the big bucks. I let my shoulders relax with relief and decided to ask my next question.

"Hey, a little off-topic, but I'm thinking about maybe ending these sessions for a while. I'm thinking that since the two reasons I started coming here are now back, maybe I should try reconnecting with them in real life versus here."

She shook her head. "I don't think that's a good idea right now. It would be unprofessional to just let you fly when you've recently fallen."

I sat back in the chair and tried to keep the rest of the session short, but she continued to ask about my feelings and a lot about Alex, which started making me uncomfortable. I kept telling her I didn't know anything more besides that she randomly stopped by and we would get together this weekend. She asked me for the details of her return and I told her exactly how it happened, leaving the electricity magic out of the story. She seemed disappointed that I didn't know more. Luckily, I looked at my watch and our time was up for today. She ended with her famous line.

"Well, you have to accept circumstances before you can grow." I got up from the lounge chair and internally I laughed, knowing that she was so predictable. Hard to believe she was getting paid the big bucks when she repeated herself.

"Thanks, I guess I'll see you in two weeks."

I was glad that was over, as I headed for my Jeep with my journal in hand. I grabbed my phone to call Jaxon.

"Hey, I'm all done with that session. What are you doing?"

"I actually was hoping that I could take you on our first official date. I mean, if you're up for it?" Jaxon asked and actually sounded shy, as if I would've turned him down.

"Absolutely... What did you have in mind?"

We hung up after we decided to meet at my house and he was going to pick me up.

I waited outside on the front porch swing. It was still early morning, so I grabbed my light zip-up hoodie to wear and grabbed my mug of freshly made coffee to sip on while I waited for him. June weather would be too hot later in the day, but early morning could still have a little chill in the air from the night before. A light hoodie and my shorts would keep my temperature perfect until the sun was more awake. Excitement grew to go on a date and I was a little nervous as to what he had planned. My stomach was filling with butterflies and caffeine, which was making me a little anxious. I knew Jaxon, though. This date shouldn't make me feel nervous. I guess it had been a long time since an actual date, though. But this was my new fresh start.

I can handle a date... I shook my head at my own feelings of stupidness.

Jaxon pulled into the driveway and jumped out of his car to go and grab the passenger door for me. That would never get old to me. He kissed my cheek, making me blush, before he headed back to the driver's seat.

"Good morning, love. Are you ready for our date?" Jaxon asked with a sweet smile but quickly cleared his throat.

Is he nervous too?

"Morning," I said with a smile and grabbed my tourmaline pendant, twisting it. "I'll admit, I'm a little nervous." I looked back at him to see his reaction. "What do you have in mind?"

"First date jitters?" He gave me a reassuring smile that

it would be fine. "I mean, technically, this is our millionth date, it's just our first one since I've "returned from the dead"." He laughed and I knew he was trying to downplay the dead part and the time away. He grabbed my hand and kissed it.

"I guess you're right. Still a little nervous, though." I shrugged.

"I'm thinking we should go to a pottery barn across the river and paint something that is already pre-made so we don't get kicked out for clay getting everywhere in the studio."

"That actually sounds fun. Yes." I said. Now I was glad I had my hoodie so that I wouldn't ruin my t-shirt with glazed paint. I didn't think I could do the whole ceramic thing, but I could definitely paint.

We drove south and over the bridge to Iowa, which was only about twenty minutes from home to Vine's Pottery Gallery. I had never been there before, but the building was so cool. It was like a hole in the wall on Main Street. The name was fitting since the brick building had a red door with green vines growing along the brick and above the door. It had a metal-made vine two-person seater red bench in front. There were Hosta plants growing on each side of the bench and a flower-hanging pot welcoming us in by the door with a "Come in to Create" sign on the welcome mat.

A young man greeted us from behind the counter. He hadn't looked up to us yet. Just welcomed us and said that he would be right with us. It looked like he was busy writing down an order. They must've had an event here last night or this morning already because the place looked like it could use a deep clean with paint on the floor and about fifty ceramic pieces painted and ready to be glazed. It must've been a kids' event. I decided to look around at the pieces while we waited for the man to finish. Jaxon joined me, walking around with me as we admired the work that had been painted.

The young man looked up while my back was facing him, but I could see his reflection through the window, so I quickly pretended not to notice his stare and faced the red bench.

"What can I do for you two?" he asked nicely.

"We are wanting to paint something pre-made," Jaxon said, looking to the empty walls. "That is, if there's anything left." They both laughed.

"Birthday party this morning," the man said as he shrugged. "It's been an early start to my day and an even longer evening of glazing awaits."

"Would you mind two more?" Jaxon asked. "It's actually our first date," he half-whispered to the man, but I could still hear him by the window.

"Absolutely! But I'll tell you right now, we don't have much to pick from. Here, let me show you what's left." He walked to the back of the room to grab the available options.

I turned around to face him and looked at what we could choose from. Poor guy was going to be busy for the rest of the day. He started to walk back to us with his hands full with the remaining three items. He started to talk as he walked back.

"Here we go. We have this fish on a rock, tentacles mug, and this fairy tea—" he explained while he looked up and fumbled with the teapot, dropping it with a loud shatter. He was looking at me embarrassed. Jaxon bent down and started to grab the larger pieces off the ground. The man froze, as he stared at me. I had never seen this guy before in my life. He was taller than Jaxon and had dark black hair with bright blue eyes and broad shoulders.

What was wrong with him? Was there something on my face? Why was he staring at me?

My anxiety started to creep over me, and I started to feel uncomfortable. Luckily, Jaxon broke the awkward silence.

"Hey, man, do you have a broom? I'll help get this swept," Jaxon said and the man's stare finally broke away from me to look at the shattered teapot.

"Oh, thanks, man. I will clean it. No big deal." The man said and looked back at me. "I'm sorry, you reminded me of someone. Kind of caught me off guard, lady. Well, my mistake, unfortunately, just left you with the fish and the mug only. I hope that is okay?"

I looked at him confused. Trying to place him, but I had never seen him before. "Yes, we will take those two. Thank you, and I'm sorry about the teapot." I said apologetically, happy since I wanted the tentacles mug regardless. "I can pay for the broken one too," I offered.

"Oh, no, not at all. I am clumsy. It was my fault," he said, shaking his head. "If you two don't mind though, I am going to lock the door and put the closed-sign up since I don't have anything left for other customers and that way I can start glazing these, while you two paint." He motioned to the clay pieces and we both nodded in agreement. "Happy first date to you both. The paints are back there already next to the brushes. Just yell if you need anything.

Make sure you do multiple coats of paint, they glaze better that way." He winked at us, handed us the ceramic pieces, and started walking to the door for the closed sign, then back to the counter to grab some of the kids' pieces to start firing them. He disappeared to the backroom to get to work.

"Do you know him?" Jaxon asked me once we were alone.

"No, I've never seen him before."

"He was looking at you like you stood him up on a date or something. You sure you didn't break his heart while I was away? I obviously wouldn't be mad; I was gone for a long time."

"No, I really have never seen him before. Honestly, I would tell you." He shrugged and we dropped it. It was time for our date day, and we were lucky to have the whole place to ourselves.

We grabbed a plate and started to pick out our colors. I grabbed black, purple, light green, light blue, and a dark blue and filled my plate with enough paint color for each. My mug was much cooler than the fish on the rocks statue, I smiled internally knowing this. Jaxon grabbed bright colors, not at all the colors I would've picked for a normal-looking fish or rocks. He was going to make a one-of-a-kind statue.

"Hey, cool, look at this," he pointed to the fish's mouth and then to the bottom of the rocks. "It's a hidden compartment. You could put a house key or something larger in the mouth here and then you lift this bottom rock for the hidden door to open and collect it. That's actually pretty genius," he said excitedly.

Okay, maybe his choice was the better pick after all.

"That is really cool! Are the colors you're picking going to match your bedroom by any chance? Because those colors are not very flattering." I laughed at him, and he came up behind me and started tickling me, as he laughed and mocked me for making fun of him.

"Hey, stop," I said between giggles. "I'm going to spill the paint." I caught my breath and dipped my finger in the purple paint, and spread it across his face. Before he could react to what I did, I grabbed the blue and got his other cheek. We were both laughing when he grabbed me from behind, setting my paint plate down and holding my arms steady to my chest. He grabbed his unflattering bright green paint bottle and squeezed a dime-sized amount out on the top of his hand while holding me still and made a green heart on my left cheek before I could get out of his arm lock.

"Hey... No fair! At least I picked good colors." I said, and we laughed seeing each other's painted faces. He grabbed my face and kissed me sweetly. The butterflies returned, and I couldn't help but smile at him.

"Come on, let's paint these masterpieces," he said as he grabbed our paint plates and we went to sit down.

We painted and let them dry, then painted another coat and let them dry again. We did that about four times before we both stood back and looked at what we had created. As much as I didn't want to admit it, his fish turned out pretty badass. I was excited to see what it would look like fired and glazed. My mug looked very under the sea themed and would be neat when it was glazed too.

In between focusing on the painting, we made small talk about life and what the future could hold. We kept the talking ordinary. There was no witch talking, just in case the worker was in earshot. He had been in the back the entire time, occasionally walking out and grabbing a new group of kids' pieces to fire up. He would glance over at us but never said anything more to us until we were ready to pay and leave.

We walked to the counter when they dried and waited for him to return to the register.

"Well, those turned out great. I will call you in a few days once they're fired and ready for pick up."

I finally looked at his name tag. *Ezra.* He was very nice, I'd be sure to leave a good review for him on their website.

"Thank you for letting us come in here. It was very fun," I said while looking at Jaxon smiling.

"Yeah, man, thank you! That was just what we needed," Jaxon said. "Her dad is going to love me when I give him the fish as a gift." He laughed and looked back at me.

"Oh yeah? Trying to buy my dad's love now, I see."

"Doesn't hurt to bribe him with gifts. I mean I am dating his only daughter," Jaxon said while Ezra looked at us both and smiled.

"Alright, you two, this one is on us. Go enjoy the rest of your day. Just write your name and number down and we will call you when they're ready for pickup." Ezra said

We both thanked him for the unexpected gift to us. Jaxon and I both wrote our names and numbers down, whoever was available first could come and grab them. We headed out of the door and back on our first date adventure.

"Where to next?"

Jaxon smiled as we jumped back in the car.

I sat down and turned around, noticing he had a small

cooler in the backseat of his car. He said he wanted to have a picnic at our abandoned field. No magic, just a picnic, he said.

The June sun was starting to get warm, I unzipped my hoodie and took it off. We rolled down the windows and drove up the bluffs toward the field. The breeze felt nice. To the left, you could see the river flowing beautifully and fast with boaters throughout. The sky was blue with a few clouds spread out so the sun didn't have any clouds to block its warmth. We made it to the abandoned road, parked the car, and grabbed the cooler. He even had packed a blanket to sit on. He had planned this whole thing and actually put effort into it. I smiled to myself, thinking that a week ago, I never would have dreamed of any of this being possible, yet here we were.

He laid the blanket down and set the cooler on it. He pulled out homemade turkey sandwiches, personal bags of chips, two sodas, and a whole bag of chocolate chip cookies. I smiled when I looked at his pre-planned date day. We ate and laid on the blanket, looking up at the newly rolling clouds in the sky. It was nice. It was everything that I needed.

I turned over and blushed when I saw him already staring back at me. "Thank you for this." His brown hair was falling to his brows and his blue-green eyes staring back at me with admiration.

"This is just the beginning. We have plenty of time for more dates." He smiled and leaned in to kiss my forehead. He pulled me closer until my head was snuggled into the nook of his neck. He smelled of sandalwood and soap. The same woodsy scent that he used to have. It was weird how certain scents could trigger a memory or a person. His scent overpowered my Verbena soap and Juniper shampoo and I didn't mind one bit. His scent would linger on my clothes, and that was another thing that I loved.

"Do you think we would've made it this long if there wasn't an accident?" I asked.

"I like to think so. Why do you ask?" He hugged me a little tighter.

"Just overthinking and all. You know me, or at least you used to." I laughed nervously, realizing that I had grown up and that I hoped that he wouldn't get bored with me.

"I'm just happy that we're making up for lost time... Freya, if it were up to me, I never would've left you alone. I promise, I never stopped thinking about you." He looked down at me with a serious expression. I looked up at him and felt my cheeks flush at his so-sure words.

"I never stopped either," I said back to him.

He pulled me atop him and started to kiss me deeply. I pushed my lips back to meet his just as fast. His arms had me encircled and seemed very afraid of letting go. He groaned and started kissing my neck. My head was swirling with excitement. He flipped me to my back gently and pulled my chin up higher so my lips reached his. My hands reached to explore his firm torso. His breathing slowed as he held in a chuckle, as my fingers traced his abs must've started to tickle, and his kisses became less urgent and sweeter. My breathing started to even out with his as I smiled back, but my cheeks became too warm and my fingers began to tingle.

Oh no!

I could feel my magic coming out to play.

How do I control this electricity?

I sat up quickly, pushing him off of me, and I clenched my fingers into fists. He could see them sparking once he looked down at them. My embarrassment grew. I could feel my emotions not letting me keep my magic under control.

"Shit!" I screamed and stood back quickly to give distance between us. The last thing I wanted was to hurt him. The electricity went to the palm of my hands, and I had to open them before a fire erupted. The electricity shot up through my palms as if I was struck by lightning, only I was producing the lightning and it was purple.

Jaxon stood and tried to come near me but I shook my head frantically. "Stay back."

"Freya! Are you okay?" Jaxon yelled across from me. His protective instincts made me go against my wishes as he closed the distance between us, grabbing my arms and holding them both up and away from both of us with his cooling hands. The magic slowed and then stopped. My hands trembled, not knowing what just happened.

"I'm so sorry, I don't know what just happened." I looked down at my hands and shook my head. "That came out of nowhere. I'm sorry." I bit my lip embarrassed and stood up, pacing back and forth trying to understand it myself.

My surroundings started to disappear again, my knees grew weak, and I saw the ground coming up fast before Jaxon caught me, but even he started to dissolve.

I was standing in a garden, and Ezra was with me. We were walking hand in hand. I told him that I wanted to show him something that I had been practicing. I looked at my hands, and started with purple electricity, and formed it into a sphere of purple. I rotated it with my other hand then turned it red. He called me 'babe' and said that he was proud of me. He said that I had never been able to change its colors before. Then, he took my hands and closed his hands around mine, and it disappeared. He smiled proudly at me, and he leaned in to kiss me.

My eyes opened wide, and I was back in Jaxon's arms. He was cradling me with true concern on his face.

"Woah, where did you go?" Jaxon asked nervously.

"I just had another vision," I said worriedly. Trying to sit myself up and hold myself together. "These are getting vivid and kind of weird."

"What happened in this one?" He asked.

"I was practicing my electricity magic thing and changing the electric sphere to a different color. But I don't even know how to do that." I shrugged. Leaving out the part about Ezra, because that was not going to happen and had not happened, I really hoped Alex could explain these visions a little more. I also really hoped that these visions were not predicting the future because I wanted Jaxon in my life. Especially since I only just recently got him back.

Ezra was a good-looking guy, but come on! Really?

Jaxon looked at me with concern.

"Hopefully, Alex can help explain these more this weekend. I don't know much about visions to be honest. I'm an Earth witch, nothing more." His lips came up in a defeated pout.

"You're not nothing, and I hope she can." I smiled at him. "Maybe we can just pretend this part didn't happen on our first date if that's okay with you too?" I asked. "I'm a little embarrassed that I don't have more control over my magic."

"You're a newbie who has just learned she has magic. I wouldn't expect anything less. I'll help as much as I can." He kissed my forehead and rubbed my arms until I started to relax more.

We spent the next few hours back on our date day. We laid under our tree in the field on the blanket and discussed what he has been doing the last year and a half. Job-related, relationships, achievements, and anything else that made me feel like I knew him again. He was quick to say no relationships since us. He had worked a few part-time jobs to keep him busy, and he finished his high school with online classes so he could work and practice his magic with his parents. He had a full-time workload with magic training, online schooling, and part-time work. He didn't have time for a relationship.

"Do you really think we would've still been together if it weren't for that night?" I asked shyly again. Not ready to hear the answer if it was not what I was hoping for.

"I think so. I mean, I hope so." He leaned closer into me and grabbed my hand, interlocking our fingers. "I know I haven't aged well." I laughed at his sarcasm.

"Oh, yeah, the masquerade mask made you more presentable in public for sure." I jumped up and ran away from him chasing me, teasing me back. Simple, fun love.

The sun had passed us overhead and was starting to set toward Iowa. I sat up and looked toward the Mississippi and watched the pink and golden sky make the river shine brighter and just stared at the beauty of the land that we lived on.

Breathtaking.

We packed up and he dropped me off at home. Kissing me goodnight. I felt like I was walking on clouds as for once... my life felt happy again.

Journal: June 9th ~

Jaxon took me on our first, well, new "first date" and it was really fun. My cheeks still hurt from smiling so much. You know, that feeling you get called a "perma-smile" where your face feels like it just got done with a tough workout, but it was a great workout, or when the muscles just hadn't been used in a long time and they are stuck that way. Yeah, they feel kind of like that. The pottery place was fun. I'm excited to pick up the finished products in a few days.

That boy Ezra was a little odd, though. He was handsome, but I had never seen him before today, and I don't know why he kept staring at me. I must've checked my reflection in the window ten times to make sure nothing was out of the ordinary. Then, to have a vision with him in it was extremely weird. I'm writing this down so that I can get it off my chest without having to tell Jaxon. I didn't want to ruin our first date any more than with my hands feeling like they were going to explode with magic while we were kissing. That was embarrassing enough.

I need to get this magic under control, I know that it's all new to me still, but I feel deep

in my bones that I was born for this. Something inside me keeps telling me to push harder, that something is coming that I need to be prepared for. My body keeps telling me that this magic path is exactly where I'm supposed to be.

I'm a WITCH! There, I said it. I'm a witch, and I'm going to figure ME out!

Chapter 11

Clara Vine, the Badass Witch

Friday was finally here after a long, uneventful Thursday night of selling tickets and vending popcorn at the Rendezvous to a few customers that came in to watch a new romantic flick that was having a sneak peek special. There was no magic play since I was training a new hire. The young kid had to tag along with me everywhere and I had to teach him everything I knew. After work, I had to shower just to get the extra butter flavoring out of my hair that I swore the smell lingered for days if not washed out. I ended up having an early night last night, knowing that I had to work today and then Alex would be picking me up.

Jaxon had agreed to spend Friday with my dad out on the fishing float, like old times. I think he wanted a distraction himself, knowing that I was about to spend the day with his ex-wife, and deep down, I knew his feelings for her never left him. He still loved her very much. Jaxon gave me a lingering kiss, which made my knees wobble and my cheeks flushed all before seven a.m., before he left for the day with their fishing gear. They both promised they were only a phone call away if I needed them.

After work was over I walked outside of the back door of the theatre after punching out to look for Alex. She was waiting in the lot for me. I jumped in her car, and we headed south about thirty minutes or so to Prairie Du Chien, which had a larger population than the town of Crystal Rock but was still on the smaller size for a city. Alex was driving and pulled over right before the 'Welcome to Prairie Du Chien' sign.

"Here, spray this on you, it's a protection spray, and I can't afford to let anyone find them because of us," she said quickly and handed me the spray. "It has Vetiver and crystal-infused black tourmaline. It's going to shield us from being found on their map."

"Tourmaline?" I reached for my pendant that Jaxon had made me and twisted the crystal in my hand. Alex looked down at my hand on the necklace and nodded.

"He made you a protection necklace before the accident. That actually makes a lot of sense now," Alex stated.

"Yeah, I guess it means more than just a silly art project then. I don't understand, who are we hiding from?" I asked.

"I didn't say yet. Let's go see Clara, she can explain things a little better. She is the other puzzle piece to this story for you."

I sprayed myself, and so did Alex. She pulled back onto the road and headed toward a house in the bluffs. The house was located on a secluded dirt path road. The only way of knowing there was a house a mile down the road was because of the mailbox at the edge of the road. We pulled up to a small cottage built into the side of a bluff. There were vines growing along the sidewalls, and a garden to the right with another to the left.

Wow, this person was really into plants.

There was a light on in the house as we got out of the car. We started walking toward the front door when it opened quickly, and the short lady with dark hair and the same oval glasses was on the other end, waving at us to come in quick. We walked in, and she looked behind us at the dirt path before coming in and closing the door. She whispered something with her hands on the door. I couldn't make it out, but the door glowed with a bright light briefly before she turned around to greet us.

"Well, let's take a good look at you." She held her hand out to me and motioned me to spin around. "Ah, yes, you have become a beautiful woman. It has been a long time. I'm sure you don't remember me... but I'm Clara, and you can call me Aunt Clara if you would like to." She smiled with very caring eyes and a soft face. She had a sincere tone to her voice, a motherly one. I guess first impressions do stand out.

"Yes, I slightly remember you actually. I was a kid, though, so it's been a while. It's nice to officially meet you."

"Your mother—" Clara started to say when I cut her off.

"She's not my mother," I said too quickly with bitterness.

"Sorry... *Alexandra* told me that we have a story to explain to you. I think you actually might think differently of her once you hear it. It's a story that should've been brought up a long time ago, but we were playing things as safe as possible for the time being with other bloodlines being wiped out. We couldn't risk it," she started, then stopped. "Why don't we go sit down, and we can discuss this family matter more?"

I agreed and we went to sit down in her cozy living room. Everything about the house seemed warm and welcoming. It was not just a house, it was a *home* and it felt nice. Clara offered us tea and mini cucumber sandwiches. I really wasn't hungry, but the tea sounded good. My stomach was still a little queasy from anticipation as to what was going to be found out today. I took the tea and sipped on it. The warm liquid was soothing to my throat.

"Well, where do we begin?" Clara spoke. "Alexandra, how about you start with the reasoning behind the Marks that we get?" She spoke with her sweet voice. It was odd, even though my stomach felt like it was in knots with the unknown, I somehow felt really calm here. I felt as if my mood went from nervous and anxious to relaxed, just like when Alex had touched my electric hands last weekend to give me a feeling of calming tranquility. But then my phone buzzed, and it made me jump. I could feel my cheeks blush when I saw who it was, and I sheepishly smiled thinking about our prolonged kiss this morning before work.

Jaxon- Hey, how is everything? Just checking in.

Freya- Yeah, we just got to our destination. She's explaining some "family history". Call ya later. K?

Jaxon- Okay, call me if you need me sooner. Fish ON!

I looked up, and Clara and Alex were staring at me, questioning my smile and rosy cheeks.

"Your boy, I presume?" Clara asked. "He's the reason

your Mark reappeared on you, at least that's what we're guessing. He broke the hideaway spell during that accident. We were trying to keep your magic hidden with a simple spell that we cast early on in life. The less you knew the better... we thought, which up until now was working out very well." Clara sighed.

"Why would you want my magic to stay hidden?" I asked, confused.

"Well, Freya, you come from a very strong bloodline of witches, and unfortunately, there are a few Immortals left that are trying to wipe us all out and be the only ones remaining." Alex started talking and looked up at me to see if I was ready for this. I was eager and ready, at least I thought so. I nodded to go on. "They have been trying to kill off our bloodlines and gain permanent immortality. With each pair of Anchors that they kill with the dagger, they gain their magic and longevity. It's sadistic and sad, but that's why they are the most powerful witches out here. They have to be around a thousand years old by now. We're not exactly sure how many are left in their clan. Last we had heard, it was just Eric and Izzy left, but of course, they have to change their names every few decades to blend in. So, we don't really know what they may go by now." As Alex was talking, my mind was firing with this new information of immortal enemies.

Was this even real life? It sounded more like a movie.

I sat forward on the loveseat, and one of my hands came up under my chin to keep my jaw from dropping while the other hand tried to lay causally on my lap like this was a normal day.... But this was much more than just a normal day. This was really happening, and I nodded again for her to continue as if I could consume more.

"When we are born, we have another witch born that will share our Mark. Usually, they are born that same month, and the most powerful ones share a birthday. They become your Anchor. The universe decides who is meant to be with who. Your Anchor could be a lover, a friend, a family member, or a complete stranger. We don't know why it happens that way, but it's just how the universe plays her games." Alex looked at Clara for clarification that she was explaining things easily enough to understand. Clara nodded in encouragement. "The Mark that we receive will match our Anchor's identically in the same location."

"So that's why Mrs. Oakes made Jaxon leave. June third is his birthday, so she thought we were Anchors. She was trying to keep us alive after the accident by splitting us up. But I never had a visible Mark."

"It seems that way, yes. Although, Margo Oakes has had a feud with Alexandra since she started dating Jim back in high school. She was never very fond of Alex." Clara stated, which I guess Margo and I had that in common. "She could have done that in a much more informative way for you, though. I am sorry for how left in the dark you were about being a witch until recently. I did not see you in a vision until this past weekend, which is why I called Alex to tell her your Mark reappeared after all these years." Clara explained. "We're assuming that Jaxon triggered your magic, which could make your Mark reappear. That would be why you haven't had any accidental magic mishaps in the past. Your full magic potential has been locked up until recently. For good reason... we thought, at least until now."

"Wait, you have visions too?" I asked excitedly to have something in common with another witch, and if she knew about mine, then maybe she could help explain how they work.

"Freya, I have quite a few tricks up my sleeve. I've had more practice than you, my dear." Clara smiled and touched my hand in a caring caress. I felt my shoulders relax and the feeling of calm came over again. "The visions work better over time as we practice controlling them."

"Hold on, is this you making me feel all calm and relaxed, or is it the tea?" I asked, laughing. It was weird, she could say anything and I felt like I could trust Clara with my life. It was too bad I didn't feel the same way about Alex anymore.

Clara smiled and said, "Yes, Alex and I have the power of persuasion as one of our specialties. I also have the visions and a few more gifts I was blessed with. Mostly a green thumb." She smiled. "And the tea is just going to help your mind relax and help you take in all of this information without feeling overwhelmed."

Woah, that was going to help my head from exploding. "Back to the overload then," I said, sipping faster on the sweet honey, magic tea.

Alex half smiled and looked away in the distance. "A few months before you were born, Eric showed up. He was there waiting for me on the porch while your father was still at work. He wanted to know how far along I was but wasn't asking for the sake of a healthy pregnancy. He was terrifying, and I knew something bad was about to happen.

When I tried to get past him and run back to my car, he grabbed me and yanked me into our house. Nearly knocked me out when he slammed me up against the wall. The room was spinning, and it was hard to concentrate on what was happening. When my head cleared, I realized that he came to threaten me. He said he would spare my life and Jim's life for the price of giving you to him. He thought Jim was my Anchor. He thought he held the power over my life, thinking that we were paired together as witches in the same house as Jaxon's parents do. He was wrong about your father, though, and the deal meant nothing to me. I would not give you up to him, and he then realized that Jim had no Mark, which made him angry. You see, Eric and Izzy paid a price for immortality. They were sterile and could not produce an heir for the legacy they had created. The price of killing innocent lives cursed them, and the universe would not let them bring life into this world. They became obsessed with trying to collect a set of Anchors to raise as their own. Unfortunately for them, no one was willing to give up their children, which is when they started wiping us out." Alex's eyes came back to me for a quick second before she looked away and continued.

"Eric left that day, and his silence was what scared me. He turned on his heel and walked away without saying a word. Eric is not someone you want to cross, considering that he is immortal and dangerous. I knew I had to come up with a plan before you were due. I called Clara and filled her in on Eric's deal, and we came up with our own plan for the day you were born." She looked at Clara, and I saw a slight smirk reach her lips, but a small tear forming at the corner of her blue eyes. "It was ultrasound day, and Clara came with me while your father was at work. It was that day we realized we were expecting not one little witch, but two of you."

I choked on my own tea and wiped my lip. "What do you mean two?" I interrupted, unsure of what she was going to say next. I couldn't tell if I was excited or freaking out due to the tea and Clara having my emotions just in a mellow mood.

Clara took over. "Freya, we had to split you guys up at birth. You two were the first set of true natural born Anchor witches both born with the Mark, not needing a near-death experience to trigger it either, and you were born under the full red moon, which is the most powerful energy force given to our kind. And to be born twins, nonetheless. It has never happened in our lifetime. Only something we were told as children by our families. Once we found out that Alex was carrying twins, linked Anchor twins, we knew nobody could find out. Not even your father, my dear." Clara stood up and continued to talk while pacing back and forth. "We came up with a plan that has not been an easy plan for anyone, but it needed to be done. If Eric would have come to the hospital and realized what you were, then he would've taken you both from the hospital and disappeared, and we would've forever been chasing a psycho and his mate to the ends of the earth to find you both. This was the only way to keep you and her alive and with us. We had to use a memory tea concoction on the nurses and doctors that had helped with the ultrasounds and on delivery day. Even with your father, unfortunately. Which is why he was 'out fishing with no cellphone service' on your birthday." Clara put her hand on Alex's shoulder, with tears glimmering in the corner of her eyes that were ready to spill over.

Maybe there was more to her leaving my dad and me behind than I originally thought.

I have a twin?

It was an insane thought that all this time I had a sibling and didn't even know. I swallowed hard and tried to stop my thoughts from overwhelming me and continue with as much information as I could learn before she left again.

"So, is my twin..." I hesitated at the new word in my vocabulary. "Is she my Anchor?" Clara looked at me and nodded gently with a smile. "Does she live here? Does she know about magic? Can she do the same magic as me?" I had so many questions that started to overflow my brain, and my mouth couldn't keep up with my thoughts. I needed the answers to come faster than I could ask. I needed to see her with my own eyes and then maybe everything would fall into place and make more sense.

Clara laughed quietly and waved her hands to slow down. "Yes, she lives here with me. Yes, and yes. Combined, you two can be the strongest pair of Anchor witches from a single bloodline in decades, if not centuries. Even more peculiar is that Jim is mundane and still produced a set of witch twin heirs with Alex's bloodline." Clara shook her head. "It's been a long eighteen years trying to keep you both safe and making sacrifices where they were needed most. I understand how you feel about Alex leaving, but she really didn't have a choice that week." I looked to Clara and then to Alex, wondering what could've happened that made her finally snap and divorce him.

What could've been so bad that you would abandon your family?

"Eric threatened Alex again. Only this time, he had me... physically. He was able to track her down with my blood that was taken with his Viking dagger that is ancient and cursed. He can drop the blood on his cursed map and it can track the Anchors location." I gasped as Clara was explaining. "He had caught me off guard at the grocery store and saw my Mark behind my ear." She paused and pointed to her Mark. It was the same swirly symbol that Alex had shown me. The Marks were so strange, they looked as if you put a sticker on and went tanning, only they didn't disappear when your skin went pale again. "He grabbed me in the parking lot with an obsession he was trying to fulfill. Once he had me, he took my blood to track my Anchor on the map. He realized that he found Alex and had finally found us both. He told Alex to meet him, or he would kill me and throw my body into the bottom of the river tied to an anchor so that I would repeatedly drown in the river until she gave herself up. Then they would kill us both permanently. That day, she decided to divorce Jim and leave you to come find me without getting herself killed. Once she made it to me, Eric had stepped away for a phone call. It was the only time luck seemed to be on our side that day... Alex broke into the warehouse and got me out of there while I took the dagger for my own safety measures. Eric came back to an almost empty room with a bloodstained map that wouldn't work without the dagger. I can still hear his furious screams to this day. Alex has been on the run, as he thinks she has it with her." She smiled and exchanged a look with Alex as she nodded. "While actually, I kept the dagger protected here, in case he ever caught up to her, then I would have the leverage to let her go for the dagger. We have taken extra precautions with the protection spells over this house and your sister so that we can not be tracked so easily. So he has not found us since, and we're planning on keeping it that way. She and I live in this cottage. And he never came back to your house because he was too busy tracking Alex and the dagger far away from here. That's why we use the protection spell on the door, the spray before entering the city, and even my pottery shop is protected, just for extra measures." She smiled and winked at me.

I looked over at Alex, and for a brief moment, I actually felt the twinge of sadness for her and her sacrifices. I supposed that running for your life to keep your family safe was a huge sacrifice, and maybe I was being too hard toward her. The thought of leaving my family behind made my stomach turn as I remembered the pain I had felt losing Jaxon after the accident. I couldn't even imagine running for my life every day alone, never knowing who or when someone was watching me.

I swallowed hard and felt my emotions trying to ignite. "I think I need just a minute." I stood up and paced back and forth in the living room, trying to gather my thoughts.

Alex had been running to protect her family, and Clara had been living invisibly to keep my twin and herself safe. Clara had the dagger that Eric needed and Eric was or is a life-sucking psycho witch who's very old and has some love-mate that wanted to steal Anchor babies and witches' lives.

Creepy.

My body shook as I thought about the faceless man of the story.

Does Clara own a pottery shop? The pottery shop that Jaxon and I went to? She must know Ezra... And I have a sister... Wait, I have a sister?

I stopped pacing and turned to face them. "So, I have a twin? Is she here right now?"

"At this point, we don't think it's a great idea to meet until we know we're not being watched," Alex stated. "Even though we have the dagger, Eric is clever beyond belief. He will find a way to get what he wants."

I nodded and turned away from them.

"And you're not staying around I'm guessing?" I asked Alex selfishly.

"I don't think it's a good idea. I lost his whereabouts a few weeks ago. I've been trying to lead him in a circle, trying to find out who his Anchor is to have leverage for when he comes."

When he comes, not if he comes.

"They are never together it seems. All we know is she goes by Izzy, which is most likely short for Elizabeth, and that their Marks are located on their left arm in a triangle intertwining with an upside-down triangle." Alex traced her forearm in the form and continued to talk. "I don't think he has given up on finding me yet. I think he's planning something." She sighed heavily. "I risked coming back here when Clara called me saying she saw your Mark reappear and everything had changed. I knew I needed to come and discuss things in person and see why or who had made your magic get triggered... I thought Eric had come for you."

She stood and crossed her arms in an awkward position, as if she wanted to come and hug me but stopped herself for my sake. I needed to change the subject and dodge the hug that I wasn't ready for. I needed more information about everything while this tea was still soothing me.

Chapter 12

The Ultimate Weapon

"What did you mean by a Viking dagger?" I asked.

Clara stood up and walked to another room. She came back with a leather sheath that she began to untie to show the glimmer of the dagger.

"The Viking dagger is legendary in the witch world," Alex became excited and speaking too fast. She noticed and slowed her voice, realizing that this was all new to me and she needed to keep things at a first-grade level for now. If she never would've left, then all of this would be a hell of a lot more normal to me.

"The dagger was created by a Pagan witch who fell in love with a traveling Viking. Of course, every curse starts with either love or heartbreak." Clara said, "The Pagan was banned from her lover's ship due to them believing she was evil and would cause bad luck to the crewmen. She may have been, but according to the legend, she just loved the man so much that to be separated was killing her. She spelled the dagger and map for her Viking lover to be tracked while he would sail. He wore a necklace with her blood in it so when she cut her hand to draw her own blood and place it over the map, she could track where he was. They didn't have a GPS back then." She smirked. "She did this for months while he would come and go.

"Unfortunately, one night while he was home, she decided to make an engagement gift for herself with his blood in a vial to feel closer to him while he was away. As she was making the vial, his blood dripped onto the map and started to spiral into a location not too far from where they lived. The Pagan witch decided to follow the map that night while her Viking was sleeping. Once she made it to the location, she found a woman who shared an identical Mark with the Viking on her forearm. Only her Viking had it tattooed while the woman had it as what we know to be the Anchor Mark. The woman was pregnant with a child, and she believed the woman was carrying her Viking's child, which is why the blood tracked the baby on the map. The Pagan witch became distraught, feeling as though she had been betrayed and her love had been unfaithful. With rage, she broke into the house and killed the woman, leaving the pregnant belly to pass on its own.

"The next day the pregnant woman was walking the street to the Viking and Pagan's house to confront the Pagan witch. The breathing, living woman, still with the child, pounded on the door until the Viking answered with confusion. He had no choice, but to confirm his love for the woman and his unborn child. He explained they were destined to be together because the God's chose them to be each other's Anchor in this world. They were the first Anchors known in the universe. They believed themselves to be gods. The Pagan witch became disgusted and enraged with black fire. She tried throwing her fire toward them, but the Viking blocked it with his glowing Mark. She dropped to her knees, defeated. She had been betrayed. She yelled incantations and cursed the sword before piercing the witch's pregnant belly again, ending the Viking's child's life. After cursing the map, dagger, and Anchor witch's futures and also ensuring infertility to the Viking's lover, she took her own life by stabbing her own heart, letting the dagger fall to the ground.

"The dagger became a curse for the Anchor witch line because we can be tracked by it. The Viking and his Anchor were unable to bear children and died. That was the curse the Pagan witch whispered before using her own blood magic to seal it. Luckily for us, the universe continued to produce Anchors after them." Clara paused. "Rumor has it that the Pagan witch lived on and bound herself to the Viking's life so she could pass with him. Using him as her Anchor too, in hopes of somehow being linked to him in the afterworld. Little did she know that consuming witches' lives with the dagger would give immortality to future witches. The dagger became the most powerful weapon of the witching world. The dagger was discovered by Eric a few hundred years back and he became aware of the power it held after killing his first pair of Anchor witches." Clara finished the story before shrugging at the last part. "Again, that was the story that was told to us growing up."

I released a breath that I didn't realized I was holding. "What the hell? Now that is the crazy witch stuff that I assumed was only in movies," I said with my jaw hanging open in amazement at the legend and disgust at how savage love could make people. *How could someone use their powers to destroy a child's life and curse a whole witch line?* Love could be a dangerous game.

"I know, child. It was a story that us witches became very familiar with. That was the one dagger that we had all been looking for over the last years to be able to finally protect us." She handed me the dagger as I turned it around and examined the handle, which had teeth attached to the bone. It was made out of the mandible jaw of some animal. Clara saw me examining the teeth structure. "It's a Hildis-vini battle boar's lower jaw. It was used for strength and support of the magical blade. It was known from the Viking or Norse mythology, but must be a real animal considering that we have a piece of history in front of us." The blade was in a sheath, so I took it out to examine it further. The blade was made of black obsidian and was inevitably sharp and unbelievably well-kept for many centuries. I felt slightly nauseous and realized this was a murder weapon, and it needed to be destroyed. My stomach felt more uneasy holding such a piece.

"Why not destroy this so Eric can't get it back; wouldn't that be a problem solved?"

"Unfortunately, that is the only weapon that is believed to kill Eric and Elizabeth for good with how powerful they've become over the centuries," Alex explained. "That dagger is our bargaining chip that he wants so desperately because he knows we can destroy them with it, but also they can track our Anchors with it. So, it is a tough bargaining chip to hold."

"Eric uses it to consume the dead's powers. When he kills without the dagger, it is merely for sport because he does not gain anything from it except for wiping out lineage," Clara said. "Magic gets absorbed through the obsidian and transfers through the handle while the canine pierces the hand that holds it. Transferring the magic unto the next while the souls stay in the obsidian blade."

My breathing had become uneven without even realizing it. This was crazy to think about, and now knowing that my family bloodline was in danger made being a witch not as cool as I thought intentionally. The thought of Alex running for her life to protect all of us was starting to make me have a soft spot for her. But a damn call or text would've been nice over the years.

Ding-Ding-Ding-Ding.

I jumped at the vibration and sound of my phone on the table and grabbed it. My fingers fumbled as I tried to see who texted me, and I dropped it onto the plate of sandwiches and they flew onto the floor.

Clumsy.

I felt like the tea was starting to wear off and my nerves were taking over.

"Shit, I'm so sorry. Where is a towel?" I asked, embarrassed.

"Don't worry about it. I've got it, darling." Clara stood and went to the kitchen with the dagger. She came back with a towel in hand and dagger-less. I insisted on cleaning up the mess I made and took the towel from her. I multi-tasked as I cleaned.

"So, do I have a certain kind of magic? I mean, am I supposed to have a specific kind of twin magic?"

"Well, nothing is set in stone. So, I guess only time will tell," Alex said while I glanced at my phone.

Aisling: Hey girl, how was the Alex thing? Is she still a bad witch or what?

Aisling: Is she still in town?

Aisling: Do you still want me to egg her car?

Aisling: Shit, are you still with her now? Don't let her see these texts!! LOL

I stared at the word witch and felt panic begin to consume me.

Does she know? What has Declan done?

Thinking quickly, but responding carefully.

Freya: LOL, Witch? Still with her actually. She's not as crazy as I thought....I'll call you later and fill you in.

Aisling: You better! :) Hey, side note, my Aunt Lynn is in town and wants to go to the Farmer's Market tomorrow with you and me and she wants to meet Declan. So invite Jaxon too, we will make it a double date! I won't take no for an answer.

Freya: Okay, I'm in for sure.

I really hoped that Declan hasn't been talking to Ais about witch stuff. I was going to kill him. She needed to stay out of all of it. I didn't need her getting involved. The thought of seeing her aunt was exciting, though. I have missed her, and it had been a while since she was last in town. Seeing her would be cool, and if she wanted to meet Declan and Aisling was letting her, then she must really like him. I wanted her to be happy. She was like my very own sister.

Sister!

My thoughts floated back to the idea of actually having a sibling.

"Can I ask to see a picture of her? My twin?" I stuttered at the word. "I guess that really hasn't sunk in fully yet. Maybe seeing is believing in this case?" I questioned still feeling very intrigued at having a real sibling and still angry that I was just finding this out now. Some things should *not* be kept secret. Especially things like, hey, you're a witch. Your mom left to protect you. Jaxon is alive. Oh, and hey you have a twin sister who has been in hiding all this time.

Was my whole life a lie?

At this very moment, it was feeling like it.

Clara walked to another room and came back with a photo album. I looked at the walls, searching for a photo of her when I realized the walls were empty, the hutch and table were empty too. There were no photographs on display anywhere. You never would know there was a daughter living here from the living room view. Clara came back with the album and sat between Alex and me and started to flip through the photos.

"Her name is Haven Vine. We had her take my last name for reliable paperwork, of course. She is brilliant and witty, very similar to you it seems. We can get you two together as soon as we know things are safe," Clara stated while turning the pages. "We need to make sure Eric does not find out."

She truly was identical to me. It was almost like looking at baby pictures of myself only with memories I did not have. No matter how much older she got we still looked the same. Newer pictures showed her with slightly shorter hair than mine, but our other features matched. It was bizarre. She had only been a town away from me my entire life. At first, I was feeling angry not knowing her, but now, I was actually becoming excited to know that I had a sister close by. Even better, now I knew who my Anchor was and that the universe paired me with my very own blood for a reason.

I glanced out of the window and realized that the sun was getting low. We had been here for hours talking about our family history and our ancestors' history. I had learned so much but still didn't feel like I knew enough about my magic. Alex and Clara said that in time, we would find out what Haven and I could really do. They were not really sure how far our magic could go, especially once we're together. My phone started ringing with my dad's piano riff playing. I grabbed it and answered it quickly to make sure he was okay.

"Hey, kiddo, just letting you know that Jaxon and I are heading to Swig and Jig to get this kid a fresh fish boil from today's catch." He said, sounding happy.

"Okay, I'm almost done here with Alex, glad you guys caught some fish."

"How is everything going?" he asked with a long sigh. I could tell he wanted to know everything and nothing at all.

"All good, Dad, I miss you!" I said to reassure him that our bond was not being replaced.

"Miss you too, Freya. Unfortunately, I'm going to have to close the bar up tonight, the new kid called in sick. So, if you want to maybe meet us here after you're done with your mom and bring Jaxon home, that would help me out."

"Oh, sure." A little disappointed that he wouldn't be home until early morning now. But it was good to have business, so he couldn't complain. Now that I was eighteen

I could start bartending if he wanted the help. I'd have to mention that to him another day.

"That's fine, Dad, save me some of that fish. I'll see you soon, love you."

"Love you too."

I looked up from my phone with a smile. Alex was staring back at me with sadness in her eyes. She had been running for the last two years, and who knows, maybe she really did miss our little family and still loved my dad. It was too soon to let my guard down with her, though. Maybe time would fix us.

"I can get you back to town if you are ready," Alex said.

"I mean, I kind of feel like I have a million questions, but it's almost like my brain is mush, and I can't seem to figure out what to ask. I know when I get home I'm going to think of more." I sighed, thinking about our time coming to an end, but was also excited to see Jaxon and my dad.

"How about I give you my new phone number, and you can call or text with questions as they come? I know you think I'm a shitty person for everything, and I hope one day you can forgive me, or at least understand where we're coming from." She looked at Clara, then her stare came back to me. "The least I can do is give you information when you ask," Alex said with a smile.

"It's definitely a start, Freya. Please give her a chance to make things right," Clara added with a nod.

"Yeah, I would appreciate the number." I hesitated for a brief second and looked at Alex before saying, "I'm sorry that you've missed the last two years with us. I hope you can stop running one day." That was all I had in me to say... I didn't let my guard down, but it was enough to let her know that I understood that she had made a sacrifice and had been living a double life. We smiled at each other, and it was then that I knew that my world had changed and I wasn't mad about it. My life was starting to make more sense.

Clara hugged me before leaving and gave me a bag of crystals with an instruction manual about how to make moon water into a tea and which crystals should be worn in my bra on what days or for what energies to attract. She was one badass witch aunt, and I was glad to have officially met her. Alex drove me back to my Jeep at the theatre. It was a quiet drive watching the sunset out of the passenger window. I couldn't think of anything else to say to her until I remembered I wanted to know about my visions and if she knew what triggered them. Might as well end this car ride with another answer.

"Hey, do you know why I keep getting these random visions? I meant to ask Clara."

"Clairvoyant, you have a supernatural gift of seeing the past, present, or future."

"Do you know how to control them? One kind of came to me at a weird time," I asked blushing, thinking about Ezra trying to kiss me while I was physically with Jaxon.

"You must be opening your mind up to the visions, otherwise they wouldn't be happening." She paused. "Actually, now that I think about it, Haven has them too. Maybe it's a twin thing for you two." Her brows furrowed. "I'm assuming that when you guys meet again, they will become more clear and help you control them a little more."

"Because my Mark will complete itself then," I answered my own question, and she nodded.

As we pulled up to my Jeep, I jumped out of the car before we had to have another awkward avoidance hug. I thanked her for today, and she looked like she was going to say more but paused and just smiled. Her smile was hauntingly beautiful, and a part of me, deep down in the crevices of my broken heart caused by her, I wanted to hug her. I knew I couldn't let my guard down yet. She would be gone again, and I couldn't get used to having a mother around because I couldn't go through the heartbreak again. My guard would have to stay up.

Chapter 13

Swig and Jig

I pulled up to the back parking lot of Swig and Jig and smiled. It made me happy, I thought about my childhood spent there to help Alex and my dad paint the walls and help him count the fishing lures and jigs at the end of the night for inventory. We lived in such a small town that the bar was never an out-of-control scene while I was around. I always felt like the owner of the place, which was partially true. I knew down the road he would put the bar in my name if I wanted it. It was kind of ironic that the girl who didn't drink may end up owning a bar. At least, I would never be too inebriated to count the cash and lures at the end of the night.

It was strange thinking that this place used to be my parents' retirement plan, how they had put every penny into it before it had become successful and Alex only had to do her realtor stuff on the side. That was why it had been hard to believe her when she was gone all the time before the divorce. After today's conversation, I'm guessing it was because she was trying to keep us safe. My head spun at the thought of the late nights she was gone before the divorce. She could've been working on trying to locate the dagger or keeping Eric away from us or raising another kid. She may have had a legit excuse. I shook my head to clear it before walking inside the bar.

Jaxon was sitting at the bar across from my dad laughing about something while drinking a soda. I smiled when I saw them interacting. It made my heart happy. No one else was in the bar tonight, which made me wonder what the rest of town would say seeing Jaxon alive and well. I'm sure my dad had already been telling everyone who walked into the bar about his return from amnesia. Which now really made Margo look like a nutcase.

Jaxon turned and saw me walking in, and before I could even get two steps in, he walked over to me and leaned in for a kiss. I saw my dad turn around out of the corner of my eye and smile. He wasn't embarrassed or upset; he was trying to give us a minute of privacy.

"How did everything go?" he asked worriedly.

"Really good, surprisingly." I said, and then whispered, "a lot of information that I'll have to fill you in on later." He smiled and kissed my forehead before we walked to the bar.

"Hey, darling, you missed a good fishing day with us." He chuckled and pulled his phone out to show me the stringer of bass and bluegills they got with pride.

"Don't worry, Dad, I'm not going to talk about her here. It went good, you don't have to even ask. She had to leave town again, so you can breathe." I winked, and he let out a big exhale that he had been holding onto, feeling relieved.

"Okay." He smiled and gestured for us to sit as he went to the back to grab me a plate of food.

We stayed and chatted about their day and how he got sunburn on his nose for forgetting the sunblock that I usually pack for him. We laughed and enjoyed the night. The bar started to get customers in, and a few night fishermen came in for new lures.

I decided it was time to head home. Jaxon asked to stay with me tonight, he felt that I shouldn't be alone after another eventful day. I was relieved when my dad was the one that suggested it.

Margo didn't seem happy when he called to tell her. I could hear her disappointment through the phone as if she used a megaphone to make it clear. I didn't understand why she hated me so much. Did she really just hate Alex for marrying my dad that much that she was taking it out on me? It just wasn't fair. I may have pretended that it didn't bother me in front of Jaxon, but ultimately, I was a born Gemini zodiac, and I didn't like anyone not liking me. Especially when the only "bad thing" I had done turned out to be fake and a cover up because of her.

We drove to my house after saying bye to my dad. On the ride home, I filled Jaxon in on everything that was said today. His jaw dropped like mine did when he found out about Haven.

"That's actually insane! I wonder if my mom knew any of that?" He grabbed my hand as we drove and shook his head.

"I don't think so, my own dad doesn't even know. It's definitely a secret of a lifetime."

He rubbed my fingers and nodded. I filled him in on the dagger and why Alex had been on the run and his jaw never shut.

"I mean... I had heard the stories of the dagger but didn't realize how close it was to us," he said. "Eric sounds like a sociopath. Let's just hope we never run into him or his woman."

I nodded and swallowed hard. "Yeah, I was pretty freaked out to hear that he had been killing witches with it... Made me question the coolness of being a witch."

He shook his head and laughed. "Trust me, the coolness outweighs that asshole... We will just be careful. I won't let anything happen to you, I promise." He squeezed my hand a little tighter as we drove the rest of the way home.

My journal was actually going to enjoy this simple day. I felt like I would have to write it down and reread it in the morning to make sure it wasn't a dream. That tea must've still been coursing through my system because I still *felt* calm.

My phone buzzed.

Ezra: Your pottery pieces are fired/glazed and ready for pickup anytime when the shop is open (P.S. they turned out great!)

I smiled and showed Jaxon the text as well pulled into the driveway. He frowned at first, asking why he didn't get the text, but of course, the man would text the pretty girl over him. Then, his phone went off too with the same text. We both laughed, and his shoulders dropped. Now I was even more glad that I didn't tell him about the Ezra vision. He seemed pretty jealous of him, even though he shouldn't be. I quickly changed the subject by telling him that he had to come to the Farmer's Market tomorrow with Aisling, Declan, and her Aunt

Lynn. He groaned at the idea of being in a larger crowd but didn't say no.

We walked inside, locked the house up and he put on a movie, and I took a deep breath and met him on the couch as I laid back in his lap to watch it, but as soon as my head hit his chest, my eyes felt heavy and my brain felt exhausted. Before I knew it, I had fallen asleep to the sound of his heartbeat and his light rhythmic chest rises under my head.

"Freya, don't freak out... I know you think this is a dream, but we need to talk. We need to get together in person for our Marks to complete themselves so these visions can be controlled."

I saw myself looking into a mirror, only it wasn't me. My hair was too short, and I didn't even own that shirt.

Haven.

Was she trying to connect with me, or was I dreaming? I looked at the mirror and realized it was her looking at me or me looking at her. It was a mindfuck. What time was it? I looked down at my watch and panicked. Wait... I was just sleeping, and Jaxon was with me... I needed to wake up. I looked around as my breathing quickened. As if Haven read my mind or body language, and she started talking again.

"No, please don't wake up yet, hear me out. Meet me by the river tomorrow near the pottery shop. We can complete our Marks then. We both need them to be whole for us to control our magic more. These visions are messing with me too. Please meet me there at sunrise."

This was definitely a dream. I felt myself twitch and finally confirmed with myself that I was dreaming. The mirror with Haven started to disappear, and my body started to fall through the floor, like in one of those dreams where you wake up right before you hit the ground. I was falling and everything around me was becoming dark, and I hoped that before I hit the ground I would wake up, but panic started to set in as I free fell.

Please let me wake up...

My eyes opened, and I could feel Jaxon underneath me still, just how we started the movie. The movie was over, and the TV screen was dark. *What time was it anyway?* I grabbed my phone to check the time. It was four in the morning, not nearing sunrise yet. My dad should be home from the bar by now. I stood up, and grabbed the blanket off the recliner, and laid it on Jaxon before heading toward his room to check on him.

Relief washed over me as I saw my dad sound asleep in his room. He must've shut the TV off when he got home. A part of me felt guilty for him seeing Jaxon and me sleeping on the couch, but I reminded myself that if he didn't like it, then he would be sure to tell me in the morning. No more secrets. Well, of course, I held a big secret from him now. I could feel the guilt consuming me just thinking about it. I wasn't supposed to have secrets from him anymore. It was our little pact. I needed to find a way to tell him at some point without him sending me to a psych ward. Just not right now. Right now, I was just happy to see him sleeping soundly and safe at our home.

I headed to the kitchen to grab a water bottle, but I jumped at the sound of footsteps coming toward me as I turned from the fridge. Jaxon came up from behind me and grabbed my hips, pulling me toward him.

"Waking up alone in your living room made me think

your dad carried you to your room or something." He laughed. "Is everything alright? You have that serious face right now." he asked. Never missing a detail.

I nodded while trying to open the bottle. "Yeah, I'm fine. Just checking on my dad to make sure he made it home from work." I hesitated about telling him my dream, but he was looking at me and I could tell he knew something was up. "I think I had a weird twin connection thing with Haven, or maybe it was just a dream," I said, feeling embarrassed. I think I was still getting used to the idea of having another human being around to hear my thoughts besides Aisling and my dad.

He grabbed the bottle and opened it for me. "What was it about?" he asked curiously before handing it back to me.

"She asked me to meet her by the pottery place at sunrise to finish our Marks." I shrugged.

He crossed his arms and leaned back against the counter. "Well, do you want to go? The sun will be up in like an hour. I can drive you?"

"You mean, you can drive my Jeep?" I laughed. "Remember, I am your ticket home."

He smiled and scrunched his nose.

"Up to you, love."

I blushed. "I don't know... I think it was just my mind playing tricks on me. Subconscious overthinking and being excited to meet her." I sighed. "Let's go back to sleep."

He smirked. "Or I can make you breakfast? Either way, it's a win for me to spend time with you." He pulled me closer and kissed me while holding me in a tight hug.

The feeling of his arms wrapped around me made me feel safe. Not that I couldn't handle myself because I was a strong, smart, independent woman, but having him around gave me butterflies. The same butterflies I thought I wouldn't feel again, or at least hadn't felt in a long time.

I smiled because breakfast and snuggles were the answer, and it worked for me. The sun was rising now, and a part of me wanted to go and check the pottery shop. Just in case she was really waiting there. It was a decent drive away, though, and Aisling wanted to meet up early for the Farmer's Market to get all the goods before they got picked over by the rest of the town. I couldn't go and I didn't want to be disappointed. I made up my mind and went upstairs to get dressed for the day of shopping.

Prairie Du Chien held their Farmer's Markets almost every weekend during the summer months, but this was the first one of the season and the biggest one they held each year. There were multiple vendors from other towns who gathered, so it was about five times the size of the normal ones. As Jaxon and I pulled up to the already busy parking lot, I spotted Aisling's car with Declan and her Aunt Lynn getting out of the car. Aunt Lynn was so pretty and looked as if she never aged. Her long, well-nourished, wavy dark hair that laid to her mid-back and tiny body frame with olive skin drew attention to her anywhere she went. She was the definition of a goddess. Aisling's whole family could've been formed from Zeus himself. I parked the Jeep and ran out to them, hugging Aisling first, then jumping to her Aunt Lynn's arms in a long hug.

"Ah, I've missed you so much! It's always so nice to see you!" I said with excitement.

"Oh, darling, I've missed you more. You have grown since I've last seen you. You have such a glow to you, beautiful as always," she said, as she kissed my cheeks and then examined me from head to toe. "Now who can this young man be?" she asked and whispered to me. "Is that your Oakes boy?"

I looked at her and nodded with a smile.

"It's a long story. One for another time." I winked at her, and she smiled in agreement.

Declan walked over to Jaxon and greeted him with some manly secret handshake. They laughed, and I heard Declan say they had their hands full with these women today. I rolled my eyes at them both.

"Hopefully, it doesn't rain before I can get to the handmade soaps! That vendor was here last year, and I finally ran out of all the bars I bought. That Verbena one was my favorite. The one I gave you too," Aisling said excitedly.

It was my favorite one too, the one I used often when I didn't want to wear perfume because it smelled so good.

Luckily today the sky was overcast with a light fog on the Mississippi due to the early morning dew. The sky looked like it would rain, but there was no rain in the forecast until later tonight. Hopefully we would be fine.

Handmade soaps, fresh veggies, flower bouquets, handmade jewelry, artwork, wooden signs, clothes, and so many more vendors. This was the market you didn't want to miss. We started walking through each tent, and today I was happy that I didn't have to pay for my Jeep so I had extra money to spend on arts and crafts. Jaxon had his arm around me as we went to the pottery tent. He pointed to a man spinning clay into a fish. I laughed and joked that his own would not turn out that cool. We kept browsing each tent, purchasing little odds and ends to support the locals.

Aunt Lynn walked back to us and handed Aisling and me each a small brown paper bag. We smiled at each other and opened them at the same time. Matching twine bracelets with Labradorite beads and an infinity symbol engraved on each. They were beautiful. As she put it on me I felt a little zap as she tied it on for me. I looked at her, questioning, but she didn't make eye contact with me. Which made me wonder if she felt that too? Or if it was just a coincidence....It had to be.

We had been walking around for a while and we still hadn't reached the end. There were still so many vendors to check out. I looked ahead and found the soap vendor that Aisling had been waiting for. I pointed it out to her, and she got all giddy, grabbing Declan's arm and went running with him. Jaxon grabbed my hand as we kept walking at a normal pace, and Aunt Lynn walked ahead a little faster to be close to her niece.

Everything seemed fine until a chill ran up my spine for a moment as we were walking by a handcrafted dagger/sword vendor. My body felt like I needed a hoodie on, even though it was already eighty degrees out. I had goosebumps and I could feel that something was off. Jaxon noticed the shift in my temperature and looked back at me.

"I'm okay, just got a random chill," I said reassuringly. "Hey, let's check this shop out." I said as I pulled his arm, dragging him with me.

The chill started to subside, but something about seeing the daggers made me think of Alex running with the ultimate weapon. I knew it was safe, but I just wanted to check out what they had in the tent. Jaxon looked at me questioningly, as if I had never been into renaissance daggers in the past. We glanced through a few, and I ran my fingers along a few of the handles just to see if anything triggered the chill. I didn't know how to be a badass witch yet, but I knew when my body felt off. That was something I had always been in tune with. Nothing felt out of place. And just like that... The chill was gone.

Weird.

I shrugged, and we kept walking. I looked up ahead and saw everyone still buying up the soap shop. I hoped she would save some for me. I chuckled at the thought of her ever forgetting about me. I knew she would never.

We were a tent away from the others when a woman with a hat and her hair in a ponytail collided with me by accident. For a split second, a hazy image of a blonde-haired woman with long braids started on the sides of her head above her ears down to her mid-back and heavy eyeliner that looked as if charcoal was used flashed in my mind. She was wearing a heavy fur coat and animal skin armbands intriguingly tied with leather. Then, in an instant, the image disappeared, and I was back to reality. The woman had run into me while her head was turned away looking behind her when we collided, causing her to drop her bag of herbs. If it weren't for Jaxon, my head would've hit the ground. He caught me and balanced me from the impact. The woman turned apologetically.

"I am so sorr—" she started and stopped. "Miss Chamberlain, I am so sorry. I wasn't looking where I was going." Isadora said almost frantically.

"Oh, it's okay. Are you okay?" The image was gone, and it was another pointless vision that led to nothing. I shook my head and tried fixed my top.

"Clumsy me, I turn my head for one second, and I make a fool of myself." She flashed a smile and fixed her hat.

"It's really okay." I smiled reassuringly. "Small town and all, I figured I'd run into half the town here. Just wasn't expecting to literally run *into* someone I knew." We both laughed.

She looked passed me and smirked. "Jaxon, I presume?" she asked.

"The one and only," he said, reaching for her hand in a greeting.

She smiled and offered her hand.

"Now I have a face for the name. Well, I better get going, can't miss the homemade honey tent up there. I hear Mr. Marcus has been selling out before noon each time he's here." She said with a chuckle and started to walk away before turning and saying, "I'll see you this week. Keep writing in that journal of yours."

I nodded and waved bye.

"Damn, that woman hit you hard. She's lucky you were so nice about it. Any other person may have shoved her back," Jaxon said.

Aunt Lynn walked back to us and looked me over as she asked with concern, "Who was that woman?"

"Oh, that was my therapist. Isadora." I shrugged. "I'm fine, really. It was no big deal."

"*That* woman is a therapist?" Aunt Lynn almost spat with her eyebrows raised.

I nodded. "She's actually pretty nice for a therapist. I don't think I really need to be seeing her much anymore, though. I feel like I'm doing better," I said embarrassed that this day was turning into a mental health assessment.

"I think you are doing wonderfully, darling. You can definitely stop seeing her. Waste of money, in my opinion." She smiled and waved her off, and we started walking again.

I looked down, and noticed my bracelet had fallen off. I showed Jaxon my empty wrist, and we both started searching the ground. He found it lying in the grass, grabbed it, and started to re-tie it a little tighter. Again another zap hit me.

What the hell? Is this infused with magic? Was Aunt Lynn a witch?

I laughed out loud at the thought. Jaxon looked toward me curiously as I shook my head. My brain had been overwhelmed lately, and maybe I was losing it a little.

We met Aisling and Declan by the soap lady's stand. Declan had his hands full with about fifteen soap bars, and he was telling Ais that he thought she had enough as she laughed and handed him another one. I bought two, and Jaxon handed Declan a bag to hold onto them with. After that we kept walking. There was a herbs and garden tent up above that I could see, which matched the bag Isadora dropped. I hoped that nothing got ruined in our collision. We started to get closer to it as I realized that the woman behind the table was Aunt Clara.

Shit!

I didn't want to blow her cover in case anyone was watching. I didn't know if I was supposed to pretend I didn't know her or not. Jaxon and I walked slowly toward the tent, and I hadn't made eye contact with her yet. She had her head down separating the veggies and replenishing the herbs that had been bought already. We kept walking and made it past without eye contact. I would have to text Alex later and see what I should do in a situation like this.

We made it a few tents away when Aisling came running up to us from behind.

She grabbed my arm and turned me around to face her. "Oh my God! Freya, you have a doppelgänger! There's a girl back there that looks just like you. Did you see her?" she asked excitedly.

What? Haven's here with Clara?

Of course, she was.

Reality set in as I realized that Aisling had no idea, or Declan and I couldn't let them find out. Curiosity was pulling me back that way to see her for myself. But I knew I couldn't blow Clara's cover. We were so close to each other. I could easily turn around and at least glance.

Couldn't I?

I didn't know what to say. I froze as I contemplated my next words carefully.

"I said the same thing, Freya didn't think so, but I did too as I pointed her out." Jaxon chimed in, saving me from an explanation.

"Woah, girl, 100%. I wish I had a look alike. You're always the lucky one." Aisling clicked her tongue and smiled.

I laughed and we kept walking.

Declan came up next to me and whispered, "Freya, that chick looked so much like you, it was kind of freaky. Are you sure that's not your Anchor? Jaxon said you haven't found yours yet."

"Nah, I don't have a twin." I hesitated at the twin part. "Besides, wouldn't I have been drawn toward her or something?" I whispered back. "Now cut it out, Aisling doesn't know about this kind of stuff." I shoved him gently away, but enough to let him know to drop it. He looked in deep thought as he backed away.

Jaxon and Declan started walking together, talking quietly about who knows what, so I started walking with Aisling and her aunt. Girl talk kicked in, and everything seemed normal again. The sun had started to peek through for a little while, but the chill of rain was brewing over the river. Aisling bee-lined to another tent, which made it just her aunt and me standing there while the boys kept walking.

"Can I ask you something?" She asked and I nodded in agreement without hesitation. "Have you talked to Alex recently?"

"Yeah, actually we spent the day together yesterday. Why do you ask?" I asked her, confused.

"Are you one of us too?" she asked, so bluntly that my face flushed, wondering if she meant witch or something that I was overthinking.

"What do you mean by that?" I asked innocently to make sure we were on the same page.

"I'm assuming that you seeing Alex again means that she had to come back and tell you things that were happening to you. If I'm wrong, then I'm sorry to even bring it up."

I froze. She knew. *But how?*

"Yes. Very new, but yes." I hoped that short answer was

enough to make her realize that I knew what she thought I knew.

She smiled from ear to ear, and I knew that I was right. She was a witch. There was something about her that I could *feel* it.

"That bracelet is to help keep you and my little niece out of trouble. It will keep you connected with her, even though she doesn't know anything about this stuff." She hesitated and looked at me sternly. "And I plan on keeping it that way."

"I agree, but you do realize that Declan and Jaxon are too, right?"

She nodded. "I knew right away. The older we get, the more in tune we get with the supernatural, my darling."

I smiled as she put her arm around me, pulling me closer. So, we had an agreement. Aisling would stay out of this. Aunt Lynn would be another person on my speed dial if needed. My circle of witches was growing each day, and I was thankful for that. Especially if there really were dangerous ones out there trying to track us down. Thankfully, Clara had that magical weapon in hiding so we had some time. As of right now, time was on our side, and I was hoping it stayed that way for a long time.

After another hour, we all had bags of goodies purchased from the locals, which was money well spent. I was getting shopped out, though, and was ready for lunch. We walked past Clara's tent once more on the way back to the parking lot, and I was hoping to get a glance at Haven, but nobody was behind the table. A small sign was up saying, "Be back in 5." Well, that was that. Another day we would meet then, and I was hoping that it was going to be sooner than later.

Aisling, her aunt, and Declan were going to part from us and grab lunch elsewhere. I hugged Aunt Lynn extra tight, knowing that I would see her again but probably not for a little while. She hugged me back for an extra minute and whispered in my ear, "If you need anything, please call me. Love you, Freya. My new little witch." I smiled and nodded.

Chapter 14

Magic Strength Training

Jaxon and I headed to the Diner to pick up sandwiches and planned on heading to the field to practice magic before the rain hit. I wanted to try and control the orb circle from my vision with Ezra. I was sure I could do it today if I ended up doing it at some point in the near future. That was the only part of the vision that I was planning on keeping true. What would happen between Jaxon and me that would bring Ezra and me together? Would I be caught in a love triangle and have to choose?

That was so *not* going to happen. Those were toxic.

Jaxon was finally back in my life in an unexpected twist, and I was not going to let another man take his spot. These visions needed to stop, or at least stop sucking so much.

We made it to the field. I stared fondly out at the abandoned field with the single tree in the center. It was becoming our regular hang-out spot.

"We need a name for this place, like a secret name so no one would know what we are talking about," I said.

"You're right!" He paused and was in a short, deep thought. "How about JFK? You know, like the president." He said and my eyebrows raised in confusion. "See, you wouldn't suspect anything, either. Take the J from my name and F from yours, sound good K? JFK." He laughed and said, "Hey, there was not much brainstorming involved."

I laughed and said it out loud. "Meet me at JFK? That's kind of weird, but it works. I would never think of a field off the abandoned road with that name. I would think of the museum. It would definitely keep this place a secret." I smiled and nodded. So, we agreed. Even though as weird as it sounded, nothing was as weird as being a witch in today's society.

"Did you know that Aunt Lynn is a witch too?" I asked.

Jaxon gasped and shook his head.

"There's no way she's a witch." He was still shaking his head. "Aisling isn't a witch, is she?" He asked, confused.

"No, just her. She doesn't want Ais to get caught up in all of this. So, I really hope that Declan doesn't involve her, either. Her aunt was pretty stern about keeping this from her, which I don't like keeping secrets from her, but I definitely get it."

"I'll talk to Declan about it too," Jaxon stated with sincerity, and I could see that he meant it.

We spent the next few hours practicing magic. I had finally mastered the leaf cyclone that he showed me the first day. I could do that easily just by thinking about it. My next mission was controlling the orb sphere and changing its color, or maybe it was an element? I wasn't exactly sure.

"So, some magic can be controlled more with incantations, words, or phrases," Jaxon started to explain today's lesson. "There are some old Latin words that help your mind control the powers... Did you take Latin in school?" He laughed.

"Right, I barely passed French our freshman year." We both laughed at my already horrible accent.

"Well, let me tell you the basics of what I know. Fire is Ignis, Water is Aqua, Wind is Ventus and Earth is Orbis Terrarum," he said with his best Latin accent he could achieve. "Those are the most simple ones. So basically, if you want to try and control a certain element that you are around you can whisper the Latin element under your breath and that will help bring that element to life. As I said, I am an Earth witch, so my main powers come from the earth. Declan is a water witch, so he is strongest near water and so on. We can still use magic from other elements, but our strengths come from our bloodborne magic."

I swallowed hard thinking about my bloodline. "How will I know? Alex said that I don't have the same magic as hers, and my dad isn't a witch, so how will I know what my strength is?"

He shrugged, "I guess over time we can figure it out."

I loved that he said "we" without any hesitation. It was a good feeling, knowing that my journey was not going to be done alone.

The clouds ahead looked very heavy and we could see rain falling at a distance, but it wasn't to us yet. I wanted to try my orb before the rain fell. I steadied my feet and tried to ground myself. Jaxon stepped back and watched closely. I closed my eyes and lifted my palm, whispering each incantation with each attempt at starting an orb. I could feel my fingers tingling, trying to ignite each time.

"Ignis," I whispered, and my fingertips burned with orange flames flickering from my palm, without the heat. It didn't form the sphere orb I was going for, though. I shook my hand and tried the next one.

"Aqua," I whispered, and my fingertips speckled water droplets, but were micro shaped and would not grow, either. I shook the droplets off and tried the next.

"Ventus," I whispered more loudly in my best Latin accent to see if it was my accent being too weak or my voice too low. A small to medium cyclone appeared into my palm, but only for a brief moment before disappearing.

"Okay, last try." I said.

"Orbis Terrarum," I said in a slightly louder yelling voice with the best Latin accent, and with that, the ground underneath Jaxon and I rumbled and the rocks started to lift near my feet. A mini earthquake felt like it was brewing underneath us. I panicked and stopped, letting the ground become flat again.

Jaxon's jaw was to the ground as he stood and walked over by me. "Woah, I almost thought you were an Earth witch, but then you stopped it because it didn't feel natural, did it?"

I shook my head. "Not really, the other three seemed more natural. That last one I think I said it too loud or something," I said, almost embarrassed, and we both laughed. "I will keep practicing them," I agreed, mostly to myself, but I said it out loud for reassurance from him. He nodded with a smile. "Let me try one more, maybe without saying anything, and just see if I can get the orb going."

I stood with my feet well-grounded and took a deep breath in, and slowly released it as I closed my eyes and focused on my palm creating an elemental orb. My hand was outstretched but slightly sideways. Jaxon grabbed my wrist gently and turned it so my palm was parallel to the sky. His hand touching me made my magic ignite. The second his touch shifted my wrist, my fingers did more than tingle, they became electric. They were powerful but in control. I opened my eyes, and the orb sphere had formed with a galaxy of colors swirling in my palm, as if it were the entire universe in the palm of my hand, glimmering and beautiful.

Jaxon's hand was still on my wrist, and I noticed my power growing. I could feel the sensation of my magic exploding inside me. Opening me to a whole other world of what was to come. Jaxon looked back at me with concerned eyes, like he was frozen in place and seemed uncomfortable. His stance caught me off guard... I was expecting admiration or a smile from him for being successful, but instead he didn't move. I immediately stopped, and his grip released.

He stood and shook his arm out as if it had just been struck by lightning.

"Well, I know where your strength is." He said, still clenching his fist to release the tingling. "You're definitely a syphon." He smiled and pulled me up in his arms to kiss me. I had no idea what a syphon was but that moment of finally knowing something was a fact instead of a guessing game made me feel whole.

The sky lite up with as the rain came crashing down with a crack of thunder overhead. The storm had finally hit us, and we needed to get out of an open field before we really did get struck by lightning.

We ran back to the Jeep, soaking wet and laughing like children. It was an exhilarating moment to finally know a big part of who I was, even though I didn't fully understand what that meant. But it was a start. Sitting in the Jeep, just waiting for the rain to settle a little before driving down the bluffs, and watching out for landslides that occasionally could happen with a strong enough storm to help it along. We passed the time listening to the storm above us.

"What is a syphon witch?" I asked curiously.

"I've read about it in our family's grimoire. They were thought to be extinct centuries ago or maybe they were just really good at hiding." He looked back at me. "But, I *felt* you take my magic before the little orb appeared." Panic began to grow in me when I thought I may have hurt him in the process. He must've noticed my shift in emotion and quickly added, "Don't worry, it didn't hurt. It just felt draining. It felt like..." he stopped himself and shook his head. "Nevermind."

"No, it felt like what? Please tell me." I almost begged.

"Felt draining... like the night of our car accident. It actually makes more sense now." He swallowed hard and looked away from me at the rain pouring down the windshield. "You syphoned my magic that day, which is probably why you didn't have a scratch on you. You must've used it as a shield or something to protect yourself," He said and looked back at me, as if knowing that he said too much.

I inhaled sharply as that pain came rushing back, of the loss I felt that night of the accident and how I wished I would've done more to protect him. I would've given my life for his. It was a sickening feeling, remembering the heart wrenching pain following that night.

"I didn't mean that in a bad way. I mean... how would you have even known that you could do that? It wasn't your fault. The accident wasn't your fault." He said reassuringly, but it was too late. I could feel a panic attack starting, my anxiety was crawling under my skin. My skin started to become clammy, and my heart raced beyond belief. Tears started to fall uncontrollably.

"I never meant for that to happen. If I could take that night back, I would," I said between sobs. "I would give anything to have a do-over that night." He pulled me as close as he could to try and calm me down. But the tears wouldn't stop and I couldn't fill my lungs with the oxygen I needed.

"Freya, please stop... It wasn't your fault. Someone was out to kill us, remember? Alex told you that. If it wouldn't have been a car accident, then it would've been some other way, and maybe they would have succeeded." He said as my eyes started to burn. "It's okay. I'm here... you're here... I'm not going anywhere," he said with such certainty.

I could feel every emotion over the last two years starting to settle as the tears kept coming, my heartbeat was slowing and becoming more even. It was a moment where all the guilt and sadness over the last two years had finally reached the surface, and all the new realities of being supernatural and my world changing was just so much to take in, that my body finally had the mental breakdown it needed to start to heal itself.

An hour had passed before we realized the rain had stopped and the sun was peeking back through. My dad was working at the bar again tonight and was going to have to close up.

"Are you sure you're okay?" Jaxon whispered as he kissed my forehead.

I inhaled deeply and nodded. Finally feeling relief in my chest.

We decided to head back to my house. I knew I needed a shower and a dry change of clothes. Jaxon had brought extra clothes with him too, luckily. We knew it was time to head back home and feel human again.

We parked in the driveway and went upstairs to my room. Jaxon went and laid on my bed as I jumped into the shower across the hall. I let the hot water flow and it was just what I needed as I let it run down my back and washed away all the tears from earlier. As the shower started to fill with Juniper shampoo suds and Verbena soap, I took a minute to just breathe in the aroma and clear my head. I felt like I was finally able to catch my breath and breathe again.

I stepped out of the shower, realizing that I forgot to bring a set of clean clothes into the bathroom. Jaxon was in my room with my clothes that I needed, but all I had on was a towel. I blushed, thinking there was really no way of getting in and out of my room without being detected. I towel dried my hair and put in some leave-in conditioner. I put on a little foundation under my eyes and some eyeliner with mascara to make myself feel a little more presentable and give me that boost of fake confidence while in a towel going face to face with Jaxon.

The door creaked open, and I hesitated in the doorway before stepping out of the bathroom and heading for my room. My cheeks felt hot, no need for blush because it was already natural at this moment. I peaked in to find Jaxon sleeping on my bed with one arm behind his head and the other on his abdomen. He legit was sleeping. I laughed to myself, thinking about how nervous I had been to walk into my own space when he was sound asleep. I walked over to my dresser and grabbed some clothes, then walked back to the bathroom and got dressed. I looked at myself in the mirror and let out a sigh of relief. I needed to let him sleep. I grabbed my journal and sat at my desk and started writing about everything that had happened recently.

Journal: June 11th ~

My days are starting to blur together. So much has happened, and I haven't had time to write anything down. Let's start with yesterday. I met with Alex who filled me in on our family history. She officially introduced me to Aunt Clara, who is a badass witch and just a really sweet person. I learned about the Anchor witch history and how it started back in the Viking ages. Crazy to think how long witches have roamed the Earth. Oh, yes, the Viking history was another story. It was unfortunate that the love story ended tragically for both the Pagan losing her life and the Viking's lover becoming sterile all because of a love triangle that ended badly. Fortunately for us witches, Aunt Clara has the dagger locked up at her home to keep them safe and away from Eric, that murderous

sociopath. That is one advantage we witches have right now, and the plan is to keep it out of his hands until I can figure out how to DESTROY it. The destroying part is the part I haven't told Alex yet. Destroying it is the only way to keep us all safe, and she will need to understand that.

Alex has been on the run for the last two years, and it actually makes sense as to why she's had no contact. I'm still mad as hell at her for up and leaving, but a part of me understands it now. If I were a mother, would I do the same to keep my family safe? I feel like I could've found a different way. Hopefully, the situation never arises and makes me choose such a choice.

Now the biggest new discovery that I've heard yet...... I found out who my Anchor is! I still don't think I've wrapped my head around it. I have a SISTER! Not just a sister, but a TWIN! She's been so close this whole time, and I never even knew. Maybe we have run into each other, and she's avoided me for our safety. We haven't officially met yet, but I hope we can soon.

Aunt Lynn was in town today, and we got to spend the day shopping at the Farmer's Market with her. She told me a secret about herself that I would've never believed up until recently. She's a witch too! I am truly not alone anymore.

Aisling has no idea, and I plan on keeping it that way.

Earlier today, Jaxon and I went to JFK (our newly named abandon field up in the bluffs) that we have been practicing at, and he realized that I am more than just a witch....I'm a___________________________________

My pen drew a line right off the paper. As Jaxon came up from behind me, and grabbed my hand to spin my chair around to face him. He didn't realize I was writing and had a panicked look for a moment until he realized it was only my journal and not a critical document of some sort. He smirked before leaning in to kiss me.

"Sorry, didn't mean to scare you. But do you mind if I take a quick shower here?" He asked.

I nervously blushed at the thought of him naked in my house, but nodded quickly and looked down at my journal with the line across the page.

Shit, the pen was permanent.

At least I was the only one who saw this thing with its imperfections and chicken scratch for cursive.

"Okay, I'll be back in a few." He kissed my forehead and butterflies grew in my stomach. It was still an unreal feeling having him this close to me again at least in this lifetime. I closed the journal and jumped on my bed while looking up at my ceiling and resting my mind.

Chapter 15

The Unknown Number

My phone buzzed from my nightstand while laying there and lit up the whole ceiling with its glowing screen. It buzzed a second time.

Unknown: Hey, it's Haven. We need to meet and complete these Marks ASAP.

Unknown: Ezra gave me your phone number from Aunt Clara's pottery shop.

My jaw dropped as I saw the name Haven on my screen. I never thought it would follow with a let's get together conversation. I hesitated and wondered if Clara or Alex knew about this or if she got my number from Ezra. I wondered if Ezra knew any of this.

Unknown: Oh, sorry. Ezra is my boyfriend. He told me you had been in this past week and he panicked when he saw you walk in with another man, mistaking you for me briefly.

Well, now that made a hell of a lot more sense. I began to guess that my vision the other day was maybe Haven herself and not me after all. I sighed with relief and glanced back at the phone. If that were the case, then I was safe to tell Jaxon all about it so that he would realize that there would be zero competition in the future with another man and wouldn't have to feel insecure or jealous any more. Although, I guess looks-wise, I was Ezra's type too.

Freya: Hey, okay. When?

Excitement grew inside me like never before. We were going to meet and complete our Marks. I didn't know if this was a planned rendezvous or a secret mission that shouldn't be discussed out loud. I contemplated on telling Jaxon.

Haven: Can you meet tomorrow morning around ten when the shop opens? That way Clara won't suspect anything.

So, Clara did not know about this meeting. It was like she was reading my mind. A small part of me felt that we shouldn't do this, but the other part of me had a heavy desire to meet her and finish this symbol on my back for full power access.

Freya: Yes, tomorrow works.

Haven: Great, and sorry about the dream thing. I didn't mean to freak you out.

Freya: That was real? I debated all day if I was losing my damn mind after that. So thanks for clearing that up. LOL

Haven: LOL, sorry. Once our Marks are complete then we should be able to control our magic better. See you then. Please don't tell Alex or Clara.

Freya: I won't.

I wanted this just as much as her it seemed. We must both be desperate enough to feel complete. I knew that I wanted to know what I was fully capable of. Jaxon came walking back into the room shirtless with his jeans hanging low on his hips, water dripping down his sculpted chest from his hair. I felt my eyes widen, and my pulse quicken. I hoped he didn't notice my fiery cheeks. I looked away before I became too tempted to fill the space between us. He walked over to me and gave me a worried look.

"What happened? What's wrong?" Him being so observant was sweet, but might get me in trouble in the future.

I shook my head. "Well, Haven texted me," I said and waited for his reaction.

"How did she... Is everything okay?" His brows furrowed.

"She got my number from Ezra at the shop... he's her boyfriend," I smirked. "She wants to meet up and complete our Marks tomorrow morning." I held my breath, waiting to see what his thoughts were on that.

"That's amazing! Boyfriend, huh? That makes a hell of a lot more sense." He smiled, and his shoulders seemed to relax a little. "Yes, finishing your Mark will probably make your training a little easier for you, even though you seem to be a natural." His smile grew and he picked me up from the bed and hugged me tight. "Wait, you don't think this is some kind of trick or something, right?" He asked as he pulled away and looked into my eyes for the truth.

I frowned and debated on it myself. "I don't think so. The vision would make way more sense if Ezra is her boyfriend—" I froze, realizing that I said too much and now I would have to explain about the visions.

"What does that mean?" He sat down on the bed and next to me with a concerned look.

"Shit, well... I was going to tell you." I fumbled with my phone out of nervousness like a child. "It's just been a busy week with a lot of new information, and I kind of forgot about it." His shoulders tensed up again. *Explain Freya, he's nervous.* "I had a vision with Ezra that I was showing him a new trick in making the sphere orb in my hand and changing its color, and once I achieved it, then," I hesitated, "he came in to kiss me."

"Oh." That was all he said as he inhaled and he half smiled. "Is that why you wanted to practice a little harder today?"

"I figured that if I could achieve the magic with you, then maybe that vision would just be nothing and not some weird future premonition without you. I don't ever want that. So, I figured if we could achieve the vision first, then maybe it would change the future universe's path, but when she texted me a few minutes ago, it all actually made sense." I smiled, realizing that was the truth. I didn't want another person taking his place. "I have an idea," I said excitedly.

Freya: Hey, just to make sure I'm not being set up... Send me a picture of what you found on the beach while walking with Aunt Clara the other day.

I held my breath, waiting and hoping that I was correct about the visions connecting and putting the pieces of this puzzle together. Slowly, but surely.

Haven: Pic image loading.....

And there it was. The proof that I needed. The purple hag stone she had picked up while walking the other day. I *had* been having visions of her, a trick the universe was playing to get us closer to each other. I showed Jaxon with a huge smile, but he still looked confused. I explained how I had a vision of this and thought it was the future me. He smiled, and his shoulders seemed to relax. He pulled me on top of him and started to kiss me.

"I believed you before the proof." He smiled and I felt his hand caress my lower back.

"Thank you."

It was getting late, and all the fresh air and rain today had me feeling exhausted. We laid in bed and had pillow talk. The kind that happens in the early or late hours in a fresh, new relationship to figure out every hidden secret needed to know to make the relationship work or to run for the hills.

My phone chimed. I grabbed it and read my dad's text, letting me know he would see me in the morning because he would have to close up once more this week. I frowned and decided that I needed to put up a help wanted sign up for him. But a part of me knew he was only working this weekend to distract himself from the fact that Alex had been back in our home.

I set my phone down on the nightstand and laid back down when my phone buzzed again. I groaned as Jaxon turned over and grabbed it to hand it to me, but paused when he saw the name.

"It's Alex... Do you want me to read it to you?" He asked with concern.

I nodded while holding my breath.

Alex: Hey, just checking in on you. If you need to know

anything more, then please text. I'm sorry for having to leave again so soon.

She was checking in on me? That wasn't like her. Well, I guess that wasn't like her the last two years, but more like the mom that I remembered prior to the divorce and abandonment. I knew she had made a sacrifice. Maybe one day I could forgive her, but that was going to take time. A text wasn't necessarily a pardon gift.

I shook my head as Jaxon watched me carefully.

"Don't say anything back. I don't want her thinking that she's forgiven," I said with bitterness. Jaxon looked at the text again and then back at me with a questioning look, and I nodded that that was my final answer. The reality was that I wanted to forgive her and wished her and my dad would be together again and start fresh, but she ruined so much and she had been gone for a little too long to just be forgiven for educating me on our bloodline. Running for her life or not, the least she could've done was send a text or call occasionally so I didn't have this fear of losing everyone close to me. I looked over at Jaxon and realized he probably had that fear too. It was a bad year, I didn't want relive it. My head was spiraling with thoughts of past, future, and present. Right now, I needed to think of the present only and not get too attached to her being around again. I laid my head back onto his chest once he laid back down and breathed in his woodsy scent.

At some point, we must've fallen asleep because when my eyes opened the sun was rising and beaming through the window, directly into my face. It was warm, but a little too bright for my liking this early in the morning. I rolled over to the nightstand and looked at the clock. Six forty-four a.m.

Ugh.

Too early to be awake that was for sure. Well, I was up now, so I might as well get a run in before Jaxon woke up too. I grabbed my running shoes and threw my hair in a messy bun and headed for the door.

Chapter 16

Fuck, I Fucked Up

It was just a little past seven when my phone switched from music to a phone call. *Who was calling me this early in the morning?* I paused and came to a slow jog, trying to catch my breath before completely stopping and getting my phone out of my armband. Isadora's name flashed across the screen.

"Hello," I answered while still catching my breath.

"Hello, Miss Chamberlain, I am calling to cancel our sessions for this week and all upcoming until further notice."

"Oh, okay." She had a tone to her voice that did not sound friendly, and curiosity got the best of me. "Is everything okay? You never cancel on me."

"Unfortunately, no. There was a break-in at my office last night, and the entire place is destroyed and will take months to fix in this little town, I'm sure." Her tone was angry and filled with bitterness.

"Oh my gosh, I am so sorry. Who would do something

like that?" I asked, utterly out of curiosity because crime in Crystal Rock was not very common.

"I haven't the slightest idea at this moment, but I will find out. I will be in contact with you when we can reschedule our next session," she said annoyed.

"Okay, good luck, thanks for letting me know. I will keep my journal updated in the meantime," I said in hopes that she would be happy that something had come from her sessions with me and that I was enjoying the writing part versus the talking part. I heard an exasperated sigh before she hung up without another word.

Who would even do that?

That small closet of space couldn't hold anything valuable enough to break in for. The lawyer's office and dental office maybe. But a therapist's closet... I didn't think it was worth it. Hopefully, the cops would be able to help her out. As annoying as she could be to me, she really was a nice person and didn't deserve that.

I made it back home and realized that my dad's car wasn't home. I knew he was staying late at the bar to close up but he would be home by now or at least let me know if he was going to sleep on the couch in his office there. I walked up the stairs to my door while another car pulled into my driveway behind me. I turned quickly but was disappointed when it wasn't him.

Aunt Lynn walked fast out of her car and met me on the front porch with a book in her hands.

Okay...?

"Aunt Lynn—"

"Freya, get into the house now. We need to talk." She had a serious and stern look on her face as she pushed up the stairs to the front door. Something was very, very wrong.

What was going on? Where was my dad? Did something happen to him?

I opened the door and realized I had stopped breathing and was beginning to feel faint before I caught my next breath. Her visit could be anything, and my anxiety and thoughts needed to shut the hell up.

"What's going on?" I yelled, feeling defeated. I knew that at this very moment, my life had been going too smooth for too long, so of course, it was time for bad news to come crashing down. That's how it always happened. My life would start going good before my world would flip into darkness again. My palms were sweaty just waiting to hear what was going on.

She slammed the book she was carrying onto the dining room table. I stared in disbelief that this early morning wake-up call was over some damn book. I shook my head and stared at her confused.

"Okay, so...it's a book?" I shrugged.

"This is *not* just any book, Freya. This is the journal you write in."

"That's not my journal." I relaxed my breathing, realizing this was all just a mistake.

"No, this *is* your journal. It's not the copy that you write in, but it copies everything that you write and lets her read it. She knows everything you have written up until last night when I broke in and took it from her before destroying the cursed place." Aunt Lynn breathed heavily as her normal composed face was in anguish.

"What do you mean, it copies? Wait... You destroyed her place?" My eyes widened with horror.

"This is a magic journal that I created nearly a thousand years ago. This is magic that I created." Aunt Lynn snapped, and my head started to feel foggy and my body started to feel clammy. I felt as if I couldn't swallow and I needed a glass of water before I passed out. I made it two steps before my legs felt like spaghetti, as my head wrapped around the idea that my journal was not a secret and that Aunt Lynn just said she was a thousand years old. I felt like I was going to be sick. I grabbed the wall to my right and started to use it for balance as I crumbled to the floor, shaking my head.

"A thousand years... It copies... Your magic?" I was mumbling the words under my breath. Aunt Lynn heard them and walked away before coming back with a glass of water.

"Drink this. Now listen, child. There is much more than you know. I don't know if she read your last entry before I got there and took it, but if she did, then they would know that Clara has the dagger at her place." She started and paused as Jaxon walked into the dining room and was staring at us both with concern.

"She? As in my therapist? Isadora?" I asked, finally connecting the dots. If she read it, then unfortunately, the damage was done, and my last entry said too much. No one would be safe once they knew we had the dagger.

"Isadora was the Anchor witch that stole Eric from me. She is a witch, and I am the Pagan from the stories I'm sure you've heard. Except that the story told misses so many details of what really happened. At least, according to your journal entry." She looked at me and waited for me to say something. "I realized who she was when she ran into you at the Farmer's Market, trying to rip that bracelet off of you."

My heart sank into my chest, and my hands came up to my head, pulling my hair out of its bun to half cover the embarrassment on my face for not figuring this out on my own.

I set the water down and seemed to find my voice. "She called me a little while ago canceling our upcoming sessions because of a break-in."

"Of course, she did. She probably thought that you broke in there and was hoping she would catch you in a lie."

"If you're the Pagan witch from a thousand years ago, then how are you still alive?" I asked bluntly.

"I linked my life with Eric before using the dagger on myself. Of course, Eric and Isadora are Anchors, so I basically became their third wheel lifeline. When they became immortal, I was able to survive with them. I don't like how it's worked one bit." Aunt Lynn then added, "Out of revenge, I took their baby boy and raised him and each child for every generation after. They didn't realize that their little descendant was an Anchor witch like them and lived a long and beautiful life after the stabbing. They sent the child down the river in a proper Viking burial ritual, but never ignited the raft." She paused and took a deep breath before continuing. "I heard a baby crying on the river a little while later and realized what and who he was, that he was linked to another child just like his parents were. I raised him to be like me and as my own. I never knew how much my heart could love another being until this child existed. He gave me a purpose and made me realize that being a parent was the best love anyone could ask for. So from then on, each generation that was born since I have watched over and been Aunt Lynn and protected them with my every being to keep his spirit alive."

I looked back at Jaxon who seemed to be processing every word. My jaw was to the floor. I quickly closed it and shook my head. "I had no idea. I always wondered why you didn't have any children of your own, but you were such a great motherly figure to Aisling and me growing up..." I took a deep breath in before asking, "Is Aisling a descendant of Eric and Isadora?"

She nodded gently. "She must not know. She will feel as if she has bad blood, and we both know she is far from bad blood. She is one of the purest souls I have ever known of every generation. She reminds me most of my sweet baby boy, and I want to keep her that way."

I nodded and understood. I realized that I had been lied to for the last two years and been face to face with an Immortal during my therapy sessions. I had been played by her. I felt so stupid. And now my own journal betrayed me, by sharing my secrets and whispering them in her ear. She knew about the dagger. She knew about me being a witch. She knew Aunt Lynn and Alex were witches. She knew everything.

Shit...

"She even knows I have a twin. Fuck! I fucked up everything!" I gritted my teeth. "What time did you break in yesterday? The last entry was written late last night, maybe she never saw it."

"Around midnight. I guess only time will tell if she tries to come after you or me or anyone you love. She is one evil witch."

I froze, realizing that my dad was not home from the bar yet and he never called me. I jumped up and started dialing his number. Straight to voicemail. I tried again. Voicemail.

What have I done?

"My dad! He didn't come home from the bar last night, and he's not answering." I yelled, not meaning to yell at Jaxon or Aunt Lynn, but I was in a panic. If they had taken him as leverage to get what they wanted, then this would be my fault. That stupid journal needed to be burned.

I ran out of the house and jumped in my Jeep. Both Jaxon and Aunt Lynn jumped in with me. Aunt Lynn had a fire in her eyes. She was ready to fight with me, and the fire in her eyes matched mine too. If anyone hurt him, there would be real consequences. He had been my only constant, and I would not lose him. I sped down the road and hit nearly every stoplight possible. Every second seemed to be minutes. My heart raced. Jaxon kept trying to call him as I drove, still nothing. Voicemail.

We pulled up to Swig and Jig, and his car was parked in the back still. A slight bit of relief washed over me, but I would not let my heart slow down to a normal pace until I knew for sure that he was safe.

The door was locked. I grabbed the keys and fumbled with the lock before Jaxon grabbed the keys and opened the door himself. All three of us ran inside and started to search the place.

Empty.

This couldn't be happening... My heart began to sink.

I ran out of the front door and looked up and down the road. Pacing back and forth in the parking lot, my hands igniting with fury and revenge, I squinted down the road one last time, hoping that I would not become a vengeful soul toward anybody. Almost choking on my breath and shaking the magic from my hands, as I saw my dad walking back down the road from the gas station with a coffee in hand. My anxiety was already so high that tears started falling from my eyes. I ran to him and nearly knocked him off his feet, spilling his coffee.

"Dad, I was so worried. You didn't come home and didn't call or anything. I—" I hesitated. "I thought something bad might've happened to you."

My dad huffed and squeezed my a little tighter. "Oh, kiddo, I'm so sorry. My phone died, and I forgot my charger at home. I've been working on the books here trying to catch up with the paperwork and lost track of time." His arms loosened from around me, and he put his arm over my shoulder and started walking back to the bar with me. Jaxon and Aunt Lynn walked out just in time for us to meet them in the doorway. Relief washed across both of their faces.

"Woah, you brought the whole search squad for me, huh? Glad to see how much you still love your old man." He laughed. I tried to laugh, but I choked on my tears as he hugged me tighter.

"Extra charger is in the bottom drawer of your desk to the left. Just so this doesn't happen again." I sighed with relief.

"What would I do without you kid?" He kissed the top

of my head, and I felt better knowing that he was safe. Now the gears in my head started to turn as I thought about the journal and how if Isadora did read my last entry, then Eric would stop chasing Alex and go after Clara. I needed to get to Haven sooner than later and come up with a plan. We walked back into the bar and I pulled out my phone and started typing.

Freya: Can you meet me within the hour instead?

Haven: Sure, behind the pottery shop?

Freya: Perfect, we might have a problem with the dagger. I'll explain in person.

Chapter 17

Nice To Meet You, Sorry I Ruined Everything

I had an hour to clear my head and figure out what I was even going to say to her. Our first meeting was going to consist of me screwing up a two-year plan that had been working perfectly until I showed up. Now I needed to come up with a solution. Great... She was going to think I was an idiot.

I needed to get home, shower, and come up with a strategic plan, that was now all on my to-do list. Aunt Lynn hugged me hard when we got back home from the silent drive and said she would be watching out for us in the meantime. She would keep me informed if any leads on Eric or Isadora became relevant, then she would call right away. That made me feel slightly better that I had a guardian witch looking over my loved ones and me.

I couldn't believe that I was fooled by a damn therapist. I wanted to know her whole story, did she even grow up in this town? Did she even know my parents? Was that man in her photo Eric or even her real husband? Her whole life was a damn lie to get information from me on Alex to find the damn dagger. I hated it.

What a bitch!

I was going to fix it. All of it.

I failed in my first month of being a witch. It didn't really surprise me, but damn, it made me mad. I needed that dagger as far away from Clara as possible. Assuming that Isadora read that last journal entry, she would know that Alex doesn't have it on the run and will be looking closer at Clara. I needed to hide it. It was my responsibility.

We walked into the empty house, and a cold chill ran through my body and made me shiver. The house felt off, maybe it was because my dad wasn't here with me, or maybe because now I felt vulnerable. Jaxon and I walked to each room and searched the whole house and made sure every window was still locked. The house was secure. I let out a sigh of relief as Jaxon came to me and hugged me tight. His kiss made me relax even more. For a brief moment, my mind stopped spinning as I enjoyed the sweet normalcy of our closeness.

I jumped in the shower, dried my hair, and put a little bit of makeup under my eyes, mascara and eyeliner to hide the tears that I had cried earlier. At least this way I felt more like a human again. I could do this. I grabbed jeans and a t-shirt from my room while Jaxon was downstairs talking to his mom on the phone. He had her on speakerphone, and I could hear the disappointment in her voice with him still hanging around me. I didn't think Jaxon realized that I was in hearing range when I heard her say, "I told you something like this would happen if you two got back together, bad things follow that girl."

I sucked in my breath and listened.

"Mom, stop! Nothing bad follows her. If anything, maybe I brought the bad back to her. She was doing great before I showed up in her life," Jaxon said.

"Oh honey, you are my good luck charm. It's not you, I can tell you that right now," Margo said to her only child, her pride and joy. Here I was... another woman in his life, and was thinking that I was ready to take him away from her. That was the reason she didn't like me, or at least that made the most sense. I started walking down the stairs to meet him in the living room. He glanced at me and smiled apologetically.

"Mom, I have to go. Love you. Oh, and by the way, Freya is the best thing that has ever happened to me," he said with a wink.

"She's right there, isn't she?" Margo asked with bitterness, and Jaxon laughed before hanging up the phone.

I walked over to him and sat. "Margo really doesn't like me, huh?"

"Nah, she's just being an overprotective mother. You know how she is." He hesitated. "Well, she's the same as she used to be. Nothing has changed with her." I needed to change the subject because the thought of Margo hating my existence didn't sit well with me considering that she had kept Jaxon away from me for almost two years already. I couldn't think about her right now.

"I think I have a plan for the dagger. It should work, I think. I'll need Haven to help." I said.

He smiled even wider and seemed excited to see what I had come up with. I was now the leader of this mission.

Well, I sort of caused the mission to start with, but nonetheless, I was going to fix it.

Jaxon drove my Jeep and we headed for the pottery shop. My stomach was twisting at the thought of taking charge of something that I just found out existed the other day. My anxiety was going to have to disappear, and my confidence was going to have to come back to the surface, even if I had to be an actress for the next few hours to get through this. Look strong, be smart, be confident.

I can do this.

At least the sun was shining, which was helping with my anxiety, at least slowed my trembling. I needed to focus on one thing at a time. I had to hope that Isadora never even read the journal. It was the weekend, and she wouldn't have been working. I didn't like waiting games, but this is one we would have to play.

We pulled up to the shop, and I took one glance in the rearview mirror before stepping out with confidence and headed for the red door of the shop. Jaxon was following right behind me. He seemed to have confidence at all times.

"Miss Freya, you made it!" Ezra said, as I walked in before he had even switched the sign on the door from closed to open. "Hey, Jaxon." He nodded to him and walked over to give him a handshake.

"Hey, Ezra, is Haven here yet?" I asked excitedly while hiding my nervousness.

"She's out in the back, across the train tracks by the river. She told me to let you know." He stared at me. "It's crazy how much you guys look alike," he said and looked toward Jaxon. "Sorry, man, if it was awkward the last time you were here. I thought my girlfriend had brought another man into the shop at first glance. Kind of shocked me." He laughed nervously.

"Nah, it's all good. I get it. I got a quick glance of Haven at the Farmer's Market, and I thought the same thing." He laughed, and they started talking about the ball game that was on today. It was my chance to slip away and meet Haven. I glanced back at Jaxon, who was watching me intently. He gave me an "are you sure about this" look, and I nodded before opening the back door.

The sun blinded me for a moment, as I let my eyes readjust to the sun reflecting off the Mississippi. I crossed the train tracks and peered down by the small beach and saw a woman walking along the water's edge. I knew immediately that it was her. I took a quick moment to catch my breath and started walking toward her. Her hair was shorter than mine, but not by much. Such a strange moment...

Alright, time for nothing.

I sucked in a breath and walked up to her as she turned around.

"Haven," I stated confidently. She smiled, and I recognized myself in her. We were almost a mirror image of each other besides our hair length, the glasses, and our dressing styles. She had on short overalls with a tighter-fitting shirt and low-top Converse. She wore glasses that made her look like a bookworm, but in one of those sexy womanly ways. She was prettier than I was, she had the confidence that I was lacking.

"Freya!" she said excitedly and hugged me without hesitation. "This has been something I've dreamt of for far too long." I felt a twinge of pain thinking about how differently we were raised. How long had she known she had a twin? How much more information did she know that I didn't? The questions started to whirl in my head, and I had to quickly stop them and get back to the reason we are here.

Be confident, Freya.

"Yeah, this is... something," I said as our hug started to end. A smile had made its way to my face, and it felt genuine. This was an extraordinary moment in my life, and I needed to enjoy it.

"Clara and Mom can not know about this. They wouldn't approve," she said quickly, and I nodded in agreement, knowing that she was right. But I wished that "Mom" was not in her vocabulary. I looked down at her necklace, she was wearing the purple hag stone she had found on the beach the other day. "So, do you have a plan for the dagger?"

My eyes drew away from the stone and back at her. "Yes... and I'm about 95% sure that it will work." I felt the doubt starting to set in."I will take the dagger and hide it at my home since the Immortals would never think that Alex would hand over the ultimate weapon to a newbie witch who barely knows what she is doing yet. Also, I'm going to try and syphon the magic out of it, so if they do somehow find it then it will be magicless. I hope." I started with confidence before ending the last sentence with doubt. She looked at me questioningly.

"Not a good idea?" I asked while shaking my head, realizing how stupid the plan sounded out loud.

"I think it's a great idea, actually. How do you syphon the magic out?" She looked excited.

"Oh." I blushed. "Well, I was kind of hoping you knew how."

"But I'm not a syphon."

"I thought if I was, then you would probably be one too?" I shrugged. Realizing how wrong I was about so much.

"I have never been able to take magic from anyone or anything. When did you figure that out?"

"Jaxon actually figured it out while we were practicing the other day."

"No way! That is badass and way cooler than my dream interfering skills. I guess you got the better power out of this twin deal," she said and smiled. "Can you try it on me? I'm curious how it works."

"I mean, um... I don't really know how I did it. I was hoping that you knew."

"Damn... Well, we are going to have to figure it out. Your plan sounds like a good one, and now I want it to work. Why don't we start with the ritual to complete our Marks and then if you don't have any other plans we can try and figure it out after." She smiled.

I felt the doubt grow but knew that we needed to complete our Marks regardless. Maybe everything would click afterward. I shrugged. "Okay."

Jaxon and Ezra started walking toward us from the shop. When they made it down by us, Haven explained what we were going to do, and everyone seemed to agree that we were doing the right thing.

Ezra laid salt on the sand, connecting it into a perfect circle. He took two pieces of driftwood from the edge of the river and laid them directly across from each other. He directed Haven and me to stand on the driftwood and combine hands across from each other in the center. We listened and stepped over the salt in a mirror image. We reached our hands out, and as soon as our hands locked, a vision started, and I felt my knees go weak. The last thing I felt was Jaxon's arms sliding underneath mine and holding me up.

This vision was not like the others. This was instead a carousel of images from childhood and growing only, it wasn't of me. It was Haven's life. I was seeing her whole story in glimpses. Her childhood was a lot like mine, full of love and playfulness. Some bumps and bruises, but mostly, life with Clara seemed peaceful. Alex was there in some images too. There was a memory I knew too that popped up. The playground with Aisling. We were all three playing with each other. Alex had been checking in on her through the years. That made sense why Alex's realtor hours were all over the place. She wasn't selling homes, she was trying to keep her home together. I could feel tears starting in the corner of my eyes. Alex was living a double life to make sure her daughters both knew her and were being well taken care of. The older Haven was getting, the more glimpses I saw of her being taught magic by Aunt Clara, probably pre-teenage. Her Mark was faded, not hidden like mine. Hers was on her left wrist, and I could see it. *Why was mine on my back?* A new age started, and I saw Ezra appear. They were dating around the early teens it seemed. Probably the same length Jaxon and I would've been together if he hadn't been taken away. High school started, and she was a brilliant student in the class and seemed to take leadership in all of her studies. She worked with Clara at the pottery shop day in and out and was learning how to tend the garden of herbs while practicing her magic. Ezra seemed to be her supportive lover who seemed to never leave her side. *Wait, did he live with them?* The images continued to this year. Haven was nominated for valedictorian and offered multiple scholarships for her science studies and research internships out of state. She was some kind of genius. I was lucky to get offered a few grants, but no scholarships like her. The images started to imbed in my mind as if she and I had lived together our entire lives and I *knew* her. *Was this same thing happening to her with my memories?* I knew mine were not nearly as lovely as hers were. Mine were darker. Then the hag stone appeared. Then the orb, Ezra, the kisses. Everything spun so much faster as my head started to tingle. Her Mark began to glow. I sucked in a deep breath. Then the carousel stopped spinning, and darkness consumed me...

My eyes opened, but the sun was blinding me. My arm hurt, it felt as if it were on fire. As if it were being branded like a cow. I looked down while my eyes were adjusting. Jaxon still had me in his arms, and Ezra had Haven in his. We were all four sitting on the sand in the broken salt circle. Ezra looked worried and I was glad that I couldn't see Jaxon's face, knowing that it was filled with the same emotions.

I looked at my arm and there it was, glowing. My Mark was complete and had moved from my back to my left wrist. It was beautiful. The swirls of a journey like an Unalome symbol being born and living with good intentions and bad mistakes turning into an endless knot at the top of my wrist, standing for being reborn and reborn again as an Anchor witch. It was small, but it was strong, and it was everything I stood for. It fit me.

I smiled and looked at Haven, who was wrapped in Ezra's arms. Her Mark was glowing too and looked identical to mine. *It worked.* Whatever she had done, worked! I could feel the magic flowing through my veins. I could feel my strength. I quickly looked around us to make sure no one was watching and put my hand out in front of me. I whispered in the best Latin accent I could conjure, "Ignis," and there it was the small flame instantly. It glowed fiery orange before I whispered, "Aqua." The flame turned to water droplets and left a cool tingling in the palm of my hand. "Ventus," the water started to turn in my palm into a twisting mini tornado. I finished with a whisper, "Orbis Terrarum." The ground shook from underneath all of us, and stones lifted from the ground effortlessly. I smiled and realized that I was in control of my magic. I didn't know how to do the syphoning yet on command, but the elements I could control more easily. Jaxon leaned down and kissed my head in approval. Haven's eyes opened, and she was smiling just as big as me. She practiced her glowing orb across from me.

"It worked!" she squealed with excitement! "I could feel all of that." She grabbed my wrist and put hers next to mine as we marveled at our matching Marks. "We are finally complete. You have no idea how long I've waited for this moment for us both!" I realized she had been waiting a lot longer than I have since she knew she was a witch long before I did. The images flashed through my head again, and I had to ask her.

"Could you see my life in little flashes too?" I asked, embarrassed.

"Only the good stuff." She smiled and winked at me, knowing well that she was lying, but she wasn't going to make a scene in front of the guys. Ezra leaned down and kissed her, passionately. I felt uncomfortable watching them, so I turned and faced Jaxon. We laughed when I realized he had felt awkward too.

We stood and dusted off the sand that had accumulated during the Mark awakening ritual. I felt strong, and I wanted to keep practicing until I could figure out how to syphon the magic from the dagger to keep everyone safe. It was solely going to be up to me this time. Clara wouldn't have to hide anymore, and maybe Alex could stop running. Haven and I could actually get together without being secretive. Life could maybe be normal again only with a twist of witch added to it.

"Hey, I know this isn't the only reason you guys came over here, but your pottery pieces really are ready for pick up." Ezra laughed, and his head nodded toward the shop. We all laughed as he wiped out the rest of the salt as if we were never here. We walked back toward the shop. He turned the sign to open and grabbed the pieces. Haven and I were talking by the back door in the employee-only section when I saw a familiar car pull up out front.

"Hey, man, what are you doing here?" Jaxon asked.

"Bro, Aisling won't stop asking for a date here ever since Freya told her about it," Declan said. I knew I recognized his car. "It's our three-month anniversary, so I wanted to surprise her with a gift certificate. Is that lame?" He asked Jaxon.

"Not at all. She's a good person. Don't mess it up with her."

"Yeah, I'm still trying to figure out why she keeps hanging around me." Declan laughed.

"Yeah, we're all trying to figure that one out." Another voice chimed in laughing, but I did not recognize it. "Is the owner here today?" The man asked, changing the subject.

"Not yet. She will be in later. Do you need to leave her a message?" Ezra asked.

"Nah, I'll stop by another time. Thanks." I walked out to them to say hey.

"Hey, Freya! Do me a favor, and don't tell Aisling I'm here. It's a surprise."

"I won't say anything. That's very romantic of you." I winked."Surprisingly, you don't seem like the date type of person," I said with a smirk, and he grinned at me with narrowed eyes.

"Yeah, well, Ais is a ten, and I'm trying to keep her around, alright?" He smiled back at me.

"Freya? As in Freya Chamberlain?" The other man asked.

"The one and only," I said, looking at the man who seemed familiar now that I saw him in person. Tall, broad shoulders, suit, and slicked hair. He looked like a lawyer and I just couldn't place him. He had good looking gentleman features, but with a hard edge to his jawline that made him intimidating.

"You look like your mother," he said and I stiffened briefly before my eyebrows went to a frown. I still preferred to hear that I had my dad's features versus the woman who abandoned me.

"Oh." I wanted to say she wasn't my mother anymore, but I bit my tongue, remembering the sacrifice she made and knowing that Declan's dad didn't need to hear my sob story. "Thanks? I think." He looked to be staring at my wrist that had the newly formed Mark, but his dark eyes seemed to be off in the distance.

Was Declan's dad a witch too? Does he see my Mark? Did he even know that Declan was one?

"You will have to tell her that Mr. Greystone says hello. It's been years."

I chuckled at the thought of seeing her anytime soon. He would have more luck than me.

"I'll let her know next time she decides to come around." I looked at Jaxon who smiled sheepishly at me. He had a better relationship with his mom than I did and I kind of envied him for that.

"You do that," he said sternly and headed for the door without looking back. Declan lingered around, waiting for the certificate.

"Sorry, he's kind of an asshole," Declan said and nodded toward his dad.

"No, he's fine," I said reassuringly.

"We're nothing alike, I can promise you that."

I smiled at Declan and shook my head to let him know that he did not have to explain himself or apologize for his dad. It was no big deal. I looked toward the door and saw that he was already sitting in the driver's seat on the phone. He looked annoyed.

I walked back by Haven, who was sitting in the office while looking through her purple hag stone at a picture of Aunt Clara on the wall. I looked at her confused. She looked back at me and handed me the stone, as she pointed toward the picture. I peered through the hole in the stone and gasped. It was a picture of her and Aunt Clara outside of the pottery shop, but when I pulled the stone away, the picture was only of Aunt Clara again.

"But how?" I asked.

"Magic, of course," she said and smiled. "She's been so careful about hiding us from the Immortals that even pictures have been hidden." She glanced at the stone in my hand before continuing, "If you are lucky enough to find a hag stone, then you will see the magic through it. Hag stones are known for seeing into the Fae or magical realm, but really, they are made in the current of rivers, and at the stones weakest point, they develop a hole. For witches, they become treasures when their weakest point finally breaks through, making them whole."

"Woah.. that's so cool. I used to collect these as a kid, but I had no idea about all of that."

"Keep it." She reached out to me and offered it.

"Oh, no, I couldn't. It's yours."

"I just met my long-lost sister. In case we ever get separated again, then at least you will have something to remember me by without the adults knowing." She winked at me, and I smiled. "Plus, I have another one."

"Thank you." I felt shy all of a sudden, like I wasn't prepared to give a gift to receive one.

"Now, let's get back to business. We need to figure out your syphoning trick." She clapped her hands together and leaned back against the wall.

"We? As in, you're going to help me?"

"Well, between me and your boyfriend, Jaxon, I think

we can figure it out. He seems pretty smart. Plus, Ezra will cover for me at the shop. Aunt Clara will have no idea." Haven waited for my response. As I thought it over, making sure I ran every scenario through my head so that we didn't mess up anything else in the meantime.

"Yes!" There really wasn't another way. I was so new at this magic stuff. I mean, I felt stronger already after completing the Mark. I looked at my wrist with admiration at the newly formed tattoo that I couldn't see when it was on my back without a mirror. Only the whole syphoning trick was a whole new ball game. I had no idea how to control it, or even start it. Maybe Haven has had enough practice to figure it out.

"What is your strength if it's not syphoning?" I asked curiously.

"Oh, I'm a healer." She shrugged her shoulders as if it was obvious. "It actually makes sense, though, if you think about it."

"What does?"

"You can take magic, and I can give it back, so to speak. Healthwise anyways. We're kind of like the Ying to the Yang and all the good stuff." She smiled. "I guess we really are stronger together than apart."

I closed the space between us and hugged her hard. "Thank you!" It just felt right. Meeting her and being with her just felt like I was right where I was supposed to be.

Chapter 18

How Does One Steal Magic?

Jaxon, Haven, and I headed to JFK. After a short, private discussion with Jaxon in the back office, we both decided that it was still the safest place to practice magic and that Haven was a safe bet to join in on the secret. Jaxon had been coming to JFK the last two years to practice his magic, and no one had ever been up there. Now he was putting his trust into me and Haven to keep it a secret. I knew she had just as much to lose as we did.

Haven drove behind us and followed us to the field. Thankfully, the sun was still shining. The field was drying up from yesterday's rain, so there were some patches of muddy water that were still absorbing back into the earth. We could either avoid those for walking or use them to our advantage for practice. I smiled, thinking about how I felt stronger already. Today would be less draining so I could focus more on the syphoning part instead of the elemental magic. We walked over to the tree in the middle of the field to grab some shade while we worked.

"So, how did you do it before, the syphoning?" Haven asked.

"Well, that's just it. I don't really know. Jaxon grabbed my wrist the last time while we were practicing, and it just sort of happened." I lifted my palms toward the sky and stared at them, willing them to work their magic.

Nothing.

"As soon as I touched her, I could feel my magic draining. Not disappearing, but weakening for sure." Jaxon looked at me and smiled with a reassuring gesture that I hadn't hurt him.

"Well, I guess we start with that. Get back into the position you were in and try it again."

Without hesitation, we did just that. I closed my eyes, and I braced myself as he grabbed my wrist. For a brief moment, my fingertips tingled, then nothing. I opened one eye, nervously looking at Jaxon who shook his head.

"Let's try it again, let me try to focus more."

The next three hours were basically trial and error, well, mostly error. Maybe Jaxon was wrong about the syphoning part after all. Nothing was working, and I really was trying. My mind was clear, I was focused, and this was definitely something that I wanted. Deep down, Alex was on my mind. The years spent running and wasted away from Crystal Rock, away from my dad and me, away from Clara and Haven. It just wasn't fair to any of us because of this stupid dagger. I needed to fix this for her. Maybe then she could come back, or at least she could stop running. I wouldn't tell her that her safety was my concern, but deep down, it was.

"Maybe let's take a break," Haven suggested, and I was

grateful for the breathing time. I was starting to feel drained. Maybe it was from the hot sun overhead, or maybe because I was running out of fuel. Jaxon must've read my mind because he piped in.

"Let me run and grab some food for us. Anything in particular?"

"Anything sounds good at this point, and water please." I smiled as he kissed me before heading toward the Jeep.

That left just Haven and me. It was such a strange feeling to have her next to me, as if it was the most natural daily routine there was. I wanted to know more than the visions supplied me with. I hoped that we have forever to fill in the rest. We went and sat under the tree to try and catch some shade.

"So, is Ezra a witch too?"

"His family was, but he never received a Mark. It's kind of a sensitive subject for him," she answered sadly.

"What do you mean, was? Did they lose their magic somehow? Can that happen?" My brows furrowed, and my thoughts started to wander.

"They were killed by the Immortals. He was only a child when it happened." She looked at me with sad eyes, but a hard, fierce look behind them. She had a plan, and it was a revenge plan.

"Oh no! Poor Ezra." I couldn't even imagine losing both parents at a young age. "I wonder why his Mark never showed up after a traumatic event like that?"

"That's just it, I'm pretty sure he is suppressing his magic. I try to have him practice with me, but the thought of him doing magic makes him sad that he couldn't have saved his parents. He was hiding in the house when Eric entered, and his mother told him to hide and to not come out until the lady with the glasses showed up."

"Aunt Clara?" I questioned, realizing that is how they met. Aunt Clara saved his life and probably took him under her wing, just like Haven. She was a superhero and saved children.

Haven nodded.

"She saved him and brought him to a mundane couple, who were having a hard time with the whole adoption process, and had them raise him as a normal child. Aunt Clara and I would go and visit him throughout the years for her to check on him. She was actually checking for his Mark, which never seemed to show. We became friends over the years and then started dating when we got older. His magic is the last thing on his mind, and that's okay." She smiled shyly. "He helps me control my emotions and lets me practice my magic with him. He's an amazing boyfriend. I was really lucky to have our paths intertwine."

"Sounds like Aunt Clara saved the day with him. She's pretty awesome, isn't she?"

"She really is." Haven paused. "You know, Mom really tried to be there for us both. She kind of was dealt shitty cards when she found out she was pregnant. We kind of put her life with Dad in danger. She never would've left if it wasn't for trying to save us all."

Here we go... I wasn't ready to talk about this. Luckily, Jaxon pulled up before I had to continue that unwanted conversation. After lunch, we planned to continue practicing. Haven asked if Ezra could join us and see if he had any ideas. Jaxon was the one to agree to him before I even had a say.

"Ezra can join us for everything. It'd be nice to have another guy around, so I'm not outnumbered. No offense." Jaxon threw his hands up in defense. "Plus, we can use him too for syphoning practice, he seems to be a bodybuilder of some sort and can probably take on a little more of a beating from my woman." He laughed, and I smirked at the thought of being able to bring Jaxon to his knees, let alone an even bulkier man.

We finished eating and Ezra was on his way up the bluffs to our secret location. I had to admit while hanging out with a new couple, it made me think of Aisling and even Declan. I felt guilty hanging out with another girl that wasn't my best friend. I felt even more guilty that my best friend didn't know that I have a twin... or that I was a witch.... or that her aunt was a thousand-year-old Pagan witch. I had so many secrets from the lady who had never left my side. She had always protected me and never made me feel worthless. I needed to call her today. I knew I couldn't tell her about the magic stuff, but maybe I could bring her up to JFK and show her some of it. Maybe have her figure it out somehow. I knew it would be risky, but I hated this big elephant in the room while we were together. I somehow needed to call the kettle black, without calling it black. She needed to know more.

Chapter 19

Secrets Don't Make Friends

The sun was getting low along the Mississippi when the four of us decided to finish for the night, without figuring out the syphoning trick. I started to think they were wrong about me after all. Maybe Haven and I weren't as special as Alex and Clara thought we were, and maybe Eric and Isadora were wrong all along. This whole thing could be a big misunderstanding and life could get back to normal. I knew it was just wishful thinking though. When I thought about it, my life had never really been normal. Even as a kid, I remembered feeling like I didn't really fit into the crowds. I always shied away from the cliques of friends and had my own small circle. I always felt like I was missing a part of me, and now it all made more sense.

Jaxon's phone had been blowing up for the last hour... I glanced every time and saw that it was Margo. When he finally answered, she told him she wanted him home for dinner and family movie night. He asked if I wanted to come along, but the thought of being in the same room as Margo was a huge no for me at this point. I wasn't a huge fan of the mother figures right now anyway, and I didn't think that being around her would make that any better.

I decided to drop Jaxon off at his house and make a pit stop at Aisling's house. I needed a girl's night. I had to work at the theatre the next day and most of the week, so tonight was my only real free time. I texted my dad to let him know that I was going to spend the night over there and I would see him in the morning. He said he was staying at the bar tonight again for the last time and then he would be all caught up. He told me that Aunt Lynn stopped by after we left for JFK and brought him food from the diner. They chatted for a little too long and he was behind on the books again. It crossed my mind that she wanted to stay with him just to make sure that he was not in harm's way with the Immortals, which gave me some peace of mind.

I really wanted Aisling to know the truth about everything. There had to be a way...

The drive to her house was short, so there was no time to brainstorm. I guess we could just hang out and see if it somehow came up in conversation. I knew it was a long shot. If the opportunity didn't present itself, then I would just drop it.

I pulled up to her house and walked inside the already unlocked door. They had always had an open-door policy in this small town, that had always been pretty safe and quiet. I walked down the hall to her room and could hear her talking on the phone to someone. I opened the door and quietly sat on her bed as she smiled and waved at me. I smiled back, mouthing the words "hey" and sat on the end of her bed. I could hear Declan's deep voice coming through the phone. My phone buzzed as I went to set it on the nightstand to charge.

Haven: I think we should move the dagger for the time being.

Freya: That's a good idea. Any recommendations?

Haven: Your house. No one would suspect you to have it. No offense LOL.

Freya: It's true, though. LOL

Haven: I'll bring it over tonight, and you hide it somewhere safe, and don't tell ANYONE where!

Freya: I won't be home until tomorrow morning. Sleeping at my friend's house.

Haven: Okay, tomorrow morning then. Thx and P.S. I'm really glad we met up today!

Freya: Me too!!!!

I smiled to myself at the thought of today and the excitement that I had about the future. Life had been pretty nice to me lately. I felt like by saying it out loud, then the universe would jinx my life again and give me hell for a while. So, I was just going to keep that to myself. Aisling was looking at me when I looked up from my phone, and had been off the phone for at least a minute or two.

"Jaxon?" She asked with a smirk.

"No, I mean, yes, it was him." I lied.

"You two are going to become inseparable again." She smiled. "I'm really happy for you, Frey!" I could tell she meant it, and the guilt from lying was lingering even more now. I groaned silently to myself. I hated keeping secrets. "What'd ya have in mind? Movie or bonfire?" She asked.

"How about both?" I asked. "Your dad still have that projector?"

She laughed and said her dad never threw anything away. She walked out of her room, and I sent a quick text to Jaxon.

Freya: I hate lying to her.

Jaxon: Go with your gut. Maybe a need-to-know basis?

Freya: Where would I even begin?

Jaxon: That is a question that I can't answer. Sorry, babes.

Of course, he couldn't answer. He'd never had to keep a secret about his magic once he found out he had it. He was surrounded by his supportive and helpful parents. Once his Mark was triggered, and I was out of the picture, he didn't even have to hide it from me. He's been practicing for the last two years and has had support and answers. He didn't have to have secrets with his loved ones.

Aunt Lynn would not be happy about this, or even the idea of me debating this. I thought keeping her out would be the best option until I was with Haven earlier today practicing and realized I felt guilty that Ais had no idea she even existed or that I knew about her. I thought to myself, would she hide something like that from me? I doubted it. She was an open book, and that was what I've always loved about her. There was no bullshit with her.

My mind sifted through each scenario, and every path leading me to either hurting her or her aunt or me hurting her because I hurt her aunt by going against her. She came back into the room just as my phone started to ring. The sound of the phone actually made me jump, and Ais looked at me suspiciously. She knew something was up.

Shit! It was Haven calling.

Ignore. It rang again. Ignore.

Shit, shit, shit...

If I answered with Ais right in front of me, then she would know it wasn't Jaxon. There was no other woman in my life besides her that would be calling me, and she knew that. Something had to be wrong, though, otherwise why would she keep calling? I took a deep breath and exhaled slowly as the phone rang again. I closed my eyes and hit accept.

"We have a problem!" Haven said with an alarming voice.

"What is it?" I asked.

"The pottery shop was just set on fire. Aunt Clara luckily had just left about an hour before, but Ezra was finishing closing the books when a woman walked in demanding to see Clara. She was manic and had a fire in her eyes, Ezra said." She paused and took a deep breath in. "It was Isadora. She knows about the dagger. She must've read the journal."

I gasped realizing that this was my fault too.

"Ezra is okay?" I asked.

"Yes, nothing that I can't heal." He had been hurt by her, which made me angry.

"We need to move the dagger now. Can you meet me at JFK?" I asked too quickly, looking up and realizing that Ais had heard every word and her eyes were as wide as the Mississippi. "Make sure you are not being followed," I added before hanging up the phone and turned to look toward Ais apologetically. *What was I supposed to say now?* This was more than just a secret, this was life or death for all of us, including her Aunt.

"Ais, will you come with me? I'll explain on the way."

Need-to-know basis, I thought, as I contemplated what kind of harm I may have just done to her. She nodded without hesitation. She trusted me, and I needed to make sure she was kept safe.

Sorry, Aunt Lynn, maybe you should've been the one to have shared your family secrets. It's too late now.

We drove up the bluffs, and for the next fifteen minutes, I shared my visit with Alex, the dagger, and even Aunt Lynn. I told her all about Haven and how it was still very new. I was driving, so every now and then, I glanced over. Her face seemed to be very composed considering that it was a lot to take in. I wished I had some of that tea from Aunt Clara to help with the overload.

When I mentioned her aunt, she froze. She seemed to be scanning through her memories over the last eighteen years to see if she had missed something that would've made more sense. Her jaw dropped when I mentioned Haven being the girl from the Farmer's Market. She had clearly seen her before I had, and a part of me was slightly jealous that day, but this very instant, I was happy getting all of this off of my chest to my best friend.

I panicked, realizing I needed to call Jaxon and tell him what was going on.

"Ais, can you call Jaxon and just let him know we're heading to JFK? Tell him Haven called."

She was calm and opened her phone without hesitation. Jaxon agreed to meet us there, just in case he was needed, even just for emotional support. Once Aisling hung up the phone, she said she needed to call her aunt. I froze, knowing I betrayed her aunt but agreed it was for the best. We were pulling up to the field, and saw we had beaten everyone else there. I decided to walk to the tree in the field and let her and her aunt have some privacy. A few minutes had passed before Aisling walked from the Jeep over to me. It was barely a second that had passed before I realized she had tears in her eyes. Clarity was occurring, and it was overwhelming. I remember feeling like her not that long ago. Her Aunt had confirmed everything I said to her. I grabbed her tight and hugged her.

"It will be okay. We will be okay," I assured her.

She nodded her head and hugged me tighter. I felt my shirt getting damp from her tears and rubbed her back like we always did when one of us needed comfort.

"So, Aunt Lynn is one too? You would think she could've lit the damn candles on my birthday cake last year when no one could find a lighter." She and I laughed at the memory of her dad rummaging through the entire kitchen without any luck. That was the very moment that I knew everything was going to be okay with her knowing the big secret.

Another set of headlights pulled up the winding abandoned road, and my eyes squinted in the dark to make sure that we were safe from other visitors. My right palm tingled with an electric orb just in case it was Isadora, or worse, Eric had followed us up here. Ais looked at my hand, and her eyes grew larger, and her jaw dropped. But I knew I was ready to protect her at all costs. The electricity grew, and it lit up the dark tree we were standing under. My breathing settled when I realized it was Haven and Ezra. I dropped my hand and let the tingling subside. We were safe.

"Ais, I'd like you to meet my long lost sister, Haven, and

her boyfriend, Ezra. Both witches." I smiled at the idea of being able to finally say the words out loud. Aisling was peering down the dirt path, eyes squinting, and ready to take on the night's new adventures.

Haven and Ezra walked over to us quickly. Haven had the sheath in hand under her light jacket, halfway hiding it, protecting it.

She brought it! Now, where would I hide it?

"You must be Aisling?" Haven asked matter of factly. They hugged quickly. "I'm sorry I had to take Freya away from you for the night. Emergency, I swear."

"I get it. My family is just as involved as yours." Aisling smiled, but her eyes didn't meet Haven's. Instead they met mine, and I nodded in agreement. Another set of lights were coming up the path. My jaw clenched as I hoped it was Jaxon, but just in case... My palms started to tingle, and I looked down at them and then to Haven, who automatically turned to see the lights, with both of her hands ready with electricity too. It felt normal, as weird as that sounded. We were in sync with one another.

Jaxon stepped out of the car, then his passenger door opened. My palms lit up, throwing my electricity into the sky to illuminate the extra person with him. Aisling ran to him and jumped into his arms before he could even stand. *Declan.* The race of my heart slowed, and I could relax a little more. Jaxon, Declan, Haven, Ezra, and Aisling were all here with me and ready to protect our families. Who would've known that we would all be united in Jaxon's and my secret field on this warm June night?

Chapter 20

Syphon or Die

The thought of my family dying because I couldn't learn a simple damn trick that was supposed to be my specialty power was kind of sickening. My stomach turned at the thought of letting everyone down. Bile formed in the back of my throat as I realized it was all on me. No one else could do it. Talk about the weight of the witching world on my shoulders. I felt like I was going to be sick... The group of us were at JFK, planning and trying to think of alternative options if I couldn't figure out how to syphon the magic out of the dagger or if the Immortals got their hands on it. I just needed a minute to breathe.

I walked away from the chatter of the group with my arms up on the back of my head, trying to catch my breath and letting my lung capacity open wider. I felt panicky, and my arms were becoming sweaty.

I mumbled to myself once I was finally alone. "Shit... How did this all turn around on me? Couldn't Aunt Lynn just be the one who could fix all this? Or Alex, or even Clara? Why me?" I groaned. "I know I'm being whiny, but come on... Like me? Why am I any more special than the other ones? I'm the newest witch, and now I had to figure this out. All of our lives depended on me." My head began to spin until I finally leaned over and heaved.

Jaxon ran up behind me and rubbed my back, he quickly grabbed my hair and held it out of my face. "Hey, hey, it's okay. Breathe, Freya." His cool hands felt good on my skin, but my mind was racing. "You're okay! I've got you... You're okay."

I knew he was just comforting me and not pressuring me to get a move on. But I knew he was just as concerned. He rubbed my back quietly until the sobs settled. My breathing became a little more even after a minute or two. Aisling walked over and was sitting next to me. Both Jaxon and Aisling were with me and beside me like the good ole days. It seemed like the past month had finally taken its toll on me with the weight of the world on my shoulders. I had to do this... I didn't know how, but with them by my side, I could get through this. Aisling handed me a bottle of water, and my burning throat started to soothe itself as I chugged it. The cold water was exactly what I needed. I poured some on my palms and patted my face down with it, then the back of my neck. I sucked in a dee breath and started to feel a little better.

I can do this. I can do this!

I stood, and Jaxon looked at me questioningly, and Aisling worriedly, but I was okay. I nodded and started heading back to the others. I could feel the eyes of everyone staring at me, but when I looked up at them, everyone looked away, except Haven. It felt like she was looking through my soul, trying to make sure I was okay. I nodded and put my hair back in a ponytail and wiped my face. It was time.

"Let's get to work," I said after a deep breath. Haven smiled and stood up next to me.

"I have an idea," Haven stated. "You're a syphon. We don't know exactly how it works, but I was thinking with a group this big of witches, then maybe we can let you borrow some of our magic to syphon from the dagger."

"The only problem is that I don't know how to do it," I shook my head and felt the defeat grow.

"I think when you were trying with Jaxon earlier you were afraid of hurting him, but now there's enough of us that if you take a little from each of us, then no one will feel drained." She nodded with a smile.

"My woman, the genius!" Ezra smiled and pulled Haven to him, kissing her softly. They both were giggling like teenage lovebirds.

"Do you want to try it?" Jaxon turned to me and asked with worry. He leaned into me and whispered, "If you say no, we can leave right now and figure something else out."

I looked around the open field and looked at each and every person with us and felt that if I didn't try it now... then when?

"Let's give it a shot." I nodded.

After a few more minutes of convincing myself, I nodded and the four of them stood side by side and grabbed hands. Aisling sat on the side away from the syphoning trick, being mundane and out of harm's way. I stood in front of them and debated for a brief moment if this was even a good idea... But I knew I had nothing else. Especially if Isadora already tried to go after the pottery shop, then what would be next? The bar, or even my dad? I couldn't let that happen.

I grabbed hold of Jaxon's hand to my left and Haven's on my right. I inhaled deeply and closed my eyes... I prayed to myself that I could do this. I let my intentions grow inside me as I started to pull at their magic as best as I could. At first, nothing happened. Then, I could feel my hands begin to tingle, and all of a sudden, I felt my shoulders get heavy with a weight that was making me feel uneven on my own two feet. The magic was flowing almost too easy. I was syphoning from them, and I could feel my strength growing. The weight on my shoulders relaxed as I looked behind me and gasped.

Aisling.

She had come up behind me to place her hands on my shoulders for support but instead her body became weak and drained too quick.

"What the hell?" I yelled. "She's human."

I tried to let go of everyone as I noticed her eyes slowly shutting. Declan released his hand and rushed to her, catching her before her head hit the ground.

"Aisling!" Declan yelled.

Once our circle was broken the syphoning trance ended with my Mark glowing and I could feel a strength of power coursing through my veins. I swallowed hard trying to settle the magic deep inside me. Everyone stood upright besides Aisling. As we all frantically waited for her to open her eyes and say anything. Seconds felt like hours as we waited.

"Did it work?" Her eyes opened, and her voice was hoarse.

"Ais, what the hell were you thinking?" I asked, grabbing her shoulders and shaking them.

"Did it work?" she asked with urgency as she tried to sit herself up. Declan helped her and held her tight with worry in his eyes. I gasped when I looked at her glowing forearm.

"Oh my God! Ais, your arm... You are one of us!" I started with excitement when I realized that she had to have a near-death experience for her Mark to appear. I had triggered it... Meaning I had almost killed her without even realizing it.

I could feel tears forming at the corner of my eyes and I tried not to blink to hold the water works in.

"Now everything makes more sense." She stared at her forearm and smiled wide, she seemed back to normal after the swift Declan catch. He was looking nervously at her forearm, and he seemed to be in shock. He truly had no idea. None of us did.

Haven went over to her and examined her Mark. Between her and Jaxon, they would be the brains of the book witch knowledge to figure hers out. The glow was starting to subside, revealing two triangles intertwined on her forearm.

"I know this symbol, but I can't remember where I've seen it before," Haven announced with her brows furrowed in frustration. Jaxon looked to Haven and then back at me carefully before speaking.

"It's an old Mark. I've only seen it in the books, never in person. Looks like we've got an ancient witch along with our blood moon Anchor twins now. Badass!" Jaxon smirked.

Declan seemed in deep thought but was smiling on the surface. I could tell something was bothering him. I looked at Aisling, who looked both excited and nervous. But I smiled, knowing no more secrets.

Haven pulled out the dagger from the sheath and peered at me, waiting for the acceptance of the job. I nodded and grabbed the dagger. It was time to try and syphon this thing and then hide it.

I held the dagger in my right hand with confidence, feeling stronger than ever, and started to pull at the magic. At first, my hand felt like it was burning, I decided to use both hands and really pull the curse from the dagger. The magic started to transfer and began to have a cooling touch. I could feel the darkness of the murderous weapon becoming part of me, hoping the feeling wasn't a lasting effect from it. I swallowed hard as I didn't like the heaviness it carried, but I would keep that secret to myself. I would have to be careful what else I consumed until I knew more about syphoning. I looked down when the dagger began to glow and then my hands lite up. I smiled when I felt the last drop of magic transfer to me. I looked at the dagger, which then stopped glowing, becoming nothing more than a simple dagger with a sheath. It was no longer a witch tracker. It was no longer a soul snatcher, just an obsidian blade with a weird handle.

I let out an exhale of relief and smiled when I realized that I had done it. But I knew I could not have done it without my friends and family here with me. *We did it.* We destroyed the ultimate weapon. I just hoped we did the right thing.

Chapter 21

Vacation Days and Stowaways

The next two weeks were spent mostly together, the six of us at JFK. Haven ended up telling Aunt Clara what happened the next day when she went to check on the dagger and realized it was gone. She said she had a vision that it had been taken, but she wasn't sure by who. That's when Haven called me, and we agreed to let her know about everything. It wasn't long after that conversation when Alex called me to see what had happened. I told her the same thing that Haven told Aunt Clara. We had syphoned the magic from the dagger, and I have it hidden safely. No one would ever suspect it to be at my home, hidden in the secret compartment of the painted fish pottery that Jaxon gave to my dad, who undoubtedly put it on display as a centerpiece at the house. Hidden in perfect sight. Of course, I was the only one who knew where it was, and I planned on keeping it that way forever.

Alex told me she would be coming through for a few days to check on things around Crystal Rock. Now that I filled her in on who Izzy was, she decided to come to town and see if she could track down Eric herself. She had real-ized that he hadn't been chasing her the last few weeks when she had come to town or to Clara's. Clara had a vision of him staying in a home quietly. She was almost sure that he was plotting something.

I started to feel better about the past two weeks, knowing that Alex wasn't running, the dagger was magic-less, the six of us were together most of the time, and that nothing had happened since finding out about Isadora. It was almost a little too eerie that things have been so quiet and basically normal, as if something far worse was coming. Working at the theatre was becoming the most normal part of my days because it was the most mundane place to be. The rest of the time consisted of practicing at JFK with the others or helping my dad with the shifts at Swig and Jig until he could get extra help. I could see the long nights were starting to take a toll on him. Jaxon had been helping cover the shifts at the bar while I was at the theatre to help out as much as he could too.

Margo had stopped in to see him working one day while I wasn't there. I guess she had a short, but apologetic conversation with my dad about the whole taking Jaxon away ordeal. Of course, my dad was too nice of a guy and didn't like to hold grudges, so he poured her a shot of bourbon and they bonded over it for a short while. Jaxon seemed happy that his mom had made an effort to apolo-gize. I guess if he was happy, then I would have to let it go.

The Colorado trip was in a few days, and I was ready for a little vacation. Part of me felt like we shouldn't be leaving, but then the selfish part of me thought that we couldn't live forever in fear of waiting for the Immortals to come after us. If we lived in fear, waiting for them, then they win anyway. That wasn't going to happen. At least, not anymore. Plus, Aunt Clara, Alex, Aunt Lynn, Haven, and Ezra would be here keeping an eye on things and making sure nothing was out of the ordinary.

Sitting behind Dad's vintage wooden desk at the bar, I looked down and saw there was a phone charger plugged in, but it wasn't his. I examined the cord and realized it wasn't even for his phone.

What the hell?

I glanced around the room to see if anything else was out of place. I opened the closet and looked at the blankets perfectly folded in the corner and the cot put back in place. The only thing out of place was the way the blankets were folded. He wouldn't have folded them hotel-style... I knew if it was his work then he would've rolled them and tossed them in the closet, out of sight out of mind. I knew just from that that someone had been sleeping in his office, and I was about to find out who.

I walked out to the bar where he was serving his friend Jack a shot of whiskey and had started to make a mixer for him. He hadn't made eye contact with me yet, and now I was starting to think it was on purpose.

"Dad, is someone staying here?" I asked with a tone that was angrier than I meant it to be. Jack looked at my dad nervously and then I knew that Jack knew something too. What was going on? Why was *I* out of the loop?

He didn't answer me and looked at Jack.

"Jack, do you know something?" I turned and asked him, and he blushed without a moment to pass. "Jack... What do you know that I don't?" I gently shoved his shoulder in a child's play way. And when he zipped his lips and sipped on the whiskey I turned to my dad. "Dad, what's going on here?" I asked again and started to feel embarrassed that I didn't put two and two together sooner.

The front door of the bar opened, and in came Alex, doe-eyed and beautiful as ever. Stunning, always beautifully stunning. *Great.* I rolled my eyes. It was her staying here. My childhood heart wanted to be excited and run to her, but my adult heart was still barred off with resentment. I looked at her and back at my dad before turning on my heel and heading straight back to the office, slamming the door hard, maybe a little harder than necessary, but it felt good.

"Why wouldn't he just tell me?" I shook my head and talked amongst myself. My blood boiling. "I thought the secrets were done. Did Jaxon know too? Jack knew! Geez, was I the only one out of the loop?" I paced in the backroom for a minute before my dad slowly opened the door and walked in by me.

"Hey, she needed a place to stay," he said sweetly, shrugging as if she hadn't ruined our life the last two years and abandoned us. As if no harm was done and all was forgiven.

"Yeah, and of course, you let her walk right back into your life without skipping a beat. You are too nice to people who walk all over you!" I yelled, feeling defensive over his fragile heart. Then, I looked at him and realized that *I* had hurt him more than she probably had. "Oh no, Dad." I needed to stop acting like a child. He was a smart man and a grown adult. He could make his own choices in life. I couldn't do this to him.

"Dad, I'm sorry. I didn't mea—"

"No, you're right. Your mom has a place in my heart, kiddo, that I can't let go of. I know you're worried, but I am okay. She just needed a place to stay. My head is screwed on straight, and my heart is still guarded. Please don't worry." That was the moment I realized that he was just being the sweet man that the town knew him as. The man who would give you the shirt off of his back. He was giving her safety, and in return, she was probably just protecting him from Eric and Isadora. I looked at him and nodded before running to him and hugging him.

"No, you are being you, and that's *not* a bad thing at all. I'm sorry..." I wiped my wet cheeks and sniffled. "Let her stay. I was just shocked." I realized that I actually meant it. It was more so comforting knowing that she was protecting him while I wasn't with him. My dad squeezed me tighter and cleared his throat.

I let him go without looking back at him and walked out of the office. Alex paused behind the barstool before cautiously sitting. I pulled up the stool next to her and whispered, "Thank you for looking out for him." She smiled back and nodded. "You can stay," I said before pulling at my tourmaline necklace and twisting it in between my fingers like a nervous child in trouble for talking back to my parents.

"Thank you," she said and grabbed the bottle of bourbon to pour herself a shot. I realized that she seemed just as nervous, if not more.

I looked down at my watch and knew that it was time to pack for Colorado. Aisling had been packed for about a month now and had our whole itinerary planned out. I was going to need to bring my hiking boots. Sounded like a lot of outdoor activities and adventures in the short trip. I was going to need a vacation from this vacation. Jaxon had talked to his parents about the trip, and Margo was not too fond of him leaving during a time like this, but then again, she never wanted him with me, so there was never really going to be a good time for him to get away from her. Declan was a one backpack kind of travel guy. If it weren't for Aisling, he would've forgotten his toothbrush and fresh socks. He was the perfect amount of forgetfulness for Aisling to plan and remember for him. She loved planning, being in control, and feeling needed.

While heading out of the bar to go home and pack for the upcoming weekend, Alex stopped me in the parking lot.

"Hey, just wanted to run it past you before I brought it up to Jim. Do you think he needs help with the bar for a little while? I mean, as long as Eric isn't making me run, then I could stay and help him for a bit if you want me to?" She was asking *me* for permission for a bar that she owned half of still. My dad never even took her name off the papers. It wasn't a bad idea. He really did need the help, and with Alex there, at least I would know that he was safe. She could use her power of persuasion to bring in some extra cash at the bar too with extra drinks. I silently laughed at the thought of that.

"That would be nice. We would both appreciate the help," I said nicely. "Do you think you are planning on staying long?" I was genuinely curious if I should get used to her being around again or if this was only a temporary thing for a few weeks. A part of me was hoping for the short term so that I didn't have to let her back in, but a larger part of me was secretly hoping for the long term so that I could have her back with me. It was a divided situation that I wasn't ready to choose overnight.

"As long as I can without overstaying my welcome." She smiled as I nodded.

"Okay." I left feeling speechless but I watched the corner of her mouth try and hold her own smile back.

Driving home from the bar, I had this cold eerie feeling that I was being watched. My stomach started to turn as I looked in my rearview mirror and noticed a set of head-lights following too close for comfort. I decided to take an extra turn down the street before my block just to be safe.

The car followed me down the wrong street. I decided to make my drive a little longer and continued down the side streets back toward the bar. I finally exhaled when the streetlights finally brightened the car enough for me to realize it was just Declan. A text or call would've been less creepy than following me.

I pulled up to my house, and he pulled up behind me and got out.

"Forgot where you lived or something?" He laughed and started walking toward me.

"You never can be too careful these days." I laughed nervously for a moment, but it was Declan so I was safe. "What's up?"

"Sorry, my phone died, otherwise I would've texted ya." So, that explained the unplanned visit.

"That's okay. Did something happen?" I asked worriedly.

"No, I just—" he paused and took a deep breath. "Can I talk to you about something?" He asked nervously.

"Of course," I waited as he stayed silent. "Declan, what's going on?"

"It's just that... Ais's Mark appeared, and I recognized it."

"What do you mean, you recognized it?" Now, I was the one confused. "What, like in a book or something?"

"It's the same Mark as someone I know."

"Okay? I'm not an expert, but isn't that a good thing then? You know who her Anchor is!"

"No, he's *not* her Anchor. There's no way!" He said angrily.

"Oh. Declan, I thought the Mark would be matching to her Anchor? I don't understand?" I admitted.

"It should be, but the person that shares her Mark is my dad. That can't be right." His breathing quickened as his jaw clenched. "I mean, they are not the same age, they can't be Anchors, right?" My eyes widened and I gasped. "I haven't said anything to him or Ais or even Jaxon yet because I was hoping that maybe you might know something more since she's your best friend. Did her aunt and my dad have a child together or something?"

"Oh..." Was all I could say.

"Oh, as in, yeah he's her biological father?" He questioned, studying my expression.

"No. Oh, as in I never saw that coming. Her father is her father 100%, and her mother is her mother 100%. Maybe it's just a coincidence with the symbol," I reassured him. Plus, she came from the Immortal's bloodline, which was the only secret that I have kept to myself, and Declan was not part of that bloodline.

He seemed to lower his shoulders and take a deep breath in and let it out slowly. I had him sit down on the front porch to catch his breath for a minute before putting my hand awkwardly on his back, patting it to make him feel better. I could tell now by the look in his distant eyes that the question had been eating away at him this past two weeks, and it was no wonder why he looked so shocked the night she received her Mark. I would've been just as panicked.

"Are you okay?" I asked.

He breathed in heavily and let out a sigh.

"Well, now I am." He laughed. "I thought for a second that I was dating my sister." He made a gagging sound, and we both laughed. "That would've been tragic, considering that I love the girl." He gasped after the words had already come out and looked at me with horror. He hadn't told her that yet, and I was not going to be the one to ruin that for him.

"Don't worry, your secret is safe with me." I smiled at him and hugged him in approval.

Chapter 22

Maybe We Should've Stayed

I finished packing my last bag for vacation, now all I needed was some sleep. Tomorrow was going to come early, and I needed to be ready for our flight. Luckily, my dad would be home tonight earlier than he had been because Alex said she would close the bar on her own. It was easy enough for her, the bar was like riding a bike, she never forgot how to run it. I guarantee the locals were happy to see her smiling, pretty face behind the bar instead of Jim's. It was time for some sleep, so I brushed my teeth and headed for bed.

I laid in bed and stared up at the ceiling, excited for a vacation, but also nervous to leave town while things were not fully taken care of. Aisling made a good point, though. The Immortals may never come for us. Even though they were immortal, they were still a form of a human... I hoped. They had forever to plot against us. We would only be a flight away if needed. I closed my eyes, and let sleep take over me.

The sky was dark. I tried opening my eyes to look around, but everything was dark. I felt cold and clammy.

Where was I?

Something was off. Fumbling for my phone for the flashlight, when I realized it was dead. Ugh, bad timing. That's it... I threw both of my hands up quickly and whispered, "Ignis," and let the fire ignite in my hands to light up the space I was in. Cold water dripped from the ceiling and rock walls.

A cave? Where am I? How did I get here?

I started walking slowly to escape this place when I heard a voice I knew.

"She has no idea what she's doing, don't worry. She's nothing special," a familiar lady's voice said.

"She better not be, if she ruins my plans with that dagger, then I will make sure to kill every person and Anchor she loves, and you already know what I'm capable of," a man's voice threatened.

"Darling, calm down. Everything is going as planned. They're leaving in the morning." The voice was meant to be calming, but sent shivers down my spine.

My palms began to sweat as I crept around the final corner to where they were talking. I slowed my breathing and lowered the fire to a dim light before placing my hands behind my back to peek around the corner to confirm the voices. I looked for the people, but all I saw was fire coming back at me. Isadora was throwing fire at me. She caught me invading their conversation, and she was trying to end my intrusion. Fuck! The fire was coming straight for me, and it was hot, too hot! I turned to try and block the heat, but my hands came out from behind my back to catch it instead. I panicked for a brief moment, but then realized that I was still strong. I caught her fire and let my palms face each other to let the fire grow to a volleyball size before feeling pissed off enough to take it and throw it right back at her.

"Impossible!" she screamed before dodging the fire and running off with the man in a suit chasing after her. I went toward them before stopping as the man turned toward me with his dark brooding eyes and strong jawline. It was dark in the cave where he stood, but the half of his face that I could see was evil. He would kill me if I stepped any closer. I breathed heavily with the fire reigniting in my hands and growing. I could feel the heat from the ball of fire, and now I was angry. Sweat started to bead off my forehead as I lifted my palms, ready to throw a second fireball at the evil man when Isadora yelled his name. "Eric, let's go!"

He gave me one last hard look before pointing his palm toward me and stealing the fireball I had in my hands. With a smirk that I could barely see in the dark, he let the fire die out and become a puff of smoke in his hand. "Weak," he said, taunting me before turning and walking away, leaving me standing in the dark alone.

I woke in a pool of sweat. I sat up in a panic and realized I was either dreaming or having a nightmare. I wasn't sure which one yet. My magic felt real, and the dream felt real... I looked down at my glowing forearm as my hands were tingling with fire trying to ignite. I shook my hands to let the energy leave them and tried to clear my head.

It had been too dark to get a real look at Eric, so there was no way I could not pinpoint him in a crowd. Isadora, no problem, but I had spent too many wasted appointments with that bitch. My hair felt as if I had just climbed out of my pool. I felt dehydrated and needed water. I jumped out of bed and headed for the kitchen. Ice cold water was exactly what I needed. I took my phone with me and walked past my dad's room to make sure he was home. I relaxed when I saw him sleeping soundly in his room.

I jumped when my phone buzzed.

Haven: A cave? What was that all about? I've been there before.

Freya: Were you spying on my dreams?

Haven: LOL oh God, no! But I did just wake up in a sweat, did you?

Freya: Weird...Yes. Where is the cave?

Haven: It's actually close to JFK. Instead of turning right for the path, you take a left up the bluffs. It's a creepy cave, but Ezra and I used to go exploring and found that one a few years ago.

Freya: We are getting ready to leave for Colorado, any chance you and Ezra could check it out and make sure nothing suspicious is going on? I can mention it to Alex too.

Haven: Yes, we will, and yes, let Mom know.

I frowned at the idea of Haven calling Alex 'mom' still. But I guess everyone was different. Maybe I was just bitter, but I was thankful that she was helping my dad with the bar for a little while. I sent Alex a text to get in touch with Haven while we're gone and check out the cave. I loaded up the luggage and checked on the dagger in the pottery fish one last time to make sure that it was still magicless.

Check, and check.

My dad had headed into the bar by the time I finished loading the Jeep. I drove to the bar and gave my dad another hug. Of course, he told me to be safe and to call him when we landed. Alex was not there yet, thankfully. That could've been another awkward goodbye. I headed to Jaxon's house to pick him up, and Declan and Aisling would be waiting across the street. They asked to just drive with us to the airport. My stomach started to turn as I turned onto his road and headed toward his home. The last time that I came down this road, I ended up seeing Margo for the first time before my world turned on me with Jaxon being alive and well. Breathe, I reminded myself, as I pulled up to his house. I walked up to the front door and slowed when I heard yelling.

"Loving her is a losing game, Jaxon, and you know I'm right. Anyone who is around that girl walks away or ends up dead. She is not who I want you around." Margo was screaming at Jaxon without knowing that I was in earshot on the front porch. I lingered a minute while the yelling between the two of them continued as I heard Jaxon defend me. I decided to try and stop the screaming by ringing the doorbell. Margo answered the door, and surprise washed across her face.

She changed her demeanor, and her fake smile was back. "Oh, Freya, how lovely to see you. Jaxon is just finishing packing. Do me a favor and make sure he calls me when the flight lands, so I know he is safe." *He* is safe, not that *we* are safe... of course. She hated me. I smiled and nodded quietly. She waved me in.

I had not been in their new home yet. It was strange standing in the entryway of a home I did not recognize with people I knew far too well. She pointed up the stairs and said that he should be down in a minute before walking angrily away to another room muttering under her breath. I stood awkwardly waiting. *Come on, Jax, hurry up.* I looked around the entryway and toward the living room at the wall full of family photos. Always just the three of them. Jaxon caught me off guard when he reached the top of the stairs and waved for me to come on up. I smiled at him and walked up the stairs.

"Sorry about her. She's always angry." He laughed and shoved it off, as if it meant nothing. Maybe to him it was nothing, but to me, it hurt.

"It's okay," I lied. "This is your room, hey? It's very... you." I smiled. The room was small with a queen bed and his TV was hooked up in his closet mounted on the wall. There was a second closet for his clothes, and a desk with his laptop. It was simple, but worked.

"Plain and simple is who I am, huh?" he asked sarcastically.

"It's simple, yes." I laughed and sat on his bed while he finished throwing clothes in his backpack.

He paused and looked at me with admiration. "This is my favorite part of the room." He pointed to a picture collage of him and me on the cork-board behind the laptop. I stood up and examined the photos from younger to now and felt my cheeks flush. "And that's my favorite part about you." He walked to me and grazed my blushing cheeks with his palm. He grabbed my face and kissed me softly. He pulled away and looked back at me. "Please don't let my mom bother you, she's just overprotective."

I knew he was just trying to reassure me that the argument I overheard meant nothing. But I still didn't like that she hated me so much. He must've realized that my head was still in overthinking mode. He pulled me closer to him and kissed me again before throwing me onto his bed. He caught me off guard when his lips traced my neck and followed to my stomach before meeting my gaze again.

"I'm ready for this vacation, I hope you are too." He said.

I smiled with flush cheeks and stood up, zipping his backpack for him. "Oh, I'm so ready! Let's get out of here." I wanted to get the hell out of their house before Margo came and ruined my day more with her glare.

Aisling and Declan were standing outside on their porch waiting for us. I hugged Aisling as soon as I saw her. Mr. Greystone was standing in the doorway on the phone. He was arguing a little too loud. Geez, I thought, I would hate to have to go against him as a lawyer. He had a very intimidating tone to his voice, and a hard look on his face, but he was very attractive. Declan must look more like his mom, though, who I have never heard much about. Aisling said that she died when he was younger, and it was only him and his dad. Hopefully, he was more approachable for her since she spends a lot of time there with Declan.

I waved to him as we pulled into the driveway. He nodded his head and went back to arguing. Declan yelled to him as they walked down the stairs to throw their luggage in. "Bye, Dad!" Mr. Greystone reopened the door and waved silently to Declan before going back inside and closing the door.

My eyes bulged at the lack of affection.

He didn't seem very fatherly. At least, not how the fathers that I grew up around were. I guess I couldn't really talk, though. Alex's and my relationship was sort of fucked up too.

Even the Oakes hugged Jaxon before we walked out. I was pretty sure Margo glared at me, but she at least said bye to me this time.

I shrugged.

Oh, well. It's none of my business. Time to go.

Chapter 23

Time To Relax

The flight was short, but flying in and seeing the Rockies made my heart surge with excitement. They were beautiful. I mean, the Wisconsin bluffs were amazing too, but these were breathtaking. I looked at Jaxon, and his eyes were larger than normal with amusement. He had never traveled outside of Wisconsin before, and this was his first time on a plane. If he was going to date me long-term, then vacationing was going to be a must. I was happy to see him excited and ready for adventure.

We all called our parents when we landed, except for Declan. He said his dad wouldn't answer anyway, that he was too busy with his clients. I let it go and didn't push the subject. We called a taxi van and headed to Aisling's uncle's cabin in Estes Park, where he left us keys to his SUV. It was noon, and we had the rest of today to adventure in the mountains and small shops.

We pulled up to the cabin and it brought back so many childhood memories. My parents used to vacation here with her parents, and Aisling and I would spend a week at a time exploring. It was such a fun childhood memory that we made sure to do it each summer until the divorce. We were lucky best friends that our parents got along with one another. Jaxon's parents never let him come with us, and they never wanted to join, so he would always stay home. So many getaways here that he missed.

I texted Haven to check on everything, I needed the reassurance so that I could let myself relax and enjoy the weekend away.

Freya: Everything okay there?

Haven: All good! Checked out the cave with Mom and Aunt Clara a little while ago and it was empty. She's headed back to the bar, and I'm headed back with Aunt Clara to finish repainting the shop. We're all good.

Freya: Great! Keep me posted ;)

Haven: Always!

I smiled at the *always* part of the text. I hoped that was true. Jaxon glanced at me with questioning eyes. I told him it was Haven and everything was all good. Everyone seemed to relax a little more once those words were said. The cabin was as beautiful as I remembered it. It had been a few years since the last time we were here, and I was thankful that this vacation was happening.

Aisling grabbed my hand as soon as we got out of the van, and we ran up to the cabin, leaving our luggage and the boys to pay for the driver. She giggled like a child as we ran into the place. It was exactly how we had left it. We both ran to the upstairs patio and embraced the view of the Rockies in our backyard. I let out an excited cheer as did she. After the boys met us upstairs with the luggage wrapped around their necks and under their arms, Aisling directed them to where they should set it down, and we all sat down on the patio a little while longer before deciding it was time to eat something, then hike up the mountains.

Declan offered to cook and I was glad he did because he sure could cook. I made the connection that that was a huge reason why Aisling was holding on to him so tight. Her cooking could burn down a town versus his cooking should be at a five-star restaurant. Jaxon helped with the side dishes, and Aisling and I talked about normal life. I grabbed the bracelet her aunt had given to us at the Farmer's Market and started to turn it thoughtlessly around. Aisling caught a glance at it and she laughed.

"You know that's a tracker, right?" She shrugged her shoulders.

"What do you mean a tracker?"

"She put a locator spell on it before giving them to us." She paused. "She wanted to make sure we were safe and that she was able to see where we were at all times."

"That is kind of stalker-ish." I laughed, but in the back of my mind, I actually felt safer with it just in case.

"Yeah, she told me on the phone after that night with the dagger."

"I'm not even mad about it. I like the extra safety precautions until things are better."

"Hopefully, it's only temporary, but at least it's a cool bracelet." We both nodded in agreement and giggled.

After lunch, we headed for a hike in the mountains, and after a few hours of exploring, smiling, laughing, and sarcastic jokes, it was time to head back to the cabin and grab the SUV to head into town for knick-knacks and s'mores. It had only been a few hours away from home, but it was a breath of fresh air and high altitude. There was a small shop in the center of the main street that was calling my name. The window decor had an intriguing look that screamed come in, and the door had an infinity symbol on it. Naturally, we had to check it out.

The bell dinged as we walked through. A short lady, mid-seventies, was behind the counter. She looked up and smiled brightly. We must have looked like young love walking through the door, and she must've thought it was cute, or she saw dollar signs walking in. The shop was old and looked like it hadn't had many customers in a while. It was the shop that got passed by on the street for one of the bigger souvenir shops. It was just a little hole in the wall.

"Hello, welcome, welcome. Watch your step, and come on in."

"Hi, thank you!" Jaxon said loud enough for all of us.

"What brings ya in? Anything special?" She asked with excitement.

"Just browsing," I answered.

"Let me know if you need anything specific." She smiled and turned to sit back down on her stool behind the counter.

The sweet little lady gave me the urge to purchase something from her. This was a small local shop, and you could tell the woman poured her heart and soul into the place. It was her livelihood. I walked over to the glass counter and glanced at the earrings. There was a pair of studs that caught my attention.

"Can I look at those ones please?"

"Ah, the moonstone studs, these are my absolute

favorite pair that I have here." She smiled and pulled the studs out from under the glass. I examined them and then turned them around to see the price, realizing they were a little out of my budget for this trip.

"They are beautiful, thank you," I said, setting them back on the counter. I decided to look through the rest of the store, settling for a t-shirt for my dad and another one for me, an over-the-shoulder bag with a matching coin purse, and of course, a keychain and magnet stating Estes Park, CO. I looked to the side of the register. She had graham crackers, chocolate, and marshmallows in a bundle for purchase. I smiled and added those to my order.

We headed out the door, thanking the lady for her shop and time, and went to the next one. As we headed into the next store, Jaxon asked for the car keys from Aisling, realizing he left his phone in the car. He insisted that we keep shopping and he would catch up. He kissed me before turning on his heel.

Aisling and I looked through the clothes rack and grabbed matching hats to buy. Declan rolled his eyes.

"What? You don't like hats?" she asked him.

"Are you kidding me? Do you think a hat is going to make you any less sexy? All eyes are on you through every door." He grinned and picked her up to spin her around, carrying her in his arms as he kissed her. She giggled and told him to put her down. She had a hat to purchase. They were that couple that enjoyed the PDA, while I preferred to not be the center of attention.

Jaxon walked back through the door and came up behind me, grabbing for my hand. I blushed as I hoped he wasn't going to make the same display of affection that they did. I breathed in relief when he didn't.

"Finding anything else?" he asked.

"Just this hat." He grabbed it and put it on my head, fixing my hair around it to fall evenly around my face. His look of approval made me blush again.

"This hat is a must. Damn! Can you ever look like a haggard witch?" I laughed at his sarcastic insult. He laughed and kissed me on my cheek. "Kidding, love."

We checked out a few more shops before heading back to the cabin to make dinner and have a bonfire with s'mores. As much as I loved adventuring, I was always happy to get back and relax. We sat in the backseat together while Declan drove us back. I felt the urge to check in with Haven but decided against it. She had promised if something was wrong, she would call me... I needed to stop over-thinking and relax.

The boys started to work on dinner while Aisling and I volunteered to start the fire right next to the kitchen on the deck. We could still talk to the boys if we wanted to. She grabbed the firewood as I went and looked for the matches before realizing that I knew how to make fire without wasting a match. I smiled to myself as I headed toward the pit. Aisling had the wood organized in a teepee formation. I walked up to it and told her to step back.

I put my palm out and felt the tingling start without having to whisper any Latin at all. The tingling turned to a flame, and fire ignited in my palm. It was cool to the touch, but had the heat of a real fire. I took it and aimed it to the center of the wood, and gently tossed it into the pit. The wood ignited evenly and started to crackle. Aisling looked back at me in amazement.

"Oh my God... Teach me that!" She grinned from ear to ear. I nodded as she sat down on the lounge chair, and I jumped across from her on the wicker couch with the fluffy cushion. While we played with fire in our hands.

Chapter 24

This Can't Be Happening

The day had been surreal. Tomorrow would be the two-year anniversary of the accident, and instead of being dead, Jaxon was sitting next to me, curled up by the fire in the mountains. Pinch me, I thought, so I can wake up from this dream. Aisling and Declan decided to head inside, which left alone time for Jaxon and me. Aisling kissed me on my cheek before walking inside.

Sitting quietly by the fire, wrapped in his arms, was the most amazing feeling. I never thought I would have a moment like this back again. I knew I was young when he went away, but there was just something so damn special about him that I had told myself over and over that this feeling would never be found with someone else. I had given up on love and focused more on a straight path to success. Then, when he walked back through my door, my entire world took a complete left turn onto a different path. A path that I was very happy with.

"Pinch me, please!" I giggled and looked at Jaxon, who playfully pinched my torso, which tickled instead.

"And now what was that for?" he asked.

"I just wanted to make sure that you were real, and this moment is real." I smiled and looked at the crackling fire.

His warm face inched to my neck, and he kissed me slowly before whispering, "Real."

My neck craned up toward the stars, closing my eyes as I embraced his closeness. The warm breath on my neck, his arms wrapped tightly around me made me feel safe. Not safe as in boring safe, but safe as in I was right where I wanted to be. Right here with him at this very moment. My breathing became uneven as my pulse quickened. I turned around on the wicker couch to face him and pulled him closer to me to kiss him. His breathing quickened as his hands drew up my back and held the back of my head with his fingers inter-twined in my hair, pulling me closer, which still didn't feel close enough. I wanted him, and I needed him.

Closer.

He picked me up, reading my mind, and carried me into the cabin in our room, and laid me gently onto the bed. His body heat was so close to mine that before I realized what I was doing, I had my hands on his shirt and pulled it over his head. He leaned down toward me and helped pull it off. His kissing became urgent, and my breathing sped up. I sat us up and looked into his eyes before grabbing the bottom of my shirt and pulling it up over my head, laying back down on the bed and slowly pulling him with me. The heat of his body touching mine was enough to make me want more.

He pulled back and whispered, "Real or fake?"

I laughed, catching my breath, whispering back, "Real."

He grinned before letting me grab his jeans, unbuttoning them. Feeling the electricity run through my fingers, only this time I was able to control it. It was excitement running through my fingertips, and I knew what I was doing. I tugged on his jeans and pulled him closer, as his lips met mine. This very moment I was ready to let my guard down... For him...

It had to be early morning because the sun was coming up, and I could see the clouds parting atop the mountain with the sun trying to warm up the sky. It was a breathtaking view from this cabin. I smiled when I looked at Jaxon, realizing we had stayed up all night. He got out of bed and walked over to his jeans on the floor and grabbed something small from the pocket. I squinted to see what he had in his hand, but he closed his palm and walked back to the bed.

He held out his hand and grabbed mine to put it under his. I looked at him questioningly.

"Close your eyes."

"Just show me," I said.

He shook his head and smiled. "Close your eyes."

"Fine." I closed my eyes and waited. The weight of a small object landed into the palm of my hand, and I hesitated for a moment to feel it and decided what it was before he said to open them. The moonstone earrings laid gently in my palm. I could feel my face blush.

"You bought these for me?" I asked sheepishly.

"Of course, I saw these the same moment you did, and when you didn't buy them, I already knew I was going to surprise you."

"Thank you." I blushed. He leaned in to me and lifted my chin, kissing me gently.

"I was waiting until today to give them to you. I know this was a bad day for both of us two years ago, but I wanted today to be the start of something good."

"Today is a good day." I smiled back and gave him an Eskimo kiss with my nose scrunched. "As long as you're with me, then it will be a good life."

His lips formed a smile along with mine while we kissed, and he laughed softly.

"No pressure or anything." I said and we laughed together.

I must've fallen asleep for a few hours because when I opened my eyes, I was alone in the room but heard the others downstairs talking and laughing. Declan was being a sarcastic asshole to Jaxon, and Aisling was egging him on. They were talking about zombies and how Jaxon should now be called a zombie for coming back to life. I snorted at the nickname that I was hoping would not actually stick. I'd rather just forget about the past and move on with the future. I looked to my left and saw a Columbine flower atop Jaxon's pillow with a note next to it that read, "Morning, sunshine, last night was definitely real (smiley face). Thank you for being you. Breakfast is ready, but take your time." I smiled at the little note and climbed out of bed to check my phone. No missed calls or texts. We had survived a night away, and no crimes were committed here or back home.

The weather app said eighty degrees for a low today. It was definitely a pair of shorts, tank top, and Converse type of day. I jumped in the shower and got ready for the day as quickly as possible. The others were on the deck with coffee and empty plates when I stepped outside ready to take on the day. Aisling jumped off Declan's lap and came to sit next to me and Jaxon on the couch.

"Are you guys ready to hike Dream Lake today?" she asked.

"I am up for whatever you guys want," I said happily, knowing we only had two more days to explore.

Jaxon leaned over to me and kissed me before asking, "Did you sleep well?"

"Very," I smirked.

Declan laughed and made an annoying cheering sound. "Ohhhh... it happened, didn't it?"

"Declan, shut up!" Aisling yelled and jumped up to smack him. He grabbed her and pulled her down by him, teasing her while playing with her hair. He was such a child sometimes, and other times he was very sweet.

"I will not confirm or deny that," Jaxon said sarcastically and looked at me as he winked. "I am not a kiss and tell type of person." And neither was I. But I would have to tell Aisling about it later on.

I ate breakfast before we headed for the trails. Over the next few hours, we saw bears, which were terrifying and amazing at the same time. Elk roaming freely, and one gigantic moose got too close for comfort. We made it to the lake and had our breathtaking moment of views and pictures before sitting on the tallest rock we could find for a break. It was such a different atmosphere from the Wisconsin bluffs and Mississippi River monsters. Though, the heat was a little too much today with the higher altitude, and I was ready to head back to the cabin and hydrate. I was starting to lose my momentum, knowing that we had to hike back down. I think we all were. We looked at each other and made a mutual agreement to head back to level ground. My phone was still quiet, which I was thankful for. A part of me started to drop my guard and feel like we were out of harm's way finally. Then, another part of me said it won't be that easy. I hesitated when looking at my blank phone and decided to text my dad to see how things were going.

Freya: Hey Dad, how is Wisconsin life?

Dad: Hey sweetie, Dad will be back soon, he's getting ice at the station. It's a hot one here.

Freya: Ok. Thanks.

I hesitated when I realized it was Alex and not my dad, but then the feeling of him being safe and being looked after by her made me happy. I decided I should stop being so short with her.

Freya: Hope you guys are having fun.

There, I thought, simple and nice for them both. That's it. The end.

Dad: It's a good day so far. I'll have him call you when he is back :)

Okay. She was trying, so could I.

We made it back to the cabin unscratched and ready to relax the rest of the hours that we had. I decided to start another fire. I loaded the pit with new logs, and Aisling dove across the kitchen counter and came running outside, announcing that it was her turn to try and light it. I laughed and told her she better not start the forest behind us on fire. She huffed and fake laughed as she held her palm out in front of her, whispering, "Ignis," before watching her big blue eyes change to embers as her smile grew.

You couldn't beat the view we had from the deck. This weekend was turning into my most favorite weekend in a long time. Well, besides the weekends spent as a kid with both my parents here when things were normal, but hey, life can be hard, and here I was getting through it. So, this weekend was a good weekend and a much-needed getaway on a dreaded death anniversary. I looked over to Jaxon, who was hunched over near the fire poking the logs to adjust them for better burning. He looked at me and winked with the grin that I had missed over the years. Declan leaned over Aisling with his shirt off, and I noticed his identical infinity symbol on his shoulder blade, matching Jaxon's. Curiosity getting the best of me.

"So, Declan, what's the scoop on your Mark? If it's not like your parents?"

"Didn't Aisling tell you? I'm adopted. My parents died when I was a kid. I was only like three or something. I don't really remember them." He paused and took in a gulp of air. "I guess I got lucky that a single lawyer wanted to play the father role, or just claim me on taxes. I don't really get it, but hey, I can't complain. The man buys me basically whatever I want and keeps to himself." He shrugged.

"Oh wow... No, I didn't know that. I'm sorry."

"Nothing to be sorry about. He's taken care of me practically my whole life, and I never went without."

"So, how did your Mark appear? Jaxon ended up with his Mark a little over two years ago without triggering it, meaning that you must've for them to appear, right?"

He looked at me and hesitated.

"I mean, we don't have to talk about it. Sorry, high altitude and all, I'm talking too much." I reassured him.

"No, it's fine." He looked to Aisling, who seemed to be engrossed in the story as well. I knew she didn't know, either, otherwise she would have told me. Plus, he wouldn't have looked so nervous to discuss it. I wondered if Jaxon even knew. I looked to Jaxon, who must have read my mind and nodded back at Declan that it was okay.

"It appeared because of my dad. He and I got into a fight when I was fifteen or sixteen years old. The fight turned into a full-on brawl. I mean, I've always been a strong little fucker... He almost had me before I threw his ass to the ground and pinned him hard as hell, causing a bloody mouth. When the blood dripped from his lip to the floor, he basically flipped a switch and came after me without his fists and used his magic against me. He basically tried to suffocate me pinned up against the wall until I lost consciousness or before he knocked me unconscious. I don't really remember which." He took a deep breath in and released it loudly. "Damn... that was a long time ago, though. I mean, it was our one and only physical fight. Honestly, I think he did it on purpose to trigger this damn thing." He grabbed his shoulder and rubbed the Mark.

"Damn, Declan, that's messed up. I didn't expect *that*," I said, feeling sorry for him.

"Babe." Aisling groaned with a sad puppy face. "I didn't know that, either. Oh my God... Your dad is such an ass. Ugh. Let's magic team up on him and kick his ass," Aisling said with determination. I could see the wheels turning as she began to plot ideas against him.

"Nah, it's over now. The best damn thing that ever happened to me really. Once my Mark appeared, he actually seemed to pay attention to me, not sure if he's scared of me now or finally respects me for being a witch too, but hey, either way, we don't fight now. It's a mutual thing."

"I have to admit, I'm glad it was you and not my mom trying to take me out for my Mark to appear. She can be one scary woman." Jaxon laughed, and Declan agreed with a bellowing laugh.

"Dude, your mom is fucking terrifying. You do not want to cross that woman. Sweet on the outside, but damn, one thing to piss her off, and you're done for." Declan exclaimed.

A quick pang hit my stomach as I thought about Margo hating me, but then Jaxon looked at me and rubbed my thigh. I knew he was trying to distract me, reassuring me it was all good, or at least I hoped he was. I half smiled as Aisling distracted my thoughts from going down the wrong path.

"I wonder who my Anchor is? I mean, I must've triggered their Mark too that night, right?"

"Yeah, that's usually how it goes," Declan answered.

"Unless maybe I'm a whole new breed of witch or just not special like you all, with a second lifeline," she said sarcastically.

"You... Not special? Please." Declan pulled her in tight for a lingering kiss, and I realized that the conversation was over as they became inseparable.

Jaxon and I headed into the cabin to give them some privacy. I heard my phone ring from up in the bedroom and walked upstairs to grab it. When I looked at the screen, I had seventeen missed phone calls from Haven and one from Alex. All within the past hour. *Oh shit.* Something was wrong. Jaxon looked at me, and his face went from happy to serious. He knew it the exact moment as I did. I unlocked my screen and dialed Haven back. It didn't even ring once before she picked up.

"Freya, we have a problem!" Her voice sounded unnatural as if she had been crying, it cracked on the last word. "They have her, they have Mom!" she yelled hysterically through her sobs.

Chapter 25

This Is Happening

It was the first time that hearing the name 'Mom' didn't make me cringe, instead I panicked and instantly regretted every rude comment I had ever said to her and the cold shoulder I had been giving her. 'Mom' meant the woman who was my rock when I was little, the one that was always by my side growing up. I hated her for leaving us, but at the same time, with her being gone, it almost made me grow up faster. She was now in trouble, and I needed to help.

The room was spinning, and I felt my phone drop from my hand before Jaxon grabbed me, leveling my weight out to sit on the ground.

"Woah, calm down. Sit. What's going on?" he yelled for the others.

Aisling came running into the bedroom and landed next to me on the ground, grabbing the phone that Haven was still talking loudly through.

"What's happening? Haven? Woah... slow down. Okay,

breathe. We will fly home now. We will be there in three hours. Do not do anything without us. Just wait." Aisling sounded so sure of herself that the airport would work with us. She didn't even hesitate. She hung up the phone and told Declan to grab the bags and throw them in the car. Then, immediately after, she was on the phone with the airlines and told them we needed the first flight back due to an untimely emergency. They listened and quickly rearranged some seats on the flight that would be leaving shortly. Everything was happening so fast and I felt like I was on auto pilot mode. I couldn't process anything but I knew we had to hurry. I stood up, still feeling disorienting, debating on what my next plan would be. My mouth was dry, making it hard for me to talk, let alone to swallow. I couldn't breathe. My phone rang again. This time it was Alex. Relief came over me, thinking that this was all a big misunderstanding.

"Mom, what's going on?" I asked quickly without thinking.

"Oh, now she's your mother. Adorable, really." It was a voice I recognized but was not expecting.

Isadora.

The bitter anger that was fuming from her tone was sickening. I wanted to scream that she was not a real fucking therapist and that my problems were not for her to know anymore.

"What have you done?" I screamed into the phone.

"Let me show you." My phone buzzed as the video call started. Isadora was standing in the middle of Swig and Jig with both my dad and Alex tied up behind her, smiling devilishly and pretending to take a selfie with them in the background as if it was a memorable moment for her.

"Here's the deal, you little bitch. Since trying to track Clara with her herbs didn't work. Clever, but pathetic witch." I gasped, remembering the Farmer's Market encounter. "You bring us the dagger back, and we will let them live. Fail, and I will kill them both, personally. Dear ole Mom will, of course, come back until we can locate Clara, but your father will meet his maker. Your choice, oh... and choose quickly. I'm getting bored of this fucking town." A man snickered in the back before talking to Isadora.

"Bored already, darling? Surprisingly, I thought you were beginning to like this place, ready to make some roots." His voice was deep and hard. I knew the voice but couldn't place it. My head was pounding.

"Dagger, or they die. It's that simple." His back appeared on the camera, a knife in hand as he walked up to Alex. My dad was knocked out, but breathing as far as I could see.

"If you hurt them, I will kill you myself!" I screamed, my voice cracking at the word kill, but my heart screaming that I would do what was necessary if they harmed my parents.

"Better hurry up, Izzy is getting bored, and honestly, so am I. Haven't killed anyone in a while," he said, too calmly, before turning the knife into a grip in his hand and jabbing it into Alex's stomach, turning it. Alex screamed, and her body hunched over.

"Freya, don't give it to him, don't come home!" she yelled with blood dripping from her mouth as she choked down the pain that was radiating from the knife still emerged into her torso.

"Stop! I will give it to you. Please. Stop! I am coming home. I will get it. Leave them alone. Please. Stop..." I begged.

"Better hope Clara is still alive," The man said with a stern voice before handing the knife to Isadora and walking toward the camera. It was then that I recognized him. I stared hard at the man with hatred before connecting the dots. The voice, the hard jawline, the slicked hair, the suit, nightmares of a demon man, the man who caught my fire. It was him. I let out a slight gasp. Eric is—

"Dad?" Declan walked back into the room at the end of the conversation. "No," he whispered, as his eyes fell to the ground and his trembling hands came up to his face. "No, it can't be him."

"Oh, hi, Declan, remember me?" Isadora came back to the screen and taunted him through the video call, taking the knife once more and plunging it swiftly into Alex's heart.

A blood-curdling scream escaped my throat as my palms lit up with fire. My whole body ignited with anger. "Mom!" Alex looked up at the camera one last time with a small smile before her head dropped to her chest and her breathing stopped.

"Off to see Clara now. Better hurry up, Miss Chamberlain, or your dad is next." I could barely hear her over my sobs and screaming. The fire in my palms needed to be released before the cabin caught fire. I could feel the magic from the dagger ready to explode inside me. The phone call ended, and I ran for the patio before throwing my hands straight out in front of me, letting my magic and anger flow through me, shooting flames in the air toward the Rockies before I felt a terrifying scream emerging from my throat as I released the flow of magic and crashed to the ground, Jaxon pulling me up to him and trying to calm me down.

Chapter 26

Home Never Sounded So Far Away

The flight home was a blur. None of us talked. Aisling rubbed Declan's back, who was bent over his seat and hadn't spoken a word since realizing who his father actually was. Eric the red, Eric the terrible, Eric the immortal witch hunter psychopath, Eric the murderous witch who probably killed Declan's parents before taking him. Oh my God... The realization hit me. Eric probably *did* kill his parents. My stomach was sick. Jaxon had his arm around me, but I felt nothing, numb to the world. My body still felt like it was on fire from the inside. *What was I going to do?* Give him the dagger in exchange for my parents and then what? What if they have already found Aunt Clara? Haven hadn't responded back to my text before we boarded the plane. I hadn't even had an extra minute to call her.

I had to trust that they were smart enough to hide or run. They didn't know where they were unless, of course, that was why Isadora broke into the pottery shop to find their address on some form of paperwork. My stomach turned. I was going to be sick. I jumped out of my seat and ran to the bathroom.

Jaxon knocked on the door before I could even close it all the way. My face fell to the toilet, and I vomited until my throat burned more than my body. My anxiety was through the roof, and in this plane, it was going into the galaxy.

"What the fuck am I going to do?"

Jaxon barged the door open and joined me in the small bathroom, with the door half opened still.

"Hey, breathe, Freya. It'll be okay. Breathe!"

"How am I supposed to do this?" I sobbed between each word. "They have my dad, and they killed my mom." My breathing sped up as a panic attack set in. I couldn't breathe. I was going to hyperventilate and the thought of passing out sounded better than reality. I wished I had never been born. This whole thing was my fault. Eric only came after my mom because of me and the power I didn't even know I had.

"Your mom is not dead. Her Anchor is still alive, and we are going to make sure of that." He was so confident in his statement. "Nothing will happen to Jim. I won't let it, I promise."

The half-opened door slid all the way open, Aisling stood there with a small bottle of mouthwash and an ice pack. The flight attendant was behind her with worried eyes.

"Flying isn't her thing," Aisling reassured the attendant who nodded and walked away. As if she had seen it all in her career.

The sobs continued, but with Aisling and Jaxon both in

close proximity to me, my heart started to relax. I tried to inhale and exhale when Aisling did to help me slow my own breathing. It was a trick we had grown up with when one of us would have a nervous breakdown. The other would help count and mimic healthy breathing. My heart started to slow. I stood and grabbed the mouthwash, gurgled in my fiery throat and splashed cold water across my face and neck.

I nodded.

We needed a strategic plan to make sure that when I handed the dagger over it was still magicless, so we would have a safe exchange. It was time to act confident and come up with a plan. Luckily for us, the plane was practically empty, and we were able to sit side by side with each other and discuss options. Declan stayed silent. Eric being his dad was a lot to take in. I'm sure he felt like he had been the one to fail and had not caught on to any signs over the years. But how could he really? Jaxon was the only one he practiced magic with, and his dad once the Mark was triggered. How would he have known any better?

The flight was about halfway done when Declan looked up and broke his silence. "Let me do it." I looked at him with an understanding of parent betrayal and studied his face. "I'll hand the dagger over while you guys get her parents away safely. Once they are safe, then I will hand the dagger over." He paused for a brief moment. "He won't hurt me. I'm still his son." His words felt broken, but hopefully, true. How could someone hurt a person who had been a son to them for fifteen years?

"I'm coming with you," Aisling demanded.

"No, I have to do this alone. I can't risk your life too."

He was right. We didn't know what Eric and Isadora were capable of, especially since they were provoked and their covers were blown. He would have to be the one to hand it over.

Every scenario possible was running through my head, and as I looked to the others, I believed that the same scenarios were running through theirs too. I took a deep inhale in and released it before looking back to Jaxon who was watching me cautiously. I half smiled, trying to reassure him that I was fine. He pulled me in closer to him, and I let my head fall into the crook of his neck. I fidgeted with my tourmaline necklace and focused on the stitching on the seat in front of me to distract myself. He kissed my head and rubbed my shoulder, which felt really nice and made me feel the slightest bit better.

We have a plan, not a perfect one, but something. Grab the dagger from the fish pottery piece and give it to Declan for the exchange. While he brings Eric to a different location, we go in for my parents and get them to Aunt Clara's for safety. They would need some kind of protection spell or locator scrambler for a while, and Aunt Clara was the only one who could do that. Hopefully, Eric and Isadora were long gone from town before realizing that the dagger was magicless. I crossed my fingers as I thought about that part of the plan.

The plane landed, and I turned my phone on instantly. My phone buzzed with texts coming through from earlier and a new one from just now.

Haven: Ezra and I are with Aunt Clara, and we will keep her safe.

Haven: Don't worry, we will be okay.

Haven: Please be safe.

Haven: I just got you back in my life and am not ready to lose you now.

The new message finally loaded. I held my breath as I opened it.

Haven: We are still at home, nothing happening yet. Aunt Clara is safe so Mom should be too.

I let out a sigh of relief as we jumped off the plane and headed for our luggage. I half smiled at the flight attendant who had checked on me while having my panic attack and mouthed the words "thank you" to her. She smiled back at me with a nod.

"Let's get this dagger," I exclaimed before heading toward the center of my hometown of Crystal Rock. A newfound strength was coming to me, knowing that we were closer to the problem and that we had a plan. Being states away and helpless was not a good feeling. I called Haven and let her know the plan. She agreed to stay at the home with Clara, out of harm's way.

Mom and Dad, I'm coming for you, hang in there.

Chapter 27

The Exchange

We had one chance to make sure this went smoothly. Aisling called her aunt to let her know what was going on. Her aunt did not like the plan but agreed there weren't many other possibilities to try. She said she would keep an eye on Declan from afar and intervene if she needed to, which made all of us feel a little more at ease with the exchange.

We headed to my house, driving faster than the speed limit and making it there in record time. There was no time to waste, a ticket was my last concern. Jaxon and I ran inside the dark house and flipped the light switches on as quickly as possible before heading to the centerpiece on the table. I grabbed the fish piece and looked at Jaxon with an apologetic look before smashing it to the ground.

"You had it in there the whole time?" He laughed.

"I figured no one would grab that ugly thing and think it was a secret compartment." I laughed back, even though this was not a laughing matter, but the sarcasm actually was making me feel a little better.

"Still better than yours." He smiled, and I laughed before we headed back outside.

"Declan, are you sure about this?" I asked him when Jaxon and Aisling were out of earshot. Declan was pacing back and forth in deep thought.

"He won't hurt me," he said reassuringly. Whether that was meant for me or him I would never know. If there was any doubt in his mind, he had a good way of hiding it. Or maybe the night's darkness made it easier to hide his facial expressions. I hugged him hard, and Aisling kissed him with tears. We needed this to work, we needed to be strong.

We dropped Declan off in the parking lot of the Willow Winds Diner. With the restaurant having cameras and Aunt Lynn sitting at a table in the back to watch the exchange, safely out of sight, he should be safe too. Eric shouldn't know that she was still alive, and tonight wasn't a night for more surprises or tempers to stir. Who knows what Eric would do seeing his ex lover, Aislynn standing in front of him after a thousand years. Would he kill her instantly for thinking she had killed his unborn child, or would he have a soft spot for her and have a moment of weakness? Either way, I did not want to find out.

We drove to the bar. The open sign was not lit up, and the place looked dark. I planned to walk through the front door, and Aisling and Jaxon would go through the back. Hopefully, it was just my parents there, but Isadora may have stuck around to make sure it was an even exchange. I kissed Jaxon before we split up. Isadora was going to pay for killing my mom. Anchor or not, that was not something that should ever happen, and it will never happen again. One last text came through as I headed for the front door.

Declan: He just pulled up, and he's alone.

Okay... Isadora had to be inside the bar. I threw my guard up, and was ready for anything. I looked down to my closed fists and opened my right hand to see my palm, letting it ignite with fire quickly to make sure I was ready for absolutely anything. I smiled when the fire ignited effortlessly. I told myself to breathe and that I am a one-of-a-kind natural-born syphon, and that I have more power than I ever knew.

I opened the door and realized the only light on was from the open door of the office. My parents were sitting tied to the chairs in the center of the room. Then I looked over and there she was. Isadora, sat at the end of the bar holding a glass of brown liquid, twirling it mindlessly.

The bitch was sitting at my family's bar, drinking my family's liquor, and torturing my family. She was going to pay for all of this. I realized at that very moment that my mom only left town because of her and Eric. *They* ruined my little family, not Alex. They ruined a lot more than just my family, and they needed to pay.

"Look who decided to finally show up," she said with a trace of bitterness. I said nothing to her, which ultimately must've pissed her off. "Excuse me, you can't even say hello? Who the hell do you think you are? I am immortal! I could kill you in a minute, or your parents, or how about the little Oakes boy?" I gritted my teeth. "He's a sexy man, that's for sure. Would be a shame to lose someone with eyes like his, and that body. Mmmm," she said, tauntingly.

"Shut up!" I yelled and brought my hands up to my sides, reigniting my fire. I was trying hard to keep my temper in control and my breathing even, but Jaxon was off-limits.

"Oh... look at the rise I got out of you now." She smiled with bad intentions. "So, here's the deal. Once Eric calls and confirms he has the dagger, I'll leave you to them. If there's any double-crossing going on, then you're all dead, and your Anchors will be next." Her smile became even wider, and a look of excitement lit up on her face.

Sadistic bitch!

Out of the corner of my eye, I saw Jaxon and Aisling peeking through the back door, and I shook my head for them to stay put. Isadora was looking at her phone and missed the exchange.

"Cute little fire trick. Mine is better," she said slyly and lifted her right hand while her left hand was holding her up on the bar. She ignited her palm into a flame that grew to about six feet off of her hand. I did not move and kept my amazed eyes as even as possible, so she didn't think she caught me off guard. I smiled back at her and raised an eyebrow to seem nonchalant. Which made her mad, she was looking for an upper hand and I wasn't giving it to her. She jumped off the bar and came face to face with me, glaring. *Shit...* she was going to kill me. *Don't move a muscle.* I could not let her intimidate me. I stood tall and smiled mockingly.

"You have something to say?" she asked angrily.

"Silence kills, doesn't it? I guess mind-reading isn't one of your specialties now, is it?" I asked innocently. "Grabbing my parents was a mistake."

She laughed. "This is only the beginning. Wait until I

kill her for good next time." She smirked when her phone rang, which pulled her attention to the bar.

She swiped her screen and placed the phone to her ear. "It's done? Good. And that boy? Alive? Really? Whatever, you're growing soft these days." She laughed and hung up the phone.

"Well, Miss Chamberlain, great seeing you, as always." She laughed. "Honestly, I don't like this look on you. I miss the broken girl you were."

"Many will, she was easy to kill," I said with pure hatred before I walked to my parents and started to untie them. She walked past me with angered eyes.

"Why Eric won't let me finish this silly little town I will never understand." She spat. "Next time, I'll make sure our semi-truck finishes the job on your man," she said, which made me turn around with fire in my hands. Before I realized it, I had thrown the fire at a closing door.

Jaxon and Aisling ran to me and helped untie my parents. My dad was wide-eyed and stared at me in disbelief. He had been awake at the last minute and saw the fire leave my hands. This was going to be a lot of explaining. I wished my mom would hurry up and wake up, so that she could explain things to him instead of me. He was still staring at me when the rope finally came undone. He may have a concussion, though, so maybe we'll keep this a secret and use that to our advantage. Or we involve him so that there will be no more secrets, which was what I would prefer.

My heart sank as I looked toward my mom, sitting slumped over with blood on her shirt. I took a deep breath and dropped down in front of her, looking up to her face while putting my hand over her heart, nothing. The wound was healed, and there was no gash, just dried blood on her shirt. I exhaled when I realized that she was going to be okay. Her chest started to rise and fall again, and she was coming to. Tears of relief started to fall as her eyes opened.

"Mom?" I questioned, still nervous that her waking up may be fake. Her hands went to her chest as she inhaled heavily and rubbed her heart before looking at my dad and then me.

"Freya," she exhaled with relief. "You're okay. Thank goodness." Her face washed over with relief. I stood up and crashed into her arms, which threw her back in the chair. Which may have been uncomfortable, but at this point, the hug was long overdue and almost a missed opportunity. Her arms wrapped tightly back around me, and for the first time in years, I felt truly complete. I think I needed it just as much as she did. Tears kept flowing as I turned to see my dad standing near the bar, grabbing a beer with Jaxon at his side.

"Can someone tell me what the hell just happened?" my dad asked sternly.

"You're going to want something a little stronger than that," Jaxon said, as he reached for the bottle of bourbon. He didn't question the drink choice. He grabbed the bottle, opened it, and started pouring shots for everyone. I wasn't a drinker, since the accident, but at this point, I could use something to take the edge off. We all grabbed a glass and threw it back quickly. The heat burned the back of my throat, but nothing burned more than the anger I had toward Isadora for what she had done to my parents.

Declan called Aisling and asked where to meet us. We

decided to leave the bar and head to Aunt Clara's. It was a safe place, then we could all be together and come up with our next plan. Eric would find out that the dagger was magicless soon and come after us. We needed another plan for when that happens.

We drove up to Aunt Clara's after we all sprayed down with our protection spray before entering Prairie Du Chein. All extra precautions were still necessary. Jaxon sat in the back seat with me and held me close to him while rubbing my shoulders and whispering, "Are you doing okay?" I nodded and exhaled a sigh of relief before looking up to him and kissing his lips.

As we pulled up to the house, we saw the lights were on and Clara was standing in the doorway. As we walked through the door, I could smell tea brewing. I hoped it was the brain overload tea that would help my dad catch up with our witch history as I realized how much he did not know. Haven walked down the stairs with Ezra, and my dad locked eyes with her. He wavered back and stumbled over his own feet. Jaxon caught him and helped him steady himself.

Haven looked to him and then to me, realizing what had just happened. Her face filled with excitement before running down the stairs to us. He looked to her, then back to me and back to her again. I could see the wheels turning in his head, and he looked like he was questioning if he had a concussion himself and seeing double.

"Dad, this is Haven. She's my twin," I said calmly. "Drink some tea, this will make a lot more sense in a little while." Aunt Clara came walking through the entryway with tea steaming from the mug.

"Are you sure that was bourbon?" he questioned Jaxon, who laughed and put his hand on his shoulders.

He nodded toward Haven. "Twin girls, Jim. It's a long story. How about we go sit down?" My dad nodded in agreement and followed Haven and Jaxon to the living room with the steaming tea in his hand, slightly trembling. It was either the adrenaline coursing through his veins or he was terrified. Maybe, both.

Chapter 28

Welcome To the Real Family, Dad

Haven and I were able to share our memories of what had happened just like we did when we completed our Marks. There was an old spell in Aunt Clara's grimoire on memory sharing, which would feel like a fast dream. We decided to let him see what he had missed for himself over the years. With the tea keeping his head from exploding, we figured it wouldn't hurt to give him his life back so he could make new memories from this point on with all of us.

Declan drove up with Aunt Lynn and joined us in the house. Aisling jumped in his arms, kissing him inappropriately in front of everyone, but at this point, no one cared. I was just happy he was safe after taking the risk he took. I looked to the living room where my dad was sitting more comfortably next to his other daughter. Alex was next to him using hand signals and describing the dagger and our history. His face seemed sad, and I decided to walk up behind him and rub his shoulders.

"How are you holding up?" I whispered.

"Considering there's been a lot to take in, I'm okay." He

turned toward me and smiled with a reassuring gaze. He turned to Alex and whispered loud enough for me to hear, "Please say you will stay this time. I will help protect our family. No more running." Alex looked at him surprised and looked up to me. I nodded in agreement to his proposal and smiled at her, putting my other hand on her shoulder. She smiled a true smile for the first time in years and leaned in to kiss him on his cheek.

"Okay," she whispered.

The moment was monumental considering how the last two years had been for us all. We may have to start running again tomorrow, but for tonight, we could be together and safe. At least, I hoped. Jaxon called his parents to let them know what had happened while we were away. I could hear Margo gasp into the phone, her tone scolding, so I walked away before I had to listen to her again.

Aisling and her aunt filled Declan in on Eric and who her Aunt was to him, also how Aisling is a descendant of the Immortals. Declan had no idea, his face was in shock at the discovery. He looked horrified that he had been living under a roof with his biological parents' murderers. I saw him look at Aisling, and sadness came over him. He stood and walked outside without turning back around. Aisling looked to her aunt, who held her back from walking after him. Someone needed to check on him, though.

I walked out to the backyard by the other garden where Declan was pacing back and forth. He didn't hear me behind him and jumped when he turned and saw me standing a foot away.

"Hey," I said.

"Hey," he said in hardly a whisper.

"Are you okay?" I asked while studying his facial expressions.

"Well, let's see, the man that raised me is an immortal murderous soul who took me from my parents after he killed them. Then, my girlfriend, who is now a newbie witch, is a descendant from them, the original pair of Anchor witches with an evil agenda, and I just handed over the only weapon that was keeping all of us safe for now. But who knows how long it will take them to recharge the weapon and come after us or just simply come after all of us for pissing them off. My dad, I mean... Eric has a temper that you guys wouldn't believe unless you have lived with him. He will come for us." He exhaled at the final sentence and brought his arms above his head before tossing them up in a defeated "we can't win" shrug.

"Hey, Declan, just breathe. Count back from ten slowly, and inhale between each number, then exhale." He mimicked my breathing while he counted aloud. "Good. Listen, it will be okay." I lied, knowing that his fears were the same as mine and I needed to have at least one of us with a calm mind. "Can I ask how the exchange went?"

"The exchange was fine. I handed him the dagger, he looked it over before handing me a bag full of cash and telling me I needed to run far away from here. Which, of course, I won't be doing." So, maybe he did have a soft spot for him after all, I thought. This had to be hard on him. He just lost the only parent he had ever been old enough to remember.

"He gave you money?"

What the hell? Was he paying him off because he knew it was over for us?

"He told me to leave Wisconsin and go start over somewhere else, to leave all this behind. Fucking crazy. I'm not fucking leaving Aisling." My heart raced as I thought about it, if he told him to run away, then that only meant that he was coming after us and he wanted Declan far away before he did.

"You don't think he will come after us tonight, do you?" I asked, now worried.

"I don't think he's the crazy one. I think Isadora is the bored one." He looked at me and closed the distance between us. He pulled me into his arms and hugged me tight. His exhale was in relief, and he let his shoulders fall. I didn't move. His hug was unexpected, and a little uncomfortable because of his height. My face was too close to his chest. He must have realized my hesitation to react. "You just looked like you needed a hug." He said and I laughed and hugged him back because he was right. I had been trying to look strong through the last few hours, but inside, I was crumbling.

"I think you needed this more than I did." I said and we both laughed.

"Shh, maybe I did. Don't judge me," he said quietly.

We walked back inside, and everyone's eyes were on us. Horror was spread across my mom's face with my phone in her hand. I paused and looked at her and my phone with a "call ended" signal flashing across the screen. Something happened, and I missed it.

"They called. They know the dagger was tampered with." It was Aunt Clara, who spoke quietly answering my burning question.

"How long do we have?" I asked.

"We've been off the maps for years up here. They have no idea where we are." Haven jumped in.

"Where's Aisling and her aunt?" I looked around the room, counting heads, and realized they were not accounted for.

"That's the problem, they just left to check on her parents. She kept calling them, but they weren't answering. They decided to drive through and check on them."

My heart sank as I realized we were no longer all together and safe.

"Shit, I'm going after them." Declan's voice boomed with anger. "He won't hurt me."

Before anyone could stop him, he turned on his heel and was out the door running to his car. I ran out of the door with Jaxon following behind closely, but by the time Jaxon reached his car, Declan locked the door and his tires squealed, which left a dust cloud in his face. I didn't like any of this at all.

Chapter 29

Moving Sounds Like a Good Plan

I paced on the front porch, waiting for Aisling to call me back after leaving three voicemails. It had been an hour, and no response. Jaxon sat on the stairs in front of me while the others were still in the house, discussing both history and plans. I could overhear the discussions going back and forth. Even my dad had a lot to say about the best options. Nothing was set in stone yet, but all I knew was the thought of leaving Crystal Rock was not on my agenda this summer. There had to be another way.

My phone rang, making me jump. I looked at the name and frantically hit the accept button.

"Ais, please tell me you are okay and everything is fine?" I asked in one breath and held it, waiting for her response.

"We are all good. Heading back to Clara's now. My aunt is going to hang back with my parents to keep them safe. They don't have Marks or anything, I checked before leaving, so we are keeping them out of the know for now." I exhaled heavily once I heard her voice. My ears were listening to her, but my brain stopped after she said they were good. Hopefully, whatever else she said was irrelevant.

"Good. Is Declan with you too?"

"Yes, he was only a few minutes behind us, which scared the crap out of me when he started banging on the door." Relief washed over me. "My parents thought we had been in a fight or something, and he was coming to apologize." She laughed. "Can you imagine Declan groveling on my doorstep in front of my parents?" She continued to laugh at the thought of him doing that would be funny, but just hearing her voice saying they were okay was a great weight lifted.

I looked to Jaxon who had been overhearing the conversation and was now smiling with relief. I hung up the phone and sat next to him on the stairs. I nestled my head under his arm and leaned into his chest. It felt safe, and right now, I needed to feel safe.

"Do you think we should leave town?" I asked.

"I've left town before, and that didn't go so well for me."

"How do we protect so many people at once on a daily basis?"

"We can't. We need to get rid of them." His voice became dark as he spoke, and I looked at him from under his arm. His face was angry and his jaw, tight. I could see the rage he was holding back.

"How do we do that?" I asked, already knowing the answer.

"We kill them."

I looked out to the front yard garden and counted the rows of herbs, anything else that was growing to distract myself from the idea of killing anyone. We were not them. We were not murderers. There had to be another way.

I jumped up from gazing at the flowers when one caught my attention in the last row and I ran toward it. I plucked it and examined it, remembering the scent of it and the little white flower at the top from my childhood. A core memory awakened inside of me when my mom and Aunt Clara talking next to these flowers one day about how it can help promote sleep. Haven and I were playing in the dirt next to it and we had to be six or seven at the time. I smiled with hope that we could use it for something. "Valerian root." I whispered to myself. If we could somehow weaken them enough with Valerian root, then maybe we would have a short chance to take them out. I had no idea how or if it would even work, but it was the first possible solution that we could use that didn't involve leaving home.

"Jax, do you know anything about Valerian root? Can we somehow make an elixir to carry with us so that if they come near us, we inject them, and they become weakened or tired? And then we—" I swallowed hard at the idea. He jumped off the stairs and walked over to the flower, picking one up to examine it.

"I'd bet between Clara and my mom they could concoct something potent. Earth magic and potions are my mom's specialty." I wanted to frown at bringing his mom into this, but we were running slim on options. I smiled and agreed to bring the plan up to them in the house, including calling Margo Oakes.

After discussing the plan with the others, everyone felt

a little safer having a hopeful backup plan, in case we were caught off guard. We would have to have the elixir nearby at all times somehow.

Jaxon glanced around the room before turning back to me. "What about infusing a necklace or ring with the elixir to make sure it's always on us? For example, your tourmaline could easily infuse the liquid, and if they came up unexpectedly, then you could pull your necklace and use it on them. Any incision or ingestion of it could make them weak. It won't kill them, but definitely weaken anyone enough to have an advantage."

"What if we scratch ourselves with it?" I asked.

"That's where my mom comes in. She can get around that by spelling them to each individual with a drop of blood. So, only yours will work for you and his for him, etcetera." He pointed to my dad, who wasn't wearing a necklace. "Well, we will get him a manly crystal to wear or a ring, that'll still do the trick." He grinned as my dad eyeballed him at the word necklace, he nodded at the ring idea instead. He still wore his wedding ring, so nothing would be out of the ordinary with wearing it when magic infused with it. I smiled at the idea of us having some sort of leverage against thousand-year-old Immortals.

Jaxon called Margo and discussed the situation, who agreed it could be easily done. Jaxon, Clara, and my mom would head to his house to get that started. Which was very nerve-wracking, considering that Eric had been living across the street from that house this whole time. Margo said the house was dark, and no one had been home. Jaxon had extra backup with both of them going with him. They would be okay and all come back in one piece.

We all gave a drop of blood with our pendants or rings, and they headed for the door. Aisling and Declan would meet them on their way back here to do the same. Jaxon lingered in the hallway for a minute longer before turning to me and waving for me to come into the next room.

"Hey, if this doesn't work," he paused and looked around before meeting my gaze again, "then we run. You and I start somewhere new, just like Declan was told to do. We can outrun them if we need to." I studied his eyes, waiting for this to be a joke. The last thing he wanted to do was to find a new home again, so why say that now?

"This will work," I said reassuringly.

"But, if it doesn't. If anything goes wrong, then I need you to promise me that you will run with or without me."

"I'm not going anywhere without you. I don't even like that you're going home without me right now."

"JFK can be our meet-up spot if anything fails, but if I'm not there within a few minutes, then you run. I promise you that when I'm there, then I will be ready to run for eternity with you."

"Let's just hope our plan works, and we don't have to run at all."

I wasn't ready for any kind of promises *not* involving him with me.

He grabbed my face and pulled me close to him before crushing his lips down on mine with a kiss that was unforgettable. It was the type of kiss that made my knees want to buckle and my lips tingled with the aftermath. "I love you, Freya Chamberlain. Remember that."

He turned and walked through the door before my lips could form the words back to him, and he was gone. My heart pounded with the adrenaline of being excited and scared. I went to grab my necklace, to twirl it in my hand out of habit, and it wasn't there. He had it with him and I felt as if a part of me just walked through that door for the last time.

Chapter 30

When All Else Fails

It had been the longest hour and a half of my life waiting for my phone to ring, sitting next to Haven and my dad, with Ezra staying busy flipping through the grimoires that were open on the table. He wanted to make sure that we weren't missing anything.

"It's going to work," Haven reassured us again for the tenth time. I looked over and saw that she was clock watching too, and I could see the doubt on her face. I knew the look all too well.

Our dad looked at her and then at me and nodded his head in agreement.

"Damn right, it will work. I am just getting my family back, and I'm not about to lose them again." He looked back at Haven and smiled wide. He had to be right. My mom and Haven were back in our lives, and we needed to keep it that way. Eric had already stolen enough of our time together, and that could not happen again.

Finally, my phone rang and I answered before I could even glance at the name. "Hello?"

"You just couldn't leave it alone, could you?" My heart stopped, and my breathing was caught in my throat. I glanced at the phone to see Aisling's name on the screen, but it was not her voice that answered back.

"Isadora," I said, gritting between my teeth with pure bitterness.

"Poor Declan couldn't listen to dear old daddy, and now he and his little girlfriend won't be coming back to your little hiding spot."

"Don't you dare hurt them," I screamed back into the phone, making Haven, Ezra, and our dad jump up and look directly at me. I pushed the speaker button and let them hear the news themselves.

"Oh... So you do value their lives? Well, then, you better come find them and fix this dagger before I use it on them."

"I don't know what you are talking about," I tried to lie and failed pathetically.

"Don't play games with me, Freya. I know you did something to it, or one of your members did, and we want it fixed, now," she yelled. Her temper was rising, and I could feel the fire starting in her eyes, beaming at me through the phone.

I could feel the sweat forming on my palms and my hand shakily trying to keep the phone steady. I tried to speak but my voice cracked when it was meant to be strong. "Where are they?"

"That's better. They're with me, of course."

"Please, where?" I asked again.

She clicked her tongue and I could imagine her smirk growing. "Even better... How about you find us in time before I kill them both? Let's see how clever you really are, girl. Tick tock." The line went dead and my stomach turned on me.

How was I supposed to find them? She was crazy. I looked at my wrist and started twirling my bracelet from Aunt Lynn before realizing what Aisling had said about the tracker. I fumbled with my phone as fast as physically possible and dialed Aunt Lynn.

"Where is Aisling?" I didn't even let her answer with a hello. This was too urgent.

"What happened?" she asked quickly.

"Isadora has her and Declan, and I need to find them now, or she will kill them." She gasped, and I could hear the low whispering of incantations coming from her lips. I prayed that she was locating her.

"You're still at Clara's, correct?"

"Yes."

"Then, she is in a high, elevated area in the bluffs, which kind of looks like it's in the center of Crystal Rock." She hesitated. "Any idea what is there?"

"She's at JFK. Thanks. I have to go."

"I'm meeting you there. Keep that bracelet on, and I will be able to track you."

"Thank you." The phone call ended and it was time to move and fast.

The sun would be up soon. We had spent most of the night awake and planning. Flying home now felt like days ago. The night was a blur, and I was grateful to have made it to a new day, but this day could be my last. Especially if I couldn't give the magic back, and of course, Jaxon wasn't back yet with our only defensive play. This was not happening as we planned, but I had to go. I had to save my best friend.

"I'm coming with you." Haven jumped up next to me.

I had no time to argue and still had no idea what I was planning on doing. "Thank you." I smiled at her, knowing that we were stronger together, but scared that us being together made us more of a target to be killed.

"Ezra, stay with our dad, and once the elixir jewelry comes back, then meet us at JFK with it. Can you do that?" Haven asked him calmly. He nodded and leaned into her, kissing her softly, but holding her face in front of him a second longer.

"If anything feels off, then you run," he said.

She nodded as she swallowed hard.

"Dad, *when* Jaxon makes it back here, tell him JFK is not safe and not to come." I made sure to say when and not if, so my anxiety could settle itself from eating me alive. He nodded and hugged both Haven and me each, telling us to be safe. His face frowned when I realized he felt defense-less, but he must know that he would be putting everyone in more harm if we have to try and protect him, magicless against magic. He needed to stay and help Ezra research. We needed to fight fire with fire, not flesh and bones.

"Hey, Ezra, can you do me a favor?" I asked before stepping out the door after Haven.

"Yes, anything."

"Hold on to this bracelet, and do not leave the house with it until the elixir is here." He looked at me confused.

"I don't understand. I thought you wanted Lynn with you."

"I can't let her aunt meet us there. Isadora will kill her

without hesitation, and I can't have Ais see that. It would end up killing her if she makes it out of this alive."

I think he understood, but he hesitated before agreeing.

"Then, you better keep Haven safe. No pressure or anything." He smirked and pulled me in a tight for a bear hug. "Remember, you two are natural-born Anchor witches, that's gotta mean something powerful."

I smiled at him, but inside, I was crumbling, trying to protect everyone I cared about who were all in different places. If only I had a magical shield that I could extend to everyone to keep safe. I barely knew how to control my own magic, though. I was getting better at it, but nowhere near ready for a battle if it came to that. I would try and reverse the syphon trick back to the dagger, but there were no guarantees that it would even work and that is what I was afraid of.

Haven and I drove to JFK in silence. She looked over to me from the passenger seat and grabbed my hand.

"We will figure this out. We can reverse the magic and then we all run like hell. I think that's doable." She said calmly. "Do you at least have your running shoes on?" She asked with a half smile.

I laughed and tried to enjoy the mood being lightened, even though it would only be for a brief moment.

"If I can't reverse it, then you need to keep your promise to Ezra and run. Do you understand?" I looked at her. "That way, if something does happen to me, then I will come back as long as you are safe too." I had never died before, and neither had she, so hopefully this whole Anchor thing worked on us too. I wasn't ready to find out.

She agreed, and we made it up to the final turn for the

field. The dirt road was more matted down now that it had been driven on more frequently. Unfortunately, Isadora now knew where we practiced. My stomach was in knots, but I knew there was no turning back. We parked a little short of our normal area to walk the last few feet and get a quick glance at the situation. A minute extra could literally make or break us. I handed her the Jeep keys, and we walked in synchronization to the top.

Chapter 31

Fighting Fire with Fire

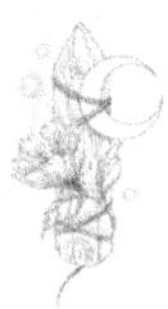

The sun was just beginning to rise at the edge of the world and let us have a little more of a view of what was to come. I inhaled heavily as I looked across the field... my field... And there she was, standing near Aisling and Declan who were tied back to back. Declan was yelling at Isadora, saying that he was going to kill her. Aisling's chin rested on her chest, knocked out but looked like she was breathing.

Haven and I walked to the edge of the field and made ourselves known by taking a fireball and throwing it in her direction. She looked up a second too early and pushed it out of her face.

"Child's play," she yelled, annoyed. "You better fix this now, otherwise your little friend will go first."

"Stop!" I pleaded when she brought the dagger near Aisling's heart. "Stop, I'm here. I'll do it."

"Now that's better." She smirked.

I ran to her, closing the distance between us. "Let her

go first. I will fix the dagger, but you need to let her go." I was not negotiating that at all.

"Not the boy?" She grinned.

"Leverage."

"Fine." She twisted her arm in the air, and the rope came undone, freeing Aisling's hands. Her unconscious body shifted, and Declan dropped his body under hers to keep her from hitting the ground.

"Ugh, young love. So fucking annoying," Isadora said in disgust. "Looks like I finally got you and your lover boy separated too. Just like old times." I gritted my teeth, and my fists clenched, but I released them. That was exactly what she wanted, a rise out of me.

Haven dropped down by Aisling and waved her hands over her head, waking her up and healing her concussion. I could take magic while she could give it. She had a true gift.

"Oh... How lovely. A healer who is identical to you. So, what does that make you?" She asked, annoyed.

"Nothing," I said with no emotion.

"I highly doubt that. Healers are unique to this world. I haven't seen one since the Viking ages, and the only other healer I knew had a twin who was—" For the slightest second, her eyes grew wide and then went back to the bitter stare. "Dead, killed by *moi*." She smiled slyly and laughed. I stepped back once and watched her carefully, wondering if she was actually a little shook by my twin. It made me think she knew something more about syphons than she was saying. The moment gave me a second of hope, despite the wicked tone that came after. She would've been a better therapist talking about syphon knowledge than trauma healing.

"Haven take Ais out of here. Declan and I will be right behind you." I spoke as if Isadora didn't exist at all, which seemed to make her angry. Aisling stood up a little woozy, and Haven helped her regain her balance. Aisling turned to Declan, and her eyes widened as she realized we wanted her to separate from him. She fell down into his arms and tried to untie the rope as quickly as possible, but Isadora grabbed her hair and threw her down the field with a strength that terrified me. *Shit, she really is strong.* I shrieked and pushed Isadora off of her. We all stood back, separated from each other and breathing heavily.

"Get her out of my face before I change my mind."

I nodded to them to leave. Aisling's eyes filled with tears. "Go!" I yelled at them both. They turned and started walking slowly away. Haven pulled on Aisling who kept reaching back for Declan.

Isadora's phone rang and she smiled before accepting a video call.

"Is it done?" Eric asked. She turned it around to face me and waited for my response. I looked at the man staring back at me with slicked back hair and a hard jawline. My heart sank when I realized where Eric was. Jaxon's house came into view and my brain started to rapid fire as I tried to hold myself together. Our plan A just got ruined.

"It will be." I grabbed for the dagger and closed my eyes, willing every bit of magic I had taken to go back to its rightful place. I felt my hands trembling from fear, not magic. I had no idea what the hell I was doing. I felt the trembling intensify, which made my whole body tremble harder and my legs gave out from under me. I felt weak in a time that I was supposed to be a savior. I fell to the ground with the dagger flying from my hands to Isadora's feet. She leaned over and picked it up, examining it closely while Eric watched from the screen.

"Well?" he asked.

Then I heard Margo yell through the phone.

"Freya, run! Jaxon is on his way... Run!" she yelled loudly before a clap sounded. Mr. Oakes screamed at Eric to leave his wife alone. I looked up at the hit and saw that they were tied up together, beaten and bruised. My head spun wondering how long had Jaxon been gone? Was he close to me?

"You had your chance to save them, Oakes. You were supposed to keep her powers from being triggered. You failed," Eric said.

"Freya, I'm so sorry. For everything. Please forgive me," Margo said sadly in a whisper that screamed to me. Eric tossed the gallon of gasoline to the side and held up his palm of fire, waiting for the dagger's status.

"It's okay, we will all be okay!" I yelled at the screen.

"Oh, honey, that's not up to you," Isadora said, grabbing the dagger and examining it. "This dagger still isn't working. Last chance to fix it, otherwise what's done is done."

I grabbed the dagger again from her and willed every atom in my body to transfer to the weapon. This time my hand burned, and the dagger became hot and glowed from heat. There was no magic transferring. It was just a fire growing in my palms, making the handle too hot to hold as I dropped it again. "I don't know how to do it." I whispered as I finally broke down and admitted to the failure while falling to my knees. Tears streamed endlessly down my face. "Please, don't hurt them. Please." I begged.

"Take care of my boy." Margo's words, now were louder than a whisper, pleading to me.

"What about *this* boy?" Isadora asked Eric in disgust.

"Kill him." Eric's voice sounded lost. He was not the same man I had talked to at the pottery shop. He was evil and heartless. He would kill his own son... Biological or not, how could anyone do such evil in this world?

Eric's flame flew in the air and dropped to the floor on the screen. Fire igniting, encircling Jaxon's parents. The screen went dark as the line went dead... Tears streamed down my face faster as my hands pulled my head to the ground, my whole body began to tremble. The rocks from underneath me started to shake.

Isadora ignored the ground and started talking again.

"Well, he's no good now." I looked up in time to see Declan's face, fallen at the words from his adoptive father. His world had just crumbled in front of him, and I was the only witness. I went to stand and tried to reach out to him for comfort before realizing that Isadora took the dagger from the ground. She lunged at him, just passing my torso and plunged it into Declan's chest. He let out a gasp from a punctured lung. She twisted it heavily and lifted him by the shoulders with unnatural strength and tossed him to the ground as if he was nothing more than wasted space on this earth.

"No!" I screamed in horror. Aisling heard the scream and turned on her heel, running back with Haven chasing after her. Everything became surreal and seemed to be in slow motion. My world was crumbling, all over a stupid dagger that I couldn't fix. I stood, adrenaline rushing through my veins, and screamed, "Orbis Terrarum," pulling the ground from under me, bringing it up in the air, amazed at my own strength, and smashing into Isadora with every ounce of magic I felt I had. Her body flew halfway across the field, giving me a brief moment to drag Declan up into a sitting position before Aisling and Haven reached us to help carry him back to the Jeep. He was still breathing, labored, but breathing. Haven shook her head and tossed me her phone with a sympathetic look that I knew all too well. She put her hand over Declan's chest, trying to heal him. *Why the phone?* I asked myself before glancing at the screen, then back to Isadora. She was still halfway down the field laying on the ground, starting to pull herself back up.

"Freya... Freya!" The voice on the phone yelled at me. I brought my attention to the video call. Jaxon was staring back at me in anguish. "Freya! Get out of there! Eric is on his way, he burned my hous—" His voice gurgled and caught me off guard as my head spun. I stared at the phone, not comprehending what was happening. Blood started to pool from the side of his mouth before spurting out toward the phone as he gasped for air.

The shock hit first and then the sickening that came next was unbearable as I realized what had happened. "Jaxon? Jaxon... Jax, I'm here! Jaxon, stay with me!" I screamed a blood-curdling scream as the phone dropped from his hand and his body fell to the ground, the screen looking toward the sunrise and his breathing becoming shorter. "No! Jaxon..." I choked. "Jaxon!" The realization of his life ending in front of me took the final breath I had in me, out. My entire world crumbled and the ground from underneath me broke as I looked at the phone one last glance before I watched Eric come up to the video call, disconnecting the line. For a moment Eric looked like he was pained but then his lips straightened into a smirk.

My entire being just wanted to collapse, but so much anger ran through my veins. My Mark began to glow brighter than the sun. I turned toward Haven and screamed loud enough for all of Wisconsin to hear.

"You keep Declan alive, that is Jaxon's Anchor!"

I turned toward Isadora, who was rushing back to me, jumping into the air with her fire in hand.

I pulled the broken ground in front of me, lifting myself into the air and carrying me toward her at undeniable speed before letting my hands twirl around each other, creating a fireball larger than hers to throw back at her. A strength that seemed more natural when I finally stopped trying to control it. Her fire came toward me, but my adrenaline didn't let me hesitate to catch it and let mine grow larger. I was holding an ancient Immortal's magic and making it my own. She was going to pay for this. All of it.

We crashed into each other while my fire was still growing, and the entire field lit up in an ominous glow. The fire formed an orange fiery sphere, surrounding us in the blaze. I took my only advantage and tried syphoning her magic to weaken her. I felt the pull start before she took my head and slammed it into the ground, stopping the transfer completely.

"Impossible!" she shrieked while her hand forced my head down harder, crushing it. "I was the only syphon!" My brain fired rapidly with so many questions and scenarios that could be or should be or would be, but this was the scenario that I might die in and any syphoning knowledge she may know would be pointless. My head began to pound.

She stepped back and took the earth rubble, slamming it into me, throwing me back into the dome of fire, which burned but did not leave any evidence behind. I took the air and pushed harder against her, pinning her against the other end of the dome. She was strong, her body stood there longer than I wanted it to. She pushed harder against me. My thoughts started to cloud as I could feel pressure forming between her debris and the fire dome behind me. My lungs felt as if they were collapsing.

Fuck, she is winning.

My mind raced as I realized I had no idea what I was doing, my magic started to drain from my insides. I started to second guess my strength as she pushed harder, and my throat began to burn. My mind went back to Jaxon on the phone, the blood from his mouth was trickling down. The anger surged back to me.

He killed Jaxon. I'm going to kill her!

I felt the rage inside me burning brighter, and my hands tingled with the magic I had accumulated from the others and the dagger. I used it to my advantage. She might be ancient, but I was a syphon, and I have more magic coursing through my veins than most witches from the soul-filled dagger. I pushed the air, earth, water, and all the fire I had left in me toward her, rocking her body out of her stance and throwing her into the fire dome opposite of me.

The dome exploded as soon as her body hit, and my lungs filled with oxygen again as my body went skidding against the crumbling ground and back into the only tree in the field. It caught me from flying off the ends of the earth itself. My lungs felt oxygen depleted as I crashed into the tree. I was either dying or already dead... And everything went dark.

Chapter 32

So, This Is What Death Looks Like

My thoughts whirled... I didn't think that death would be so dark, so final. I assumed it would be bright and happy. My entire body was aching, and my head was throbbing. Death shouldn't be this painful. Life was hard, but if this was death, then take me back. This sucks, I thought while trying to breathe in any air. At least if Haven kept Declan alive, then Jaxon would be okay, and I could die in peace with knowing that he would be alive. At least he would live on with one less immortal roaming the earth. I killed her... I hoped. Now the others would have to take on Eric without me, but with the weakening elixir, they should be able to take him down. They just had to get close enough to him. I breathed heavily as the darkness consumed me. I could feel myself slipping away. These were wounds that even an Anchor couldn't pull me back from.

"Freya, open your eyes. Freya." My face felt a hard slap, my eyes opened and I realized that I was definitely still alive. My face burned and a fraction of me thought maybe death would be easier. My body felt like it had been hit by a tree... Or maybe I hit the tree. I hoped that the tree was okay. My eyes tried to focus on my surroundings as I looked at the lady in front of me. Adrenaline coursed through my veins as I loaded my hands with fire again and sat up too quickly, which made me want to pass out with dizziness. The fire extinguished into the dirt as I used my hands to hold myself from falling. I refocused my eyes, and my heart slowed. Aunt Lynn stood tall in front of me.

"Freya? Look at me. Hey, look at me!" I blinked heavily and tried to nod that I was okay. But truly I was far from okay, really, but I was alive.

Alive!

Jaxon...Oh my God, where's Jaxon?

Is Declan alive? How long was I out for?

My head began to pound, and I realized that the crumbling pieces of land were still crumbling. I looked behind her to check for Isadora. I didn't see her, but JFK was destroyed. The only thing left standing was this singled-out tree that we were under, it was all of what was left of Jaxon's and mine. My heart sank as I saw how destroyed it was, but we had bigger problems than that right now.

"Where is she?" I asked, mumbling. My entire body, including my jaw, throbbed.

"Whatever you did to her, she's knocked out." She looked me up and down, examining my injuries. I didn't even want to look at my own bruised body. I already knew the damages. I pretended I was okay, but I knew my body could not take another hit like that.

"What now?" I asked.

"We're taking her with us, she will be a good leverage

piece to Eric. Whatever elixir they concocted should help keep her in this coma state for a while until we can get to Eric too."

"And Jaxon?" I asked shakily.

Her eyes pierced into my soul, anything other than he's okay was going to kill me. She shook her head, "I don't know. Alex and Clara have him."

"His parents?"

She shook her head again, this time no words followed. Tears welled up, understanding what had happened because I couldn't fix the dagger. I knew I was the one that killed his parents. How was I ever supposed to tell him that? It was all my fault. Margo was right, loving me was a losing game. Only this time, it was their lives that were lost. Bile built in the back of my throat as I turned and heaved acid from my empty stomach. My ribs throbbed at the too quick of motion.

"Sit still until Ezra gets here with the healing tea. You will be back to normal in a few minutes." When she said his name, the memory of the bracelet came back to me.

"How did you even find me?" I asked.

"Your dad made Ezra call me. He told me where to go, and when I noticed you weren't moving on the map, I realized what you had done." She sighed. "I would've given my life to protect you, Freya. You are just as much family to me as Aisling is."

"That is the problem, I didn't want *you* dying for *me*," I said sharply. "Aisling needs you."

"She needs *you* more." She smiled. "I won't always be here for her, and she will need you to take that place when I'm gone."

"You're immortal like them, you will outlive me." I tried to laugh before stopping myself and whimpered in pain. I held my breath until the pain subsided.

"I am linked to them." She looked at me with sad eyes. "Once they are gone, I will be too." My head had not wrapped itself around that information, and my eyes shot to her quickly.

"Then, we can't kill them!" I yelled.

"You will, and you must! When the time comes... you kill them both." Her face hardened, and there was no sign of sorrow. "I have lived long enough. I am ready."

"There must be another way! There has to be something."

"I have spent a thousand years trying to find a way and failed each time. It's okay. I want them gone more than I want to stay. They are evil, and I have done all I can to help raise good descendants from their bloodline. I think I've done a damn good job." We both smiled as tears slid down both of our cheeks. "You can't tell Aisling, otherwise she won't do what is necessary."

"What do you mean?"

"Blood magic, my dear. Her blood is the only thing that can kill them. If she knows about me being linked to them, then she won't go through with it, and we both know what needs to be done to protect everyone else." I knew she was right, but my heart sank at the idea of her no longer being in this world, our world. I have known her my whole life, and she had been such an amazing family and friend to me. There had to be another way. Time was running against us, but there had to be another way.

Chapter 33

All or Nothing

The tea started to kick in, and my body started to feel a little more comfortable. The bruises were beginning to heal before my eyes. Pretty soon, I would be ready for anything. We drove back to Aunt Clara's with Isadora unconscious in the backseat and Aunt Lynn hovering her hands over her, whispering incantations, to keep her that way. Ezra drove the car carefully. He left my dad at the house with an extra car in case of an emergency. If anything went wrong then my dad was supposed to drive far away. He didn't like it, but he wasn't going to complicate things.

"She said something about another set of Anchor-born twins in the Viking ages. Do you know anything about them?" I asked, replaying everything in my head and trying to distract myself from Declan and Jaxon's conditions.

"Twins who were Anchors?" She thought hard for a moment. "None that I knew of, personally."

"Hm... Okay." I swallowed hard. I let my mind race with images of Jaxon again. I *needed* him to be okay.

"Why, darling?" she asked, which brought my attention back to the car ride.

"Isadora said one twin was a healer, and the other was something else but never finished her story." I shrugged. "She was probably just messing with my head."

"A healer?" Her eyebrows furrowed as she became deep in thought. Her eyes closed and she scanned her images in her head. Her eyes opened abruptly. "The only healer I had heard of was supposed to be only a story, years before Eric and I had been involved. The healer was killed by her fraternal twin. Of course, it was just rumors that stirred a town a few miles away from me at the time. They were not Anchor witches, either, or she would have come back to life."

I thought about how weir that was... Twins, but not Anchors? Why would the universe not pair a set of twins? Unless there was more to the story. A part of me wanted to wake Isadora and find out more about syphoning and her words, but that would be way too dangerous. With her unconscious and dead soon, I guess that would be it.

Syphoning... She did say that. Didn't she?

My brain started to put pieces together from the altercation.

"Is Isadora a syphon?" I asked after being reminded of her last words. Maybe it wasn't real after all. My head might've been playing tricks on me.

"There's no way. I would've known," she said and shook her head before refocusing on her task.

My phone rang, which made me jump, breaking my deep thought.

"Haven, how is he? How are they? Please." I held my breath waiting for the only response my body could handle.

"Declan is stable for now. He's in pretty bad shape, but I think he will be okay. Aunt Clara and Mom are on their way here with Jaxon now."

"Did you give him some of that healing tea?"

"His lung was punctured pretty bad. It needed a little more than just tea. There was a fragment piece lodged into his lung that kept reopening the wound and restarting the healing process. I finally got it out and resealed it. Time will tell."

Time was one thing we didn't have. With Isadora in our hands, who knew how long it would take Eric to come for us. We had his Anchor. He would come. He would kill all of us if we didn't get to him first. We needed to bring him away from her and weaken him. Aisling couldn't know that her blood magic needs to kill him, but also will kill her aunt. We needed to do this quietly. Aunt Lynn wanted to get a letter together for her before everything would happen. We didn't have much time.

"Hello... Earth to Freya!" Haven announced over the phone again. She cleared her throat. "Freya!"

"Sorry, yes?"

"Jaxon just got here; he has the elixir jewelry in his pocket. He did the impossible." I smiled at the last part before feeling sadness come back over me, hoping that he would wake to see the elixir work.

"Just promise me that you are doing everything to keep Declan alive, so he can live too."

"Of course." She paused. "They don't call me the

healer for nothing." She laughed, trying to lighten the mood.

"Thank you."

We were getting closer to the cottage in the bluffs when the realization hit me that I would see Jaxon, breathless in the house that was supposed to be our safe zone. My stomach curled until I reminded myself that he wasn't gone. At least, not yet. As long as Declan pulled through, then so could he. Every fiber of my being hoped so.

My body was beginning to feel more normal again. But I could feel the magic from the dagger coursing more strongly through my veins after the explosion of the fire dome. I really hoped that I would stop feeling so strong with stolen magic. My body was beginning to feel like it had consumed a hundred dead Anchors and they needed to be released. The magic was not meant to be in one place. I could feel the others trying to escape from me. They were meant to be back in their rightful homes, or with their rightful descendants. This amount of magic was too dangerous for one person. I was a new witch with centuries of dead witch's powers coursing through me. It couldn't be good a thing. It felt as if the fight with Isadora triggered something inside me, inside the magic to wake up, and I didn't like it. I needed to reverse this, but how?

Now was not the time to bring it up to anyone. We had so much more going on that I should use the extra magic to our advantage, then figure out how to get rid of it or make it go dormant again. The cottage was in view as we climbed the last hill. I inhaled heavily and released it.

I walked toward the house as my dad came running out

toward me, examining my body and checking my eyes for a concussion.

"I'm okay, Dad," I said quietly.

"I'm just making sure. You are still my baby girl." He hugged me tight. "Jaxon is—"

"I know, Dad," I said with tears forming and a sob that I choked back. Not wanting to hear the words again and reliving in my past.

"Breathing." He paused and hugged me tighter. "Jaxon is breathing!"

I pulled away from him and looked for bullshit in his eyes. He was being honest. I jumped back and ran for the house. I opened the door faster than I meant to, and it swung back and hit the wall, leaving a small dent that I made a mental note of fixing it later. I had other priorities on my mind. Haven pointed upstairs as soon as she saw me. My feet aimed for the stairs. I opened the first room, nothing. Empty. In the second room, no one. Last room I opened the door slowly and peeked around the doorway. There he was, laying on the bed, being tended to by Aunt Clara with my mom sitting by his side, holding his hand. His eyes were still closed, but my dad was right. His chest was rising and falling. I let out the breath I had been holding and dropped to the side of the bed opposite of them, slowly grabbing his other hand, making sure I wasn't hurting him in the process.

"He's gonna be alright, my dear," Aunt Clara said calmly. "We can thank Haven for that. If Declan wouldn't have pulled through in time, then this could've been a different story." She half smiled, seeming exhausted, but happy he was alive. My mom stood up, giving me her chair to take and sit next to him. I hugged her tight as she kissed my forehead before she headed downstairs with the bowl of bloodied bandages and stitching material. Even though he was alive, he would always have that scar as a reminder. We were lucky to be Anchors who had second chances, but the scars remained, and I was sure some were more haunting than others.

I sat next to him and carefully rubbed his arm as Aunt Clara walked out of the door, closing it behind her. He was breathing, and that I would be forever grateful for. I looked around the room, realizing this must be Aunt Clara's room. It was very Clara-like. There were plants along each of the windows and crystals setting on top of the soil. The bedspread was floral, and the whole room looked like it was from a gardening magazine. I realized that I was trying to distract myself from what to say to him when he wakes. *Did he know about his parents? Do I tell him? How am I supposed to get him through this? How does anyone?*

"I thought I told you to run," he whispered faintly.

I looked at him and saw his eyes open, staring back at me. My heart soared and relief washed over me. I smiled and laughed nervously, not knowing what else to do.

"I'm not going anywhere without you, besides you left before I could tell you that I love you too," I said softly, standing and kissing his lips. He caught me off guard and pulled me down next to him, nestling my head against his new-forming scar on his chest. He winced for a brief moment before he exhaled slowly.

"I knew we'd be together again." He said with another wince as he adjusted his body.

"Does it hurt?"

"Nah," he shook his head, brushing off the truth. "But it must be healing because... Damn, it itches." He smiled when I looked up to him.

"I'm so sorry I wasn't there for you."

"You were right where you were supposed to be. Besides, I still have your necklace, so it felt like you were with me all along." He pulled it out of his pocket and placed it back over my head. I glanced down at the newly formed elixir tourmaline pendant and half smiled back at him, happy to have it back with me, but it was now a reminder of the reason why his parents were probably killed in the first place.

"It's okay," he said.

"What is?" I asked, confused.

"I know what happened... I know about my parents." I heard his voice crack at the last word before he looked up toward the ceiling, trying to hide his sadness and be strong.

"I am so sorry. I should've gone with you or done something more." I choked back tears.

"Don't do that. It all happened so fast. I couldn't even get there in time." His chest rose ruggedly with a lump in his throat. I leaned closer to him to try and take on some of his sadness. I knew it wouldn't take it away, but maybe to help with the burden. I pulled my syphoning magic through, trying to help his emotions, knowing that they were not magical and grief was a thing that would just take time.

"Jaxon, I—"

"Let's just do what needs to be done." He paused and I looked at him with another confused look. "We're going to kill them." He inhaled sharply. "For Ezra's and Declan's and now mine. They are done tearing families apart." He had a look to him that I had never noticed before. It was a dark look. I couldn't blame him, he had just lost his parents. I just hoped that the hate would rise one day and not make him a vengeful, bitter man. My heart hurt for him. The emotions were going to be too much for him. He was such a kind soul, and this was darkening him every minute that went by. He had no idea what killing the villains actually meant for Aunt Lynn. I couldn't let him have all that blood on his hands. I needed to take care of it myself.

I laid with him a minute longer before I noticed his breathing becoming more relaxed. I looked up at him and realized he was sleeping. Good, I thought, he would need to recover. I stood up and kissed him softly, trying not to wake him. I needed to get downstairs and come up with a plan that didn't involve him before he woke up and did something reckless. I walked toward the door and looked back at him one more time.

I joined the others who were gathered in the living room, discussing what to do next. Isadora was now heavily sedated, and the women were working on a spell to immobilize her until Eric could be found. If we killed her now, then she would just come back until we killed him too. We had leverage by having her, but that also put us in danger. We were playing with big fire now.

The tea I had drunk was making me feel strong again. The magic was coursing through my veins, and I felt ready to work with any plan we could think of. I wanted to end this before Jaxon woke up. I just didn't like the outcome for Aunt Lynn. Of course, I was the only one with that knowledge, and I didn't like that, either. I glanced toward her in the kitchen, sitting at the table writing a letter. The letter that would be meant for Aisling. The letter that I would have to give her once her aunt was gone. It just wasn't fair... There had to be another way. We just needed more time to come up with another plan.

Unfortunately, time wasn't our friend today. The front door came flying off its hinges and flew into the staircase with a gust of wind, pushing it harder into the home, the windows shattered along the first floor. We all jumped as I turned toward the open doorway and gasped. Time was up. He was here.

Chapter 34

All I Have

There he was, standing halfway down the driveway with a fireball forming in his hand. Our eyes met as he lifted his fiery palms from his sides and let the fire grow. He was going to burn us out of our safe place. Without thinking, I ran out in front of the house with my arms up, pleading for him to calm down.

"Where is she?" he asked angrily, a voice that would forever haunt me. He was going to kill us all. I breathed heavily, collecting my thoughts and carefully trying to plan this conversation out in my head.

"She is safe," I held my breath, hoping that it was an answer that would slow his fire.

"Not good enough," he yelled and threw his fire at me.

I caught it, which surprised even me, but pissed him off even more. His face hardened as he became the demon man from my nightmares. His hard, cold stare with a distinct jawline, and eyes that were ready to kill. The second fireball came flying at me before I could recoup from the first one. I closed my eyes and put my arms up, trying to cover my face from burning. I waited for the impact, but nothing happened. Instead a cool, misting effect came over me, and I looked up to realize it was my mom shielding me with a wall of water.

"I've got you, honey." She smiled at me, and I looked at her with an appreciation for the help. Aunt Clara joined her, as did Haven. The four of us stood parallel to him, blocking the house filled with our loved ones. Ezra and my dad, magicless. Aisling, a newbie. Declan and Jaxon were in the process of healing, and Aunt Lynn was finishing her goodbye letter.

I looked to the other ladies who joined me, my family, and we nodded before the water wall came down. We all had our palms at our sides in synchronization and headed for Eric. Our palms glowed, each with a different element to take him on. Mine glowed heavily with a fiery orange, which when I looked at the others, I thought of my purple hag stone from Haven. And the flame changed color to match it before my eyes. I smiled when I realized that my barrier between magic and me was no longer there, holding me back. I was right where I was supposed to be, and I *knew* what I was doing.

At the same time, each of us let out a scream of release and started throwing everything we had at him. Eric began to crumble underneath the power and started to kneel on the ground. He was slowly weakening. For the briefest moment, he glanced up and made eye contact and I thought we had a chance before he smiled.

Fuck.

Advantage gone.

The entire ground shook from underneath us and sent

me halfway across the yard into the garden, destroying an entire row of plants. I looked up quickly, ignoring the bruises wanting to breakthrough. Everyone was scattered apart from our once strong stance. Haven stood at the same time that I did. Our mom and Aunt Clara struggled to recoup as quickly as we did.

Eric ran with a supernatural speed over to them, who had landed near the house, and grabbed Clara. He filled his palms with a water orb and shoved it to her face, making her gasp for a breath as she choked on the water. He was drowning her right in front of us. He took his other palm and faced it toward our mom, drowning her. We were on land, and he was making them choke on the Mississippi. Haven and I glanced toward each other before running toward him with more power than we had ever practiced with. Breaking his stance and making the water evaporate, the women gasped for air, keeping their faces toward the ground and coughing up water.

He turned toward us and blinked heavily when he realized he was seeing double now that we were close to him. My hands shook for a brief moment before I realized we had caught him off guard. We needed to use that to our advantage. I raised my shaky palms and steadied them before lifting shards of glass from the broken windows, bringing them up behind me with his eyes staring in disbelief. Releasing the energy I had been holding onto for too long and letting them fly toward him, knowing full well that it wouldn't kill him, I needed him weakened enough to get closer and syphon his powers. We would need Aisling's blood to kill them both for good, and she wasn't out here yet.

The glass flew fast, slicing through the air, aiming for his entire being. He pulled his hands up and stopped them from hitting him, inches from his face. Only one got through, slicing his left arm, causing blood to trickle down his rolled-up white sleeve. His arm dropped, releasing the advancing of the shards, and touched his arm, running his palm over the gash. He looked up angrily as Haven picked the shards up again and lifted them toward him with success. About half of them cut into his arms and legs, and one just missed his carotid. He dropped to the ground, and I thought that this was it, his moment of weakness. I ran toward him, my palms ready with a fiery orb, just in case. I looked at Haven who was pinning him to the ground with gusts of wind, and he was struggling to get past her grip. I realized that we were heading down blood road, and I just hoped that we were on the right side of it.

I reached him and pulled my necklace off, breaking the chain, ready to embed it into his skin and release the elixir to knock him out. My arm went up over my head and hung there, the necklace dangling. He was controlling my arm, overriding my own body's intentions. He looked up to me, still being pushed down by the tornado on top of him. He took his other hand and aimed it toward Haven, knocking her off her feet and flinging her backward into a tree, hitting her head. Without hesitation, he grabbed Clara and Alex and scattered them against the other trees nearby. All three of them were now unconscious. There was only me, standing in front of him, unable to move.

No!

He stood and grabbed my throat, lifting me up, choking me.

"You really thought you could kill me? *You?*" he laughed demonically as I gasped for air with my hand still raised in the sky. "And your twin? She's nothing, just like you."

"I... Will... Kill... You!" I choked out, trying to get out of his grip. I looked up to the pendant and tried to release it to my other hand, but his mind grip was too strong. My hand stayed frozen. I moved my other hand to his arm, trying to forcefully remove it from my neck before suffocation kicked in. Aisling ran outside and paused when she saw me hanging in the air while my legs thrashed against Eric, trying to get him to release me. My mind was beginning to get cloudy.

"You are nothing special, just a girl," he continued. "I should've killed you and your twin while in the womb, you worthless witches. Just like your mother and her friend."

The word *special* triggered my exhausted brain into remembering that I was special. I stopped trying to free myself from his grip and tried to syphon his magic. The pull was there, but he was fucking strong. I felt like I needed more oxygen to do it. I gasped, trying to catch a single gulp of air.

Nothing.

Aisling walked out to the yard and raised her arms crisscrossed together over her head. She let out a scream before bringing her arms down to her sides, letting something bright green explode from inside her. Knocking Eric and I both over, breaking his hold on me and my pendant. Aisling marched toward Eric with her hands pushing magic hard against him, knocking him further away.

Woah, where did that strength come from?

Once he was out of sight, she looked at me and smiled.

"Where did *that* come from?" I asked with my nearly crushed windpipe.

"My aunt gave me her magic," she smiled widely.

"She did what?" I asked again in disbelief. Aisling thought she was just being a giving person, but really, she was setting herself up for death. It was a parting gift. My heart sank, but I was happy to be rescued.

"She transferred her magic to me. Some old spell in a book." I half smiled back at her, and we looked out toward where Eric had disappeared. He was emerging from the woods, coming back toward us.

"I need to syphon his magic to weaken him and then you need to—"

"I know, she told me I need to use my blood on this blade and kill him with it. She said my blood is the only way." I half smiled and nodded my head in agreement.

Ezra ran out toward Haven and carried her into the house. She was breathing when he went past us with her. Alex and Clara were slowly getting up, seeming disorientated. It was up to Aisling and me to take on the strongest Immortal walking this earth. I looked at her and nodded.

"Thank you," I said calmly to her. "Are you sure about this?"

"Never been more sure. Let's finish this!" she said before facing back toward Eric. We started walking to him together. The distance between us was closing, and he had not made a move against us yet. Both of our palms were ready. Mine with fire, and hers with a dark cloud of magic that I did not recognize.

"Who are you?" he stopped and yelled from his position. He stared at her now glowing triangle Mark, and his eyes widened.

"The girl that is going to kill you," Aisling said with hate.

"Impossible." he wasn't talking to her, but to himself. "Ais?" he yelled, haunted. Aunt Lynn already knew that he was talking to her. He recognized her magic. She walked to the doorway with her head held high and made her way to us, but stayed behind us enough to stay protected.

"How?" he asked her.

"Magic," she said back, smiling.

"Ais, I—"

"Don't!" She said cutting him off. "How did you find us?" His face softened as he stared at her. He seemed to have a weakness after all.

"Isadora is my Anchor, we are drawn to each other, Ais." He paused, and his eyes looked sad, or this was one hell of an act. "I've waited a thousand years to tell you how sorry I am. If only—"

He was interrupted by what seemed to be a tsunami coming toward him. He shielded himself, but he was a second too late. Declan had stepped out of the house, and rage filled his eyes. He was healed physically, but mentally, he was broken because of this man. I pushed the others out of the way when I saw Declan coming fast toward him. We needed to move and now.

The two of them started to throw fists, non-magic ones. Just anger-filled fists. I had never seen Declan have such rage.

"You should've ran before," Eric said between blows, "Izzy found you."

Declan laughed, pure hatred filling his voice. "You told *her* to *kill* me!" he screamed and came down on him with another blow to the head, which finally brought Eric to his knees, spitting blood. The fight stopped for a moment, and both men stepped back, staring each other down.

"Isadora doesn't give a shit about you, I did," Eric yelled.

Declan became hysterical. "Ha, you *did*? As in, *don't* anymore? Fuck you!" Declan yelled and the moment of silence broke when Declan went after him with magic.

We didn't have long to come up with a plan. Declan couldn't do this alone much longer.

"Ais, we need to get to him now while he's distracted. I will weaken him with the pendant and try to syphon while you get blood on that blade. Your blood will kill him. You understand?" She nodded and sadness washed over me, but I couldn't let that happen right now. We needed them gone. It was time.

"Let's go!" I said.

We ran toward the men fighting. My mom was getting on her feet and scanned the situation in the yard. I saw her quickly check Aunt Clara's pulse and came running toward us. *This is for Jaxon's parents.* My magic tingled in my hands, and I gave it everything I had before crashing into Eric with such a force that could have exploded the town. The hundreds of Anchors were on my side for this one. I could feel them pushing me faster and harder against him. They were fighting for their lives too. I smiled to myself, thankful for the help.

The ground rumbled from underneath us all, but I stood my ground as I pushed him hard, further away from the house, further away from Isadora. Aisling ran up next to me and started pushing her new dark magic even harder against him. Between the both of us, I could feel his arm trying to reach through the forcefield to grab us. Let him, I thought, then I will syphon him to nothingness.

His arms grabbed each of our throats, slowing the magic field and bringing us to a halt midair. I gasped briefly before smiling. He was right where I needed him.

"You bitch!" he exhaled through exhaustion. "When are you going to learn? You can't beat me, you are nothing!" His voice boomed through the bluffs.

"You're wrong," I choked. "I'm a syphon!" My hand had already gripped his arm and was syphoning his magic and his grip was becoming weaker. I smiled even wider when I saw the fear in his eyes. "You should've left us alone." I pulled his magic harder. "Jaxon's parents, Declan's, Ezra's, and then you come after mine!" The magic was coursing through my veins as I felt him becoming weaker still. "You started this... Now we're ending this with your own blood." I smiled heavily toward Aisling, and she pulled his weak grip from her neck before taking the blade from his back pocket and carving her arm to let it soak with blood. Eric's eyes went from mine to her arm in confusion.

"Remember when Aislynn killed your unborn child? Instead, she raised him to be a better man than you. *All* his descendants."

As my syphoning was beginning to feel complete, he dropped to his knees and looked at her sadly before whispering, "No."

I took my pendant and lodged the tip as far in as I could

to the side of his neck. He winced as the elixir glowed, spreading through his veins. Aisling grabbed the blood-filled blade and went to stab him in the heart to end this. When I saw Aunt Lynn standing at the porch, nodding her head and looking up toward the sky, arms raised in acceptance, fear consumed me. I thought of a world without her and how Aisling would live with the fact that she killed her own aunt. My heart sank as I yelled, "Stop!"

I pushed the blade out of her hand, wiped it clean, and took my hands, coursing with his own magic, making me unbelievably strong, and brought them to Eric's neck. Looking at his weakening, powerless body, staring down into his eyes.

"You are done!" I yelled in his face before snapping his neck and letting him hit the ground.

Aisling panicked with fear and confusion. "I have to finish this... Freya, why would you stop me?" We stood side by side, catching our breaths.

"If you kill him, your aunt is linked to his life... She'll die too." I said sadly. "There will be another way." I took her shoulder and pulled her in for a hug. She had saved my life today, and she was willing to kill her own bloodline to save us all. I had to stop her. She was Aisling Meadows, the sweetest, most outgoing, lovely girl, and my best friend, and I couldn't have blood on her hands.

"What do we do now?" she asked with tears starting to form.

"We find another way." I smiled at her as she looked to her aunt, who was running toward us with my mom.

Chapter 35

There Is Always a Loophole

We sat on the front porch of Aunt Clara's, recuperating from the long night and morning. My dad sat next to my mom with his arms wrapped tightly around her, as if afraid that if he loosened his grip, she would be gone. She nestled her head into his shoulder and seemed to finally be able to relax without looking over her shoulder, on the run. She was safe. Next to her was Aunt Clara with Haven close by her side on the wicker couch and Ezra sitting in front of them, seeming to be protecting them from any danger. Declan had his arm around Aisling, who had her head leaned into her aunt's neck on the top step of the porch, which somehow the house was still standing. A new doorway would have to be made, but we had forever to fix that. Jaxon was by my side on the bottom step, cradling me tightly in his arms, as if I were the last piece of reality that he had to hold on to. My heart was heavy at what the future was going to hold for all of us, but at this very moment, we had the two Immortal Anchors immobilized in the cave from my dream, and sealed shut so no one would find them. They were not dead, but they were not alive, and I intended to keep them that way.

Syphoning the last drop of their magic from each of them felt good at the time before sealing off the cave. It felt like a very powerful thing to do and wrong, but it had to be done. I could feel the good and evil magic inside me, trying to overtake each other, but at least the good felt stronger. Hopefully, the Anchors' and Immortals' magic inside me would eventually tire themselves out one day, and I would just be Freya Chamberlain again.

I hadn't mastered the syphoning yet, so who knew how long things would stay magicless, but the elixir in the jewelry was embedded into both of them. Aunt Clara collected enough Valerian root to make a concoction to help with the sedation spell. The seal should be unbreakable. It took all of us to get the spell right to seal it, so that should stand for something. That cave would have to hold, there was no other choice.

I went to reach for my pendant out of habit, to twirl it as my mind wandered, but of course, it wasn't there. Jaxon noticed my movement. "I will make you a better one," he whispered in my ear.

"I don't want better. How about the same?" I said softly and looked at him, his smile wide. I immediately smiled back, unsure if I would ever see that smile again. We had a long road ahead of us, but together we could get through anything.

It had been a few weeks since our world was first flipped. Our bodies were healed, our egos were still a little bruised, and Jaxon was grieving, finding ways to cope with the damages. He had been staying with us since his house was burned to the ground. The police were able to save the safe from the ashes, which made him happy. The safe contained his family's grimoire and a few family photos. It wasn't much, but it made him happy.

Our house had been pretty full this past week with my mom back with us. The adjustment with her being back had gone a lot smoother than I thought it would. Almost as if she had never left. I smiled when I looked at my dad and saw him smiling. He was happy which made me happy. The house was starting to feel like a home again, at least to me. Jaxon, on the other hand, was happy to stay with us, but he seemed to be wanting space too. My phone rang as I was sitting in the dining room with my parents. They were planning an expansion on the bar to give them a project to work on together again.

"Hey, come meet me at JFK." Jaxon's voice came through the phone, excitedly.

"But it's destroyed. Jaxon, I told you that." He hadn't been there to see it, but I knew he would be heartbroken to see how unrecognizable it was.

"Would you just get over here? Don't make me come and get you." He laughed.

Something had him in a good mood, and I didn't want to ruin that.

"Okay, but don't say I didn't warn you."

I drove to JFK with the windows down to let the breeze pass through the Jeep. The cool Mississippi mist gave the air a chill, usually not too pleasant, but today was supposed to be a hot one so the cool breeze was the only thing that was going to keep today's temperatures manageable. I got to the top of the hill and parked. I walked slowly out toward what was expected to be our destroyed field, our safe zone, and stared in disbelief when I looked up.

Jaxon was standing in the middle of the field, using his Earth magic to put the pieces back together. Large boulders, dirt, and clay chunks were being lifted across the sky and placed back together piece by piece. I looked at him with shock and amusement. He smiled wide and set the piece of land down that he was working on and walked over to me. He kissed me gently and grabbed my hand, pulling me faster to the tree that was still standing strong. I squinted my eyes at the object under the tree. Something was sticking out of the ground, but I couldn't see what it was. As we got closer, I read the sign in bold letters. "SOLD" was handwritten on the store-bought sign.

I looked at Jaxon in confusion, "I don't understand."

He smiled.

"I went to Town Hall and bought the deed to this piece of land. They gave me a fair price once they realized who I was. The lady at the counter looked like she had seen a ghost when she saw me. I guess the amnesia story hasn't fully spread around the town yet."

"You own this place?" I smiled once I realized what he was saying.

"*We* own this place. I mean, if you want to. We can build a house up here, that way we can give your parents some space, and we can have our own?" He inhaled slowly, waiting for my response. He seemed nervous.

"That... Sounds amazing!" I said excitedly, knowing that we would still be in Crystal Rock and could be close to the homes we grew up in.

"I figured we could start fresh up here. I know my

childhood home is still standing, but I think something new is what I need."

I nodded in agreement and jumped into his arms with excitement.

"So, *we* own this place?"

"Yes, *we* do."

I kissed him hard and started to feel like our future could finally begin.

With the cave sealed off and the Immortals still immobilized, we were safe. The dagger was safely stored with me. I didn't want Aisling making decisions without me, and just in case anyone else ever came looking for it, they would have to go through me and my entire family and friends of witches to get to it. Of course, I checked it every day to make sure it was still magicless, which gave me peace of mind that my syphoning trick was still working on them. I knew that it was safe, but a part of me, deep down, worried that my stealing magic method was only temporary. As long as the dagger stayed useless, then I knew that Eric and Isadora were staying magicless in the cave without actually having to check on them too. All I could do was hope that my syphoning magic was permanent. Only time would tell, but for now, I was going to live my life with the people that I loved and not worry about tomorrow.

I nestled up with Jaxon, who was sitting with his back to the tree at our new future home. I laid my head on his chest, looking over the mended field toward the Mississippi. We had a long road to recovery ahead of us, but with him by my side, anything was possible.

"Thank you, for being you," I said to him, reaching for his hand to hold above mine with his palm open. I let my fingers tingle under his and let the orb of light transfer through my palm and up over to his to let him hold the fiery orb. Smiling at how easy my magic was becoming, I looked up to him and nodded toward his palm again. He watched it change from orange to purple and then to every color after. He looked at his hand in amazement before leaning into my neck and kissing me softly. He turned his hand and closed the space between them, letting the orb vanish and interlocking our fingers.

I could feel his radiant smile coming back to him as he whispered into my ear,

"Always."

What's next?

See what happens next in the sequel Secrets & Thyme
Because is it ever really over?
For more information on the series check out the author
website for future updates:
https://stephanievorwald.wixsite.com/website

About the Author

Stephanie Vorwald is the author of the Witches & Immortals Series. She found her passion for writing long before she achieved writing 'The End' for her debut novel. She loves writing fantasy books where she can create her own world of magic in everyday, ordinary life. When she is not writing, she is a Registered Dental Hygienist. She loves being a mother to her kids and having family time.

facebook.com/StephanieVorwaldWriter

tiktok.com/@stephanievorwaldauthor44

amazon.com/author/StephanieVorwald